# Christmas Penn[y] Original Sketc[hes of the] Season
By George Manville Fenn

# Chapter One.
## Cutting Times; or, A Frost and Thaw.
### One—Freezing Sharp.

Twenty years ago, Hezekiah Thornypath was in Luck's way—so much so, that Luck kicked him out of it. Hez went up to London to make his fortune, and he took his wife and children with him to help to make it: Hez meant "to make his crown a pound," as the old song says, but he did not. Either times, trade, or Hez's management was bad; things went contrary; and, as though it were a punishment for marrying against old Thornypath's wish, Hezekiah's few hundred pounds melted away, troubles came upon him, friends forsook him, and when he considered that his affairs could be no worse, he had to fetch the doctor, who came, shook his head, and in a few hours Hez and his wife were weeping bitterer tears than they had ever shed before, for the rigour of death was fast stealing away the beauty from the features of their youngest child.

The house looked sad and sombre with the blinds drawn down; footsteps were hushed, and voices were heard but in a whisper—how needlessly Hez too well knew, as he gazed, with his weeping wife, upon the little sleeper. The world looked in advance one dreary desert, while hope seemed to have parted from them for ever. No friendly word of comfort was spoken, no whispered consolation—they were alone in the great city, and the tears that fell had no earthly witness.

A few days dragged slowly past, and then the lid of the little painted deal coffin hid from aching eyes the tiny spirit's cast-off robe. Blinding tears, breasts heaving while the thrilling words of the Apostle fell upon the grieving parents' ears, a last long look at the deep cold grave, and a catching of the breath as the earth fell heavily upon their infant's breast, and then, slowly, sadly, hand-in-hand, away from the little grave.

Three months passed away, and the shabby mourning had grown more rusty—three months of sorrow and struggles for the bare necessaries of life—and then again the slow, creaking step of the doctor; the same anxious faces watching the hard-drawn breath and fevered countenance of another little sufferer—watching with aching hearts, and moaning in the bitterness of their spirit at their helplessness, their utter impotence to give relief. Gazing with awe at the wild eye, unearthly look, and startled mien; ever and anon trying to soothe the child, whose spirit seemed to hold communion with another world. The same sad, sad scene: the creaking step departing, with the assurance, "nothing can be done;" and then, by the gloomy light of the wretched candle, the shades of that deepest night were seen to gather upon the little brow, as the eyes were closed in the sleep whose waking is into life eternal.

Through the crowded streets again, to the crowded habitation of the dead, a shabby funeral, with shabby mourners, hardly noticed but by the children, who cease their play and cling to the churchyard rails, or follow the sad procession amongst the mouldering graves. Another little coffin close beside the first in the cold, black earth, while hearts filled to bursting mourn for the lost ones, drinking deeply of affliction—of those bitter waters of Marah; and then on again, toiling through life's weary way.

Months of struggling—months of privation and misery; and after a day spent in a vain effort to gain employ, Hez slunk through the gaily-lighted streets of the West End, shrinking within himself as though it were dishonest of him to be poor, and to show his haggard face amid so much wealth. Christmas was at hand, and the gaily-decorated shops were thronged with merry faces; the streets, too, were crowded, vehicles were loaded, and railway-vans groaned beneath the weight of the presents they were bearing away. Boys home for the holidays, visitors from the country, busy purchasers and sight-seers, hurried through the teeming arteries of the mighty city; and the light of many a roaring fire danced upon the window-blinds, or sent its curtain-shaded radiance glowing across the road, telling of home and comfort, and the welcome awaiting those away. Soft flakes of snow were falling fast, and deadened the footfalls of those he met. A little farther on, strains of music greeted his ear, and a voice arrested him for an instant as he heard the words of a song well-known in happier days. Again onwards, to pass a merry party of young men, laughing and happy. Everything betokening comfort, wealth, and the festivity of Christmas, met his eye; but no misery save his own, for the bitter night had sent all others hiding down in courts and alleys, seeking in their darkness' for shelter from the winter's icy breath. Hez groaned; for he thought of past Christmas-days, and now of the present, with his one beggarly room in a court; of his patient, long-suffering wife, and half-starving children; of the dire pressure upon him, and his impotence to ward off the troubles. Want had him tightly in her clutches, and, with the thought of his misery, he looked down upon his wretched garb in despair. He had sold everything that the traffickers with poverty would buy; little by little, furniture, plate, watches, books, clothes, the little trifles interchanged in brighter days, all, all had gone; and now Hez hurried back to his lodging, knowing that he could not stir again in search of employment but as a shoeless beggar.

Hez and his wife supped that night upon the luxury he took in with him—a hot potato; the two children lay asleep in their corner when he returned; and bare and wretched as the back room was, lighted only by a rushlight, there was still one bright ray to illumine its darkness—love was there; and the same fond smile welcomed Hez back, as greeted him in brighter days; the same arms—albeit thin and attenuated—clung round his neck, and the same gentle face was laid to his, as when, in the full career of prosperity, he had returned to a comfortable home.

Christmas-Eve, and things at the worst: the tide of prosperity floated away, and Hez's bark stranded. A bitter night; no furniture to sell; no coals; no fire; and three weeks' rent in arrear. A few hours before, and a message came, that the landlady wanted to see Mr Thornypath; when the poor fellow encountered the storm of abuse in waiting for him; to listen to the threats of bailiffs, and finally, as no money was produced by the wordy warfare, to receive notice to quit. It was ten o'clock, and Hez sat by the empty grate upon a broken stool; the children with their mother were asleep upon a mattress stretched in the corner of the room. Poor things, they had cried with the cold, and their mother, trying to lend warmth to their little chilled forms, in her weariness and misery slept by their side. Hez had knelt down, and kissed away a half-dried tear from the pallid cheek, as he had added his ragged coat to his wife's scanty covering. It was a bitter, biting night, and Hez felt half stupefied with the cold; the pane of glass which the children had broken was badly stopped, and through it the chilly blast rushed in. Earlier in the night there had been an organ in the court; but the man gave in after playing half a tune, and shivered off, thinking of his own sunny land; some musicians, too, and a carol singer, had been to the public-house hard by; but their strains raised no response; and now, Christmas-Eve though it was, the occasional tramp of a policeman, and the hum of the distant street, were all the sounds that greeted the ear.

Hez sat upon his stool and mused, unmindful of the cold that crept beneath his ragged shirt, and pinched him until it left blue marks upon his flesh; unmindful of all but the half-muttered words and sighs of his sleeping wife, when he would lightly cross the room to re-adjust the wretched coverlet, and listen to her breathings, as though afraid that she might leave him in her sleep. Hez sat and mused: the bygone came back, and the thinker saw himself as child, boy, and man.

Then he recalled stormy interviews with his father; insubordination and defiance; the smarting of a blow upon his flushing cheek; and then, married life, and still happiness for a time; years of sunshine, and his barque floating gently along the stream, which now bore him for a time upon his way. Then the recollection of others' pains; the affliction, ruin, and distress he had witnessed, where adversity had been bravely battled with for long, long years.

A black cloud shrouding the man's soul: why should he suffer thus? what had he done? where was his sin? should wife and little ones bear the offence of the father?—suffer for his disobedience? Thousands around were in opulence; and he, willing to fight for his daily bread, eager to seize the work that should give him the labourer's independence, pushed to the wall by the hundreds striving to grasp the coveted food-procurer. Why should he not take what stern fate denied? must he sit and watch his little ones' agony, or apply as a pauper for parish relief? What was honesty to him now? he must have gold—gold—not to satisfy greed or the avarice of possession, but because it was the life of all most dear to him. Glittering stores of life-blood—wife's, children's life-blood—breath—lay in the windows close, at hand; could he not clutch the spoil, and let them live and be happy once more? "Thou shalt not steal!" What whispered of theft? It was no theft, but duty; the right of a strong man to grasp the possessions of the weaker, as kings made conquests. Gold, jewellery, wealth for the taking, and then in some country home to forget once more this hideous act in life's drama. "Thou shalt not steal!" Hush, conscience, hush! Man must live! But not by bread alone. Not one sparrow should fall to the ground without He willed it so! But life—life for the sleeping ones; life for his long, long-suffering wife—for his prattling children! Must he keep laws and see the famine-pinched cheeks, the blue lips, and listen to wailing cries for bread? Had he not waited and hoped—hoped still against the crushing desolation that pressed upon his weary brain? But why not die? Why should they not all sleep—sleep together? A little charcoal and the door well closed; the chimney stopped; and then, with them gently sleeping, without a struggle, wafted away from this weary life to eternal rest. His would be the sin; and they, poor, gentle, loving hearts, would be tenderly led by the hand of Mercy to their Father's home. Life! what was life but one great sorrow? They, poor sleepers, would not suffer. But what was that? A merry gentle laugh and a few half-muttered words from little golden hair, nestling close to her mother's breast; prattling words of playful glee; some happy dream playing round that little flame of life. And should he crush it out? slay as a murderer that tiny innocent? to hear no more the music of its mirth, the ringing silver of its laugh, and the broken, half-framed words and sentences of its lips—words so sweet and playful that the child itself would peer through the golden tangle that overhung its bright blue eyes, and laugh—merrily laugh—to hear its own attempts. Those blue eyes, pure in their light as the heaven reflected in their liquid depth. Must this be so? God—God forgive the thought! They should live—live to bless him yet, for his secret should be his own.

The grate bar—the broken poker! Enough: they would suffice. He would go—go at once; but stay, he must wait awhile; his wife had moaned in her sleep, the wind had rattled the window, and he felt numbed with the cold. He had thought too much; but he was now relieved and determined.

### Two—Down to Zero.

Fleet Street. The wind whistling down the river lanes and moaning through the courts. The night far advanced, and a thin section of the moon rising behind the distant cathedral. Stars bright, and sparkling like diamonds through the keen frosty air. The gas within the lamps quivering in the chilling draught, and the policeman passing a figure cowering in a dark alley near Temple-bar. The warder of the night passes, and a single vehicle rattles by directly after, the horse's breath rising like a vapour; and then wheels and footsteps gradually fade upon the ear as they pass, echoing down the long street. The bareheaded, coatless figure emerges from its concealment, and looks around. All still as death, and no eye upon its actions but the stars of heaven, as it were, spirits looking down to chronicle what passed. The rattling of a shutter bar—the grating noise as of iron upon iron, mingled with the crackling of woodwork; the figure wrenching and tearing with maniacal fury at the firm fastenings, while huge drops of sweat roll down his face. More resistance; more noise; but the figure, straining with the might of a giant, again and again, till the iron snaps in the frosty air; and then, wrenched out by its protecting bar, an iron-sheeted shutter lies upon the pavement. To dash in the thick glass, and, with bleeding hands, to seize watches, chains, trays of rings, and sparkling jewels, and force them into a bag, is but the work of a few moments, and, grasping with both hands all that he can clutch, the figure turns to flee, just as the sharp report of a pistol rings from the interior of the shop. The glass shivers, but the figure is untouched, and grasping the stolen treasure, darts along the pavement, hardly avoiding the blow aimed at him by a policeman. Away down the well-lit street, followed by sounds that lend speed to the enfeebled frame, for, joined to the shouts of the alarmed inmates of the house, the policeman's rattle sends its harsh whirring alarm-notes through the still night air. Onward, clutching the booty to his breast, and panting as the pursuing steps sound fainter; a race for more than life, and the street nearly passed, when another enemy darts from a side court, and grasps the fugitive's arm. There is a sharp struggle for a few moments, and the policeman falls, stricken to the ground by an iron bar, and the figure dashes on again. But the alarm has spread as he turns down Bridge Street, where the sharp air seems to numb the limbs of the runner. Rattle after rattle and shrill whistles are heard, and the figure stands for a moment undecided, wiping the half-frozen drops from his brow. Again onward, with enemies springing up on all sides, and shouts ringing in his ears; panting up the steep slope of the old bridge, but at the top two more enemies. Beaten, wearied, fainting; no hope; escape closed; prison; felon's dock; transportation; a starving wife and children; and a dishonoured name—all crowding thoughts, rushing to the brain to add anguish to the moment, as, still clutching his ill-gotten booty, the despairing wretch, with a last look around, climbs the heavy stone balustrade, gives one wild shriek, and parts the air in a plunge down into the dark abyss of rushing waters. The waters part to receive him in their cold embrace, and then the struggle for life—for breath—above water—borne away by the swirling eddies, and dashed against the sharp buttress; gliding along by the slimy stone, and hurried through the arch, to be caught by the back eddy, and swept into still water, and borne down by the heavy booty. One glance at the bright stars, with the stream bubbling at his mouth; arms failing with beating the waves; and then the tide roaring in the drowning wretch's ears, spreading his long hair for a moment upon the surface, and then closing above his head—the concentric rings swept away, and all cold, dark, and familiar once more—the gas in the court shining up through the window upon the ceiling, and wife and children asleep upon the floor.

Cold and stiff, Hez staggered to his feet; a heavy dew was upon his brow; a deep groan burst from his breast; and, sinking upon his knees, he covered his haggard face with his hands, and, by the side of his sleeping ones, a prayer of thankfulness welled forth from the depths of his heart that it was but a dream. Overwrought nature could bear no more, and at last, sinking beside his sleeping wife, that happy oblivion, given alike to rich and poor, closed his eyes once more in rest.

### Three—Rays from the Crystals.

The bells rang forth merrily upon that Christmas-morn; the sun shone out in unclouded splendour, and danced in vivid flashes from the snowy covering of the house-tops. Water frozen in the bedrooms, and, far off in the country, the rivers ringing with the pick-axe blows to break the massive ice. Birds upon the house-tops setting all their feathers up perpendicularly, and looking as if they had put in an appearance against the cold by donning an extra suit. There was a crisp feeling in the air that sent the blood tingling through the veins, and gave a rosy hilarity even to the porters of the gate-ways about Lincoln's Inn; for they seemed to drop their pounce and parchment air for the time, and beat their breasts, and stamped about the fresh-swept pavement with such an air of jollity, that people turned round to look at them; and one wayfarer gave it as his opinion that the Court of Chancery was dead, and the porters had received the news of a pension from a grateful country. The policemen, too, for once looked good-tempered; and one was actually seen to smile upon a ragged urchin going surreptitiously down a slide.

It was Christmas-morning, but there was plenty of business going on: the poulterer's boy from round the corner showed ears that looked like raw beef; but he had a broad grin upon his countenance as he puffed along, sending his vapoury breath on high in little clouds, and evidently happy, although laden with a tray of "Aldermen hung in chains;" and fat and plump those turkeys looked; rich, too, those sausages, but freezing hard in the sharp air. The greengrocer up Hez's Court was doing a powerful stroke of business in potatoes and greens; oranges, parsnips, and sticks of celery and horse-radish disappeared like magic. "'Taters at three pound tuppence" went off like shots; and, as for the penny a pound "flukes," there was great fear lest they should not last out, for the "floury Regents" were almost sold off. People seemed to have run mad after greens at "five-pence the market bunch;" and the master of the shop had been heard to say to his wife, that "if it hadn't ha' been Christmas-day, he'd ha' kep' open all church time!" But it was Christmas-day, as anyone might have seen by the bareheaded butcher-boys taking home the mottled beef that they could not find time for on the previous night; for trade was so brisk that there was no occasion to cry "What d'ye buy, buy, buy!" every moment being taken with weighing and cutting up.

It was Christmas-day; and, for once in a way, London seemed disposed to forget all the troubles of work-a-day life in the full enjoyment of the festive season. "Clang-clash" went the bells. One, two, three, four, five, six, seven, eight, and then backwards and forwards, and in and out, chopping and changing, dodging, bob-majoring, tripling and doubling, and rolling out their peals in every way connected with campanology; until they all went off together with a mighty clash, as though they had gone mad with delight because it was Christmas-day. Many were the puddings that, tightly bound in the well-floured cloth, had been plunged into the seething copper, as soon after six o'clock as cook could get the water to boil; and many were the happy hearts collected from far to eat of the tiresome old cloying, surfeiting, sweet, lovable, festive dish.

Saint Dunstan's church-clock had just pointed to half-past nine, when a stoutish old lady in a black silk dress, ditto bonnet, bright-hued shawl, a basket of the celebrated old check pattern, and bearing a genuine stag-horn handled gingham umbrella, secured round its waist by a piece of black tape, and much resembling its owner in bodily proportions—a stoutish old lady struggled between the knees of the passengers from the very bottom of the first "up" Kensington 'bus that morning; and then tried the patience of the key-bugle playing conductor to its fullest stretch while she sought for the money to pay her fare. Of course the 'bus had stopped before the stoutish old lady had expected it, or she would have been prepared, and she said so; while, by a series of the most terrible contortions she contrived to force her hand through the lumber-room full of pin-cushions, nutmegs, orris-root, scissors, bodkin-cases, pearl buttons, thimbles, stilettoes, etcetera, etcetera, which the stoutish old lady called her pocket, and extricated from its snug, warm place, at the very bottom, the flat tin-box which was her purse; and also, as a matter of course, which would not open at any price, till the old lady grew almost purple in the face, when off flew the lid—"spang"—scattering sixpences and shillings half over the road. But it was Christmas-day, and the conductor must have had just such a jolly-looking old soul for his own mother, for he good-humouredly and nimbly hopped about and picked up the scattered coins, put the old lady "all square agin," and then, upon the strength of its being Christmas-morning, gave the motherly-looking old soul a sounding kiss upon one of her puckered cheeks, and hopped upon his perch before the old lady could get her breath.

The passenger, who was no other than Mrs Cripps, clear-starcher and laundress, of Kensington Gravel Pits, had walked some distance up Fetter Lane before she had recovered her equanimity, when a pleasant-looking smile began at one corner of her mouth, at the side where she had lost most teeth, and gradually overspread her mottled old face, till she looked like what she was—such a true specimen of a comfortable old English dame, that a fat butcher standing at his door, with a face red as his own beef, looked as if he would have liked to take the old lady under the mistletoe hanging so temptingly with its pearly berries outside the greengrocers over the way. But he did not do it; and, directly after, a shade crossed Mrs Cripps's countenance as she turned up a court to the left. She walked up and down it several times, as she said to herself, "to get breath," but in reality to try and rid herself of a nervous trembling that would come over her, and make her old hands shake so that she could hardly hold umbrella and basket. Truth must out; and at last the nervousness so increased that the dame went into the "Rising Sun," and again brought the tin-box into requisition to pay for a glass of gin; and thus fortified Mrs Cripps turned into the shabbiest house in the court, pointed out to her as Number 9, where she puffed and panted up the stairs until she reached the second floor landing, leaving out the customary summons of two rings at the second bell, so as "to take them by surprise."

For three or four days Mrs Cripps had been in a state of great excitement; for she had found out that Master Hez, whom she had nursed when a baby, and her dear bairn, Miss Celia, whom she knew before the little darling was as tall as her umbrella, were in London and very badly off. The old lady, who had settled in the great city's suburb at the death of her husband, an event which had taken place many years before, hugged herself with the idea that she could now repay an old debt, and determined to try and get them to dine with her on Christmas-day. A real north country goose was obtained expressly for the occasion; the raisins were stoned and the suet chopped over-night, and before starting that morning the old lady had seen the pudding in the copper, and left her *aide-de-camp* with full munitions and instructions for carrying on the management of the *batterie de cuisine* until her return with "company to dinner."

In her homely way the world had prospered with the old lady. The best parlour was, though perhaps no example of refined taste, snug and comfortable; and if any one could brew a good cup of tea in the best china teapot it was Mrs Cripps. Rumour said something about dividends, and periodical visits to the Bank. Be that as it may, Mrs Cripps had a comfortable business of her own; and heavy was the load of linen—clean or dirty—that the man with the rough pony took backwards and forwards from "the squares."

It was some time before the visitor to Pounce Court could summon up enough courage to turn the handle of the door and enter the backroom, "to take them by surprise;" but when by a mighty effort she did so, the surprise was not with them, but returned upon herself. Poor Mrs Cripps, she gave a sort of hysterical gulp as she closed the door behind her and hurried across the room to greet Hez and his wife; but she had not gone many steps ere she was overcome by what she saw, and, sinking upon her knees, she burst forth into a wild fit of sobbing and weeping, rocking herself to and fro, and moaning at intervals—"My poor bairns! oh, my poor bairns!"

She had cause; seated side by side, cold, gaunt, and hunger pinched, Hez and his wife watched with famished eyes their two children eating the bare crusts which their last pence had purchased. There was no fire in the room; scarcely a bit of furniture, and cold gusts of wind rushed through the ill-filled window. But Mrs Cripps, though fat, was gifted with energy; her hand dived into her capacious pocket and brought forth a large blue cotton handkerchief, and in a moment her eyes were wiped; and as the astonished family gazed upon her she scuffled back to the door, and was gone. In a few seconds, however, she was back again to fetch her basket which she had left upon the floor; was gone again; but only to return and fetch the great gingham umbrella which stood leaning against the table, with its large stag-horn hook gazing in a pensive way into a broken saucer.

Few minutes elapsed before the silence was again broken, when heavy steps were heard ascending the staircase; the coal man gave his customary shout at the door, and half a hundred weight and some bundles of wood were deposited in the cupboard; while before Hez's wife had recovered from her surprise, in puffed Mrs Cripps, with a loaf under her shawl, and the big basket in such a plethoric condition that the handles would not half close.

A portion of the outer sunshine seemed to have crept into the room, or to have been reflected from Mrs Cripps's face; and what with attempted smiles, and the efforts required to gulp down an occasional sob, that lady's countenance was a physiognomical study. The umbrella was soon crowned with the big black bonnet, and stood up in a corner, the shawl hung up on a nail, the gown skirts pinned up all round, and the old lady bustling about the place as though she belonged to it. Twice only had she to run up in a corner to bury her face in the big blue handkerchief; but making a cheerful fire, and picking out the most nubbly coals, getting the kettle on in the most eligible position for heat, and fanning the blazing wood with the dust-pan, took up so much time that the old lady soon forgot to sob. The odds and ends of cups and saucers were then arranged upon the table; and the children, with eager eyes, watched the disgorging of the big basket, until they clapped their little hands with delight in anticipation of the coming banquet. Rashers of bacon, fresh butter, eggs, coffee, sugar, all were there; and then the kettle gave two or three premonitory snorts by way of clearing its throat, and to announce that it was going to sing; whereupon the elder girl was enlisted into Mrs Cripps's working committee, and set to do duty as toaster of a rasher of bacon before the now cheerful fire. Plates were put to warm; the small saucepan rummaged out, and a piece of rag drawn tightly through a hole in the bottom. "Tos it yuns!" as Hez's little one informed the dame after she had seen it herself and temporarily repaired the evil; and then eggs were placed in it, upon the hob, all in readiness; so that, what with the brightness of the fire, and Mrs Cripps's smiling face, the bare and not wretched room began to wear an aspect of unwonted cheerfulness.

Everything was progressing to a satisfactory state of readiness; and now the demands upon the old lady's time were multifarious: the kettle was sputtering and boiling over into the fire; the bacon was nearly done; the coffee required tossing in and out of a tea-cup; the eggs wanted watching while they seethed their prescribed three minutes and a half; and then there was the bread and butter to cut and the butter wouldn't spread, but kept coming off in great crumb-lined flakes. But perseverance overcomes all difficulties, and as Mrs Cripps had plenty of that virtue in her composition, she surmounted all her trials, and set the two children to work with an egg each, and some bread and butter, before she turned to the elders.

Hez and his wife had hardly moved since their visitor entered the room, but Mrs Thornypath was weeping tears of thankfulness upon her husband's shoulder; while the latter, with feelings of mingled gratitude and wounded pride, sat with head half averted, until his old nurse approached with so apologetic an air, such a union of respect and pity, withal such tenderly, motherly words, that Hez completely broke down, and burying his face in his hands, he wept like a child.

Poor Mrs Cripps, she was thirty years old when Hez was born, and she was thirty years older than he still; in her eyes he was but a boy, and, sobbing aloud, she knelt by his side, and parting the long hair from his forehead, the good old soul kissed him tenderly, and wiped his eyes with her big blue handkerchief. But the sun came out again all over Mrs Cripps's face, and dissipated the cloud that was lending gloom to the festive morn; whispering words of comfort to the stricken couple, Mrs Thornypath brightened up; and Hez, passive as a child, let them lead him to the table, where the old lady presiding beamed upon them all during the repast.

But it was Christmas-day, and Mrs Cripps's plans had not yet reached fruition; so, after the breakfast, she retired with Mrs Thornypath into a corner, where, during a long discussion, the latter lady seemed trying to beg off some arrangement that the other was proposing; but she was speedily conquered by her energetic adversary, who, watching her opportunity, attacked poor Mrs Thornypath in her weakest point, and carried the day by saying it would "do the dear children good." Mrs Thornypath then crossed over to her husband, who was leaning against the mantel-piece, and whispered with him for a minute; when he, poor fellow, glancing at his clothes, sorrowfully shook his head. But it was of no use; Mrs Cripps reinforced the attacking party, and poor Hez, completely beaten, gave a silent acquiescence to their entreaties.

There was now a busy interval of preparation, when a heavy footstep was heard upon the stairs. Hez gave an involuntary shiver as a loud rap was heard at the door, and then, without waiting for an answer, in stalked a stout, red-faced woman—the landlady—who, having gained scent of the new friend who appeared upon the scene, thought this a favourable opportunity for renewing her importunities. She had come with a speech all ready made up, and began:—

"Now, Mr Thornypath, about this here rent?"

Hez was about to reply, when Mrs Cripps confronted the intruder, and with the most cutting politeness said, "Pray, mum, have you brought your receipt?"

This was hardly what the landlady had prepared herself for, so she replied in the negative, when Mrs Cripps, with the same show of politeness, requested her to fetch it; and after backing the red-faced woman out, stood waiting her return; for Mrs Cripps was ready to face twenty Mrs Prodgers, and give them all a bit of her mind. This feeling was also strongly shared by the lady in question, who had determined also to make the second floor back a present of the above popular portion of a quarrelsome person's thinking apparatus; but upon her return, very much out of breath with her ascent, in spite of Hez's remonstrances, she was paid in full, and before a sufficiency of lung inflation had taken place, the closing door cut short all attempts at recrimination.

Mrs Prodgers was one of that class of householders who so abound in our thickly-populated neighbourhoods. She took a house with the intention of making all she could out of it, and not such a very unbusiness-like proceeding after all. But it is the cause of a vast amount of misery amongst those who are compelled to seek a house close to their daily avocation. They are obliged to live upon the spot, and so, in the scarcity of abodes, pay whatever rent is demanded, always a most exorbitant one, and this they contrive to pay while work holds out, but the first drawback places them at the tender mercies of their Mrs Prodgers, when their life becomes a burden, and too often that most real of all distresses, a distress for rent, sweeps away the little hardly-gained furniture. In many cases, however, Mrs Prodgers, through her over-reaching, finds that her tenants have left suddenly, leaving "not a wrack behind." Would it not be better to receive a moderate and well-paid refit?

A boy out of the first-floor back soon fetched a hackney coach, and into it Mrs Cripps hurried all her party, to be conveyed by her to the "Gravel Pits." There was plenty of delicacy, too, in the old dame, for she could not see anything upon the journey but the children, nor attend to anything but their wants, and so by degrees Hez's shame and wounded pride, that so far had covered him with an icy reserve, melted before the genial dame. The bright morning, and the merry faces of his children, listening to the details of the pudding that awaited them, these, too, tended to bring to his remembrance the dream of the previous night, and to show him that one loving, honest heart on earth was more than a match for despair. The streets were full of happy faces, and to Hez's eye everything appeared already to wear a brighter aspect. "Try again" seemed to ring in his ears, and during a temporary stoppage the greeting of one rosy-faced old man to another, "Merry Christmas and Happy New Year to you, my boy," seemed to thrill through him. Why should it not be a happy new year to him too? And with the thought the saddening, vacant, helpless look vanished from his countenance, driven away by the spirit of energy and determination; his carriage became more erect, and this unwonted aspect was communicated to her who had divided with him the troubles of the past.

Mrs Cripps still kept too busy on the front seat with the children to observe what passed opposite, but somehow or other a very large tear trickled slowly down her nose, until it descended "plash" upon the hand of the child she held in her lap, making the little thing ask in her wonderment "what made it yain there?" There was too much to point out to the children for any notice to be taken of what took place, and when at last Hez and his wife each held out a hand to the dame, the former felt that there was no cause to fear humiliation, for the hearty, honest pressure, accompanied as it was by the motherly, loving smile, showed the full extent of the existing sympathy, and how little need there was for wordy thanks.

#### Four—The Sun's Influence.

There never was such a goose before! never—brown, crimply, fragrant, and luscious, as—as—as—there; nothing else will compare with it—luscious as roast goose. The cooking too: one turn more would, nay must, have spoiled it; and as to the consequences of one turn less, they were not to be thought of. It was just, to do Mary justice, "done to a turn," and Mrs Cripps was put out of her misery; for, as she had told Mrs Hez in confidence, she had had her doubts; but they were all cleared up, and the old lady's face shone and looked for all the world like the pippins that had composed the sauce. Such mashed potatoes, beautifully worked all over the surface into elegant designs with a fork, and showing brown where they had been to the fire; while just under Hez's nose, and sending forth a maddening jet of steam, was a tureen full of supplementary gravy, and sage and onions, in case the great levy that lay within the internal regions of the goose should fail. There was a big brown jug of the brownest stout; bread of the whitest; greens of the greenest; and the table had all the best cut glass on, so as to give the effect to Mrs Cripps's six silver table-spoons. There was a real oak Christmas log upon the fire, crackling away and sending whole regiments of soldiers flying up the chimney, when poked for the gratification of little Goldenhair. Hez's eldest child, too, had had a peep in the sideboard cupboard, where there were oranges, apples, figs, nuts, decanters, and all sorts of unheard-of treasures. But at last the whole party were settled at the table; Mr and Mrs Hez top and bottom, and Mrs Cripps and the children taking the posts of the visitors.

There never was such a goose before. "Ciss-s-s-s" at the first plunge of the carving-knife a fountain of rich brown gravy spurted right across the snow-white table-cloth, and right into the salt-cellar; and then there was such scraping and rubbing up of the mess, only ending in making bad doubly worse; but at last the carver's duty was well performed, the choice morsels distributed, and Mrs Cripps idle, from the fact that she really could not force more mashed potatoes or gravy upon anyone.

At last, when summoned, Mrs Cripps's Mary came in to change the plates, and brought with her such a fragrant scent as could only have belonged to a Christmas pudding; and, sure enough, it directly afterwards made its appearance, with sides bursting open to disclose the richness within. It had been on the boil for six hours; and what with the piece of holly stuck in the top, and the wine-glassful of brandy set blazing in the dish, there never could have been such a luxurious pudding before. As to the children, they again clapped their hands with delight, but otherwise gave silent testimony of their admiration by being helped three times, and eating as only children can eat pudding.

But the best of dinners must have a termination, and so did this one; and when the hearth had been swept up, and the treasures of the cupboard shone upon the little table; and whilst the fire-light danced in golden hues within the old-fashioned decanters, full of old-fashioned home-made wine, the chairs being all drawn up round the fire, Mrs Cripps began to tell her visitors of her savings; and how that she had two hundred pounds in the bank; and it not being likely that she would want it for many years to come, it was her wish that Hez—"dear Master Hez"—should take it to begin the world with afresh, and pay his old nurse again when he could spare it. And when Hez and his wife would not hear of such a thing, the old woman grew quite angry, and took the upper hand, saying, "that they were children and ought not to dictate to an old body of her years, and that she would do what she liked with her own money," and last of all pretended to get in such a passion, that the visitors were obliged to be silent.

At last, when the early winter's eve was closing in, when the ferny foliage began to appear upon the frosty panes, and before the candles were lighted, Mrs Cripps, who had been for a long time very silent, suddenly asked Hez if he remembered the story he used to read her, years ago, out of his little book, about the mouse helping the lion out of the net. Hez replied in the affirmative, and saw again within the glowing fire the image of his tiny, bygone self, perched upon a tall chair, reading to his comely nurse. While his nurse, old, but comely still, fondly putting her hand upon his shoulder, reminded him, too, of the dreary Christmas-eve when she had come to his father's house—to her old master—wet, cold, and weary with her long walk from the distant village; how that weeping and sobbing she had come to beg the stern old man to lend her money to save her husband from ruin, and their little home from being broken up; how that Hez's father had refused—harshly refused—saying that he had too many ways for his money to waste it in helping idle people; and how, when turning heartsick to the door, a little hand had seized hold of old nurse's gown, telling nurse not to cry, for Hez would give her all his money; and forthwith thrust his little box, containing two new pennies and a lucky sixpence, into her hands, setting her weeping more bitterly than ever; bringing her upon her knees by his side to sob over and kiss the noble-hearted little fellow, till a stern voice had called him away; but only to come rushing after her again with the money she sought clasped in his little hands. "And," concluded the dame, once more sinking upon her knees by the side of Hez, "I thank God that I can show my dear boy how many years I have remembered his kind—kind act!"

It was growing very dark in the little parlour, and Mary was getting very impatient to bring in the tea-things; but her patience was tried for some time longer, and when at last, unsummoned, she took them in, and lit the candles, the children had fallen asleep upon the sofa, and "missus's" eyes looked very red.

### Five—What Followed.

Hez had found the long lane had a turning in it at last, and the roadway of that turning was smooth and easy to travel upon—so easy that he soon left all the frost and thaw far behind, and got well on in his journey of life. He used to say that a blessing went with old nurse Cripps's money, for success attended his every venture with it. He is now a man of some note in his little country-town; and it is a fact patent to all that a helping hand can always be found with Hezekiah Thornypath by those who merit it.

I spent a few days with him at Christmas-time, some three or four years since, and there, in the snuggest corner of the room, sat a very old, white-haired dame, pretending to be very busy knitting, propped up in her easy-chair, with one or another of Hez's numerous youngsters on the watch to pick up the constantly-straying worsted and needles. There was always a smile upon the old lady's face when any such act was performed for her—a smile that grew brighter still when Hez approached to say a few words.

Christmas-night had come, and a merry day had been spent. The old lady had smiled and looked pleased when Hez talked of never having been able to get such another goose as nurse Cripps gave them that day, years ago, for dinner; and that, for all his money, he had never seen such a pudding upon his table as the one he partook of at Kensington. She had sat in state, too, while having her health drunk by all the family; and feebly she bent forward to "wish Master Hez a merry Christmas." At last the party was collected round the fire, the evening was fast giving way to night, and quiet conversation was taking the place of the merry laughter and games of the afternoon. Hez and his wife sat on either side of Mrs Cripps, and had risen to once more wish the dame "a merry Christmas" before she left them for her early-sought couch. They had been talking of bygones; and, sitting with a hand grasped by those she had loved so long, the poor old lady suddenly lifted herself up, but only to fall back again in her chair as though asleep.

In the midst of the excitement, I aided Hez to carry her to her room, where she lay for days just gently breathing, but never again conscious. Watched night and day by loving friends, she passed away without a sigh during the still hours of the old year's death, with only a growing chill to show that her sleep had deepened in intensity, and that here she would wake no more.

## Chapter Two.
### Corns.

"Diet, sir; Diet, decidedly. Now you'll take this to John Bell's, in Oxford Street, and they'll make up the prescription; then you'll go on to Gilbey's—crooked-looking place, you know; just as if they'd built the house somewhere else, and then when they wanted to put it in its place found it too big, and had to squeeze it in. Well, there you'll order a few dozens of their light dinner claret. No more '20 port or fiery sherry. Taboo, sir, taboo. Light wine in moderation. Diet, sir, diet. *Good* morning."

I looked at the bristly-headed physician, who handed me a sheet of note paper with a big capital B, two long blurs, a rough blotch, a few spidery ink splays, and an ugly MD at the end of a few inky hooks-and-eyes, which I received in return for the twenty-one shillings I left upon the table; and then muttering the one word "diet," I stood in the hall upon a horrible stony-looking piece of floorcloth that quite struck cold up my legs. Here I was confronted by the footman who ushered me into his master's presence—a blue-coated, crestless-buttoned wretch with two round grey eyes that said "shillings" as plainly as any mute thing could; but I was angry, and determined to come no more: so giving the fellow only a sixpence, I hobbled away and stood in Saville Row.

Diet, indeed; why no man could be more moderate. And what's half a bottle of port for one's dinner? Why, my grandfather, sir, took his two bottles regularly, and, beyond an occasional fit of the gout, was as hale a man as ever lived. Why, he'd have lived till fourscore safe if bad management and country doctors had not drawn the regal complaint into his stomach, where it would stop. This was coming to a physician for advice. And then what did he do when I told him of the agonies I suffered?—smiled pleasantly, and said it was my liver; while when I hinted at my corns, what did he do then but metaphorically tread upon them, for he laughed.

Now, putting dyspepsia on one side, I appeal to my fellow-sufferers, and ask them, Is there any torture to be compared with the infliction of corns? Headache?—take a little medicine and lie down. Toothache?—have it out. Earache?—try hot onion. Opodeldoc for rheumatism; chlorodyne for tic; colchicum for gout. There's a remedy for nearly every pain and ache; but what will you do for your corns? Ordinary sufferings come only now and then, but corns shoot, stab, twitch, and agonise continually. What is the remedy? Plasters are puffs; bandages empty promises; the knife threatens tetanus; caustic only makes them black and smarting; while chiropodists—. Mention them not in my hearing, lest my vengeance fall upon your devoted head. Where can you put your feet to be safe—at home or abroad? Why, your very boots are sworn enemies, and the battle at putting on or pulling off makes the thought of the operation produce beads of cold perspiration upon one's ample brow. Who can be surprised at one's lying long in bed of a morning when tortures await, and you know that just outside the door, by the side of the large white jug whose water grows less and less steamy, there stand two hollow leather cylinders loaded with fearful pains to be discharged at your devoted feet.

There isn't a sensible shoemaker on the face of the earth. I've tried them one after the other until I'm tired of them. One recommends calf, another kid, another dog-skin, and another "pannus corium," and my feet are worse than ever. I won't believe in them any more, though they do show me lasts made to my feet, and insult me with hideous nubbly, bunkly abortions carved in wood, which they say represent my feet—my feet, those suffering locomotives. I'll take to sandals, or else follow the advice of the Countess de Noailles, and go barefoot like the old hen in the nursery rhyme.

I could suffer the bodily pain if it were not for the mental accompaniment, and the total want of pity and compassion shown by people. Only the other day, going down one of those quiet cab-stand streets, one of the idle wretches that I intended to engage shouted out to his companions,—

"I say, old 'uns, here's Peter Pindar a-coming."

"Who?" shouted another.

"Cove as turned pilgrim, and went with peas in his shoes," cried Number One; while, writhing with agony, and gnashing my teeth, I shook my stick at the rascal.

"You scoundrel," I cried, "it's my corn,—it's not peas."

"Then get it ground, sir," groaned the fellow; when I was so vexed that I took the omnibus instead, or rather the omnibus took me, and as soon as I had entered, I was shot into the lap of a stout elderly lady who looked daggers at me, and revenged herself by putting her fat umbrella ferrule on my corn at every opportunity. I believe it was Mrs Saunders herself, the friend of Mrs Bardell, of Goswell Street. And oh! what I suffered in that vehicle! Would that I could have performed the operation recommended by the conductor—a man with a gash across his face when he laughed—to put my toes in my pocket, or go and dispose of my troubles at Mark Lane.

It was of no use to try: every one who came in or went out of that 'bus, either trod upon or poked my worst corn with stick or umbrella, and then in the height of my anguish, when my countenance was distorted with pain, a stout, wheezing old lady opposite must "Drat my imperance," and want to know whether I meant to insult her.

I hobbled out of the place of torture as quickly as I could, and stepped into one of those mud trimmings the scavengers delight in leaving by our pavements, covering the glossy leather with the foul refuse, so that, naturally particular about my boots, I was reduced to the extremity of having a polish laid on by one of those young scarlet rascals, who kneel at the corners of the streets.

"Black yer boots, sir," cried first one and then another, but I could not trust to the first I met with, for he looked too eager, the next too slow, while the third seemed a doubtful character, so I waited till I reached a fourth.

"Do you see that slight eminence, you dog?"

"Wot that knobble, sir," said the boy.

"That eminence, boy," I said, fiercely. "That covers a corn."

"All right, sir," said the boy, "I won't hurt it. I'll go a tip-toe over him, you see if I don't. I often cleans boots for gents as has corns, and I'm used to 'em, and—"

"Yah-h-h-h," I shrieked, for it was impossible to help it, and at the same moment brought down my umbrella fiercely on the little scoundrel's head. Fancy my feelings all you who suffer, for it must have been done purposely; just as the young ruffian was grinding away with an abomination of a hard brush—a very hard brush, so hard that there was more wood than bristles—he looked up at me and grinned while I was perspiring with fear and pain, and then with one furious stroke he caught the edge of his brush right upon the apex of Mount Agony, causing me to shriek, seize my half-cleaned boot with both hands, and dance round upon one leg regardless of appearances, and to the extreme delight of the collecting crowd.

"Don't you do that agen, now come," whimpered the boy, guarding his head with both arms, and smearing his black countenance where a few tears trickled down.

"You dog!" I shouted; "I'll—I'll—I'll—"

"Oh, ah! I dessay you will," whined the boy; "I never said nothin' to you. Why don't you pull off your boots then, and not go a-knockin' me about?"

Of course I hurried away with my boots half-cleaned, and so I have to hurry through life—a miserable man, suffering unheard-of torment, but with no one to pity me. Time back, people would ask what ailed me, but now they "pooh, pooh" my troubles, since it is only my corns. I would not care if people would tread upon me anywhere else, but they won't, and I feel now reduced to my last hope.

Did not somebody once say, "Great oaks from little acorns grow—great aches from little toe-corns grow"? How true—how telling! But there, I give up, with the determination to bear my pains as I can, for I feel assured that no one will sympathise with me who does not suffer from corns.

## Chapter Three.
## A Ghastly Deed.

In Portsmouth harbour the good ship lay,
Her cruising ended for many a day,
And gathered on deck while receiving their pay,
   The sailors most thickly were mustered.
The Jews on the wharves were all eagerly bent
On supplying poor Jack, while most likely by scent,
There were sharks by the score
On all parts of the shore.
Both he sharks and she sharks enough, ay and more,
To devour poor Jack,
When they made their attack,
   And there on the land they all clustered.

Only think; from a cruise of four years returned,
And paid in clean money! No wonder it burned,
And Jack's canvass pockets were ready to give.
But, there: not so ready as Jack who would live
To the top of his income - the very main truck,
And when to the bottom of pocket, why luck,
Would never turn back
On poor happy-faced Jack,
Who never said die
In his life. And would try
To face any storm if his officers spoke,
Or the wildest of sights that the hurricane woke.


Now Dick Sprit was a sailor,
Tight and bold in a gale or
A storm. He would cheer in a fight,
'Mid the bullets' flight,
And sooner than hear any praise or flattery,
Would have run his head in a "Rooshun" battery.
Now Dick his pockets had ten times slapped,
His fingers snapped, and his trousers clapped;
He had thought of his home and the Christmas-time,
The long shore days 'mid the frosty rime.
He had gone on shore, run the gauntlet well,
'Scaped the Jews' oiled words and the grog-shops' smell.
The night was cold and the way was dark,
What mattered when Dick was free of his bark,
And with kit on his back, and stick in his fist,
His pay in his pocket, and cheek full of twist,
He started off for his six miles' tramp
To his native spot, spite of snow or damp.

Dick twisted his twist, and he flourished his stick,
And vowed he could fourteen footpads lick,
For in war or in peace, a scrimmage or spar

Is heartily welcome to every tar.
The night was cold and the way was dark,
And the town lights shone here and there like a spark,
As merrily on through the snow Dick tramped,
Though he certainly wished that the way were lamped.
   But what was that when with four years' pay,
   And a leave of absence for many a day,
   With the old folks waiting their boy to meet,
   Their sailor lad who, now fleet of feet,
   Hurried along o'er the crunching snow,
   As the thoughts of home made his heart to glow.


Some three miles past, and the sailor now
Paused by a hedge where the holly bough
Grew thick and dense, and though dim the night
There were memories many within that sight,
For the days of old came hurrying by,
And that Christmas past when he said good-bye;
While then came the thoughts of years soon sped,
Of the distant climes and the blood he'd shed,
Of the battles with storms in the ocean wild,
Of the torrid heat or the breezes mild.
But now once more he was nearing home
After his four years' tiring roam;
And with bounding heart how the night he blest,
And thought of the coming days of rest.

Some three miles past, when his blood was chilled
By a shriek which through every muscle thrilled;
He stood for a moment, and then could hear
The sounds of a struggle and trampling near;
Panting and sobs, as of mortal fight,
While from over a hedge gleamed rays of light.
Dick's feelings were wrought to the highest pitch;
His bundle he dropped, gave his slack a hitch,
Then tightening his grasp of his sapling oak,
With a bounding rush through the hedge he broke,
When hard by a cottage a lanthorn's light
Cast its flickering rays on a ghastly sight:
With gory features and blade in hand
Two ruffians stooped and their victim scanned;
As over the struggling form they leant,
Dick paused no more, but his sapling went,
Cut one - cut two on each villain's head,
Thud like the fall of a pestle of lead,
And then they fell with a deep drawn groan,
While Dick leaned forward on hearing a moan,
But suddenly turning, he ran like mad,
And breathlessly muttered, "'Twas really too bad.
Be blest if he ever did see such a rig
As to topper two lubbers for killing a pig!"


And Dick was right, for 'twas really no joke,
Though our sailor lad here had no "pig in a poke;"

But though courage should merit the best of our praise,
There's a certain fair maiden whose limpid eyes' rays
Should be shed on our mind when we think to engage,
And not in our hurry go blind in our rage;
Discretion should lead us, or else every whit,
We may turn out as blind as the sailor - Dick Sprit.

## Chapter Four.
## Come Back.

"Ha-ha-ha-ha! ha-ha-ha!" laughed Shadrach—Shadrach Pratt, light porter at Teman, Sundry, and Sope's, the wholesale and retail grocers in the City. "Ha-ha-ha!" laughed Shadrach, stopping, with one foot on the wet pavement and the other in the snowy slush of the kennel, to slap his thigh, and say: "That's a good 'un, that is—'What do the Arabs of the desert live on? the sand which is there.' That *is* a good one, rale grit. Ha-ha-ha!" laughed the little man. "I'll ask 'em that after dinner to-morrow."

Who'd have thought, to see the little fellow go skipping along through the wet, splashy snow, that there were holes in the sides of his boots, and that one sole had given up the stitches that morning and gone off, being not buried, but suffering the fiery ordeal of burning, curling about upon its funeral pyre as though still alive? Who'd have thought that he had had no dinner this Christmas-eve, and was now off, post-haste, to his home in Bermondsey (*pronounced*Bummonsey), to get dinner and tea together—a hot meal of bloater and bread-and-butter—with orders to be back in an hour at the latest? for it was busy tide with the firm, and whatever Shadrach's duty may have been at other times, he was heavy porter now decidedly.

Over the bridge, round the corner, down by Tooley Street warehouses, famed for suffering from an ailment that must amongst buildings answer to the Saint Anthony's fire of the human being; down past sacking, sailcloth, and rope warehouses; and down past marine stores, and miseries enough to give a man an ultramarine tint; and then home in the pleasant and unsalubrious locality of Snow's Fields. Snow there was in plenty—muddy, slushy snow; but the only field visible was a large field for improvement; but then, as Shadrach said, "How handy for business!"

"Here's father!" was the cry, as the little man rushed in, hugged his wife, and had his legs hugged at the same time; and then he was in the warm place by the tea-tray, toasting his steaming boots, and watching the water being poured into the hissing, hot earthen teapot.

"Now, then," said Mrs Pratt, "they've all had their teas; and you're not to touch them, or give them a scrap. But have you had your dinner?"

"No," said Shadrach; "only stayed my stomach with half a pint of four ale and a hot tater, at one; but I've brought a bloat—There, bless my soul! I always did say the tail of your coat is not a safe place, and if I ain't been setting upon it. What a good job it was a hard-roed 'un. Not hurt a bit. Who'll toast it?"

"Me—me—me!" chorussed some six or seven voices; and then the most substantial-looking of the family was picked out, and she began toasting till the fish began to curl its head and tail together, when the toaster happening to turn her head to watch the distribution of "dog's bits" (ie scraps of bread-and-butter), the bloater glided from the fork, and had to be picked from the ashes and wiped.

But it was not so very gritty when done, and only made Shadrach think about the Arabs and the sandwiches; though, after distributing so many scraps, father's share of bloater, or grit, was not large; and then up jumped the refreshed head of the family, and prepared for another start.

"'Tain't much, eighteen shillings a week, with a family, is it?" said Shadrach, counting the money out in his wife's hand; "but, never mind, there's lots worse off."

Mrs Pratt gave a shrug, as much as to say, "And lots better." But, smiling again, she told what preparations had been made towards the next day.

"There, I can't stop," said Shadrach; "you must do it all. Goose, you know! Wait till it's quite late at Leadenhall, and then you'll get it cheap. They can't sell them all out."

Mrs Pratt seemed to think that the goose would make a fearful hole in eighteen shillings.

"There's coals, and grosheries, and vegetables, and bread, and butter; and Ginger's boots are in a sad state, and,—and—"

Certainly, Ginger's boots were in a sad state; but that was not of much consequence, according to the Countess de Noailles; and if she advocated bare feet amidst the aristocracy, she would have little pity for Ginger—domus name of Mr Pratt's fourth son; for Shadrach was given to nicknaming his children in accordance with the common objects of his life: hence "Ginger," "Pepper," and "Spicy" were familiar terms for as many children.

"But didn't I, eh?—the Christmas-box?" said Shadrach, pinching his chin and looking innocent.

"Why, an old cheat!" cried Mrs Pratt, rushing to the door, and finding a brown paper parcel resting behind the bulky umbrella upon her clogs; and then, amidst a volley of cheers, bearing it to the table, which was directly surrounded by chairs, climbed upon by an escalading party, and it was only by dint of great presence of mind that Mrs Pratt saved the brown paper citadel by hurriedly opening it, drawing out a pound of raisins, and bribing the attacking party by giving them a plum apiece.

"Ta ta! I'm off," cried Shadrach, with glistening eyes, as he hurried out and banged the door after him; but only to climb on to the window-sill by means of holding on to the water-butt and nearly pulling it over, when he could peep through a hole in the shutter and see his wife hold up to the eyes of the exultant children the Christmas-box regularly given by Teman, Sundry, and Sope to their *employés*. There was a pound of raisins, and a pound of currants, and a ditto brown sugar, a ditto lump, an ounce of spice, and a quarter of a pound of peel; which was the last packet opened, when Shadrach leaped down and hurried away through the dirty street.

But it was fine now overhead, and the stars began to twinkle brightly, while the slushy roads were fast growing crisp; but not crisp enough to prevent moisture from creeping through into Shadrach's boots.

"Because they live on the sand which—law!" cried Shadrach, "what a pity we can't live on sand; what a lot the little 'uns do eat." And then he stopped short for a minute to hear some street singers spoiling a carol, and heard the reference to a babe in a manger; and then somehow, as he trotted on, Shadrach could not see very clearly for thinking of two lambs lost from his humble fold: one sleeping in its little grave with the pure white snow covering its breast, and the bright stars like angels' eyes watching it; and the other—"My poor, poor bairn!" sobbed the little man, hurrying along; and then he was elbowing his way through the throng on London Bridge, eager to get back in time.

"That's the worst of music," said Shadrach; "it allus upsets me. Ah! yah! where are you running to, you young dog?" he cried to a boy who, yelling out "I would I were a bird," blundered on to the little man's favourite corn, and made him limp the rest of the way. "Not that sort of music, confound him. Would he was a bird, indeed! Pity he ain't got his neck wrung for him. Ha! ha! ha!" laughed Shadrach, taking a long breath; "how bracing the wind is off the river! why, I do declare if I couldn't over posts or anything to-night."

But there was no room for Shadrach to run or over posts, for the streets were thronged with busy, hurrying people. The roadway was crowded too; and everywhere it was plain to see that Christmas was here. It was quite a blessing that some of the laden railway-vans did not break down, for there would have been an absolute block; while, however it was possible for all the presents on the way to get to their destination in time, no one could say. Shops and people, ay, and weather too, all spoke of Christmas: people looked hearty and genial; the shops looked generous; while, though the weather felt cold, it was not a griping, nipping cold, but a warm, dry cold that made the slush hard and firm, and whispered of blazing fires and brave old English comforts.

God bless it! I love a Christmas-night; and, when I say a Christmas-night, I mean any night in that jovial, happy tide, when men sink the care and money-hunting to spread enjoyment around; when the hand is open, either for a loving, brotherly pressure, or to aid a poorer brother; or, better still, the fatherless and the widow. The hand open? ay, and the heart too; for there seems to be breathed around a spirit that softens the hard crust, so that it

15

is open to any emotion, be it such as begets mirth or tears. Who can say what it is?—that loving, happy exhilaration that comes over us, and makes a man even kiss his mother-in-law roundly. Why, it's the very time to get your salary raised, is Christmas; and now the secret is out, I know I shall never be forgiven by the heads of firms, who will be pounds out of pocket in future. Who ever kicked a dog at Christmas; or prosecuted a thief? who ever gave a beggar a penny without a blush for the smallness of the sum? God bless it! though it comes so soon year after year to tell us how by twelve months our span of life is shorter, and that we are nearer to the long sleep. God bless it! and may its genial breath softly waft the incense from every frugal hearth in our land, and rest in love where the poor prepare their humble feast—ay, feast; for the simplest Christmas dinner is a feast sprinkled by the torch of "Christmas Present." There's something stirring in the very air, and the bells sound as they do at no other time—they go home to the feelings, and call up from the past the happy emotions planted in our hearts by God; but which a busy life and rude contact with the world have caused to flee away and hide. Back they come though, till, in the wild delight, eyes sparkle, cheeks flush, and hands grasp hands in the fulness of heart to give a squeeze often accompanied by a twinkling eye, where a tear will force its way. Holy—sacred—are those reunions—those family meetings; and sad is it when a seat becomes vacant; but is not that loss a bond to bind those left the tighter, as wishing each other "a merry Christmas," as I do, they say—"God bless it!"

Is there such a thing as a kind of magnetism in life by which spirit whispers to spirit, and by some occult warning we know that those we love are near? Or why should old Shadrach start and shiver as he passed some one in the throng, and then mutter to himself very thoughtfully—"Poor Polly!"

But it was a busy night, and what baskets did Shadrach lug about from Gracechurch Street. East, west, north, and south—here, there, and everywhere. Light porter, indeed! why, we won't insult him. But he didn't mind, bless you, though he groaned and grunted under his load of Christmas fruit; and there was something merry to say to every servant lass who lightened his basket. Toast and ale, and egg-flip too, were waiting when eleven o'clock struck, and though Mr Sope wanted to keep open another hour, and Sundry said half an hour, old Teman, the head, said "No! regular hours were the thing, and it was not fair to the young men; and that if the Queen herself came from Buckingham Palace and wanted a pound or two of fruit, she should not have it after the shutters were up."

It would have done your heart good to have seen Shadrach rattle up those shutters, as the boy down stairs held them up to the roller ready for him to take.

"Ter-r-r-r-rattle" went the shutter as he dragged it over the roller, and then "flip-flap-bang," it was in its place. "Ter-r-r-r-rattle" went another, and nearly knocked an old gentleman over, but he only gave a leap, skip, and a jump, and laughed. Two shutters up, and that big, nodding Chinese mandarin with the bare stomach is covered up. "Ter-r-r-rattle," and part of the big China punchbowl covered. "Ter-r-r-rattle," and the whole of it covered. At it again—and the squeezy almond-eyed lady hidden. At it again, nine shutters up. At it again, skipping about as though he had never walked a step that day, but just come fresh out of a lavender-and-clover bed ready for work, after lying by for a rest. "Ter-r-r-r-rattle-bing-bang-bump." He did it that time: knocked the policeman's helmet off, and sent it rolling along the pavement.

"God bless my soul," said Shadrach, aghast at such an assault upon the law of the land, but the policeman only laughed, and old Teman only laughed, and called the bobby up to the door, while he fetched him a glass of egg-flip himself, and wished him "A merry Christmas."

"Bang—slap—slip—flap—crack—jangle—jang—jink jonk—jank!" There they are; the twelve shutters up, and both iron bars; screws rammed in, and all tight; and Shadrach not a bit out of breath. Shop closed, and no Queen to beg for a pound or two of fruit and test old Teman's loyalty, as he ladled out the flip to his dozen men, when, wishing he could have poured his share into his pocket, Shadrach said "Good-night!" and was off homeward.

Plenty of people in the streets yet, but London Bridge seemed empty on the west side when Shadrach reached it, and then stopped at the first recess to look over at the rushing river. A bright, calm, light night, with snow lying here and there in patches; here upon pier or barge, there upon roof, and all glittering in the light of the full moon. Lanthorns here and there where vessels were moored, and lamps in lines upon the distant bridges. Frost laying hold of everything; but warmed with exercise and the genial draught, Shadrach felt not the cold, but knelt gazing over at the hurrying tide, and comparing it, perhaps, with his life. But there was something else upon his mind, something that kept bringing a shadow over him, and kept him from hurrying home.

At length he stepped down, and walked slowly across the bridge towards the Borough; but then, with a strange, thoughtful, undecided step, he crossed over and sauntered back towards the city again; and at last stood leaning once more over the parapet, gazing at the glittering river, till he started, for the clocks began to strike twelve. There were the faint and distant tones, and the sharp, clear sounds of those at hand, mingled with which came the heavy boom of Saint Paul's, till the last stroke had fallen upon his ear, when with a half-shudder of cold, Shadrach once more stepped down and commenced with some display of vigour his homeward walk.

There was scarcely a soul to be seen now upon the bridge, but as he reached the middle recess, Shadrach paused with a strange, tumultuous beating at his heart, for there, in the same position as that in which he had so lately leant, was the figure of a woman, evidently watching the rushing river.

"Could she be meditating self-destruction?" Shadrach thought. "Could he save her? But why should such thoughts come when he had often and often seen women of her class in the same attitude?" he asked himself the question, and could find no answer, except that it was so sad to see a homeless outcast there upon a Christmas-eve.

"Poor thing—poor thing!" muttered Shadrach to himself; and then, going up and speaking in a husky voice: "Had you not better go home, my girl?"

"What?" cried the girl, angrily; "home? There's no home for such as I."

"But the night—the cold—and—ah, my God!—Polly!"

Shadrach had advanced to the girl, and laid his hand upon her shoulder; when, starting, she turned hastily round and confronted him beneath the lamp; a mutual recognition took place, when, with a bitter cry, the girl darted away, while her father staggered and fell, striking his head violently against the granite seat.

But he soon recovered himself, slowly got up, looked hopelessly round at the deserted bridge, and then walked with feeble, uncertain steps in the direction of home.

The old Dutch clock upon the wall had given warning that it was about to strike one; the fire was low, and the candle burned with a long snuff, as Shadrach Pratt and his wife sat beside the fire silent and tearful. There was an open Bible upon his lap, and he had been essaying to read, but the print looked blurred and confused; his voice was husky; and more than one tear had dropped upon the page where it said—"I will arise and go to my father," and again where "his father fell upon his neck and kissed him;" and there was sorrow that night in the humble home.

The candle burned down, quivered in the socket, and then went out; the fire sank together again and again with a musical tinkle, and then ceased to give forth its warmth; but through the two round holes in the shutters the bright moonbeams shone, bathing the couple with their light, as slowly they knelt down, and Shadrach repeated some words, stopping long upon that impressive clause—"As we forgive them that trespass against us."

"And you'll leave the back door unfastened, Mary?" whispered Shadrach.

Mrs Pratt nodded.

"And forget the past if she should come?"

"Ah, me! ah, me! my poor girl!" cried the mother, thoroughly heart-broken, and for the first time since her child forsook her home showing any emotion; "what have we done that we should be her judges?"

The moonbeams shone brightly in as the couple rose, and after listening for a moment at the stair foot, Shadrach walked to the back door, opened it, uttered a cry, and then fell upon his knees; for there, upon the cold snow, with her cheek resting upon the threshold, lay the lost one of the flock—cold, pale, and motionless, but with her hands outstretched, and clasped together, as if praying for forgiveness. Stretched upon the cold snow by the door she had stolen from two years before; lying where she had crept, with trembling hands, and quivering, fevered lips, whispering to herself that she would die there, for she dared ask no entrance.

Need the story be told of that Christmas-day, and of the joy in that poor man's home—of the sick one weeping in her mother's arms—of the welcome given to one the world called lost! I trow not; but let us skip another year, and then stand in the same room, in the same place, and at the same hour, as with a bright light in his humble, ordinary face, Shadrach Pratt, a man not addicted to quoting Scripture, takes his homely wife's hand, and whispers—

"More than over ninety and nine just persons which need no repentance."

## Chapter Five.
## Upon Christmas-Eve.

And I've found that out that it isn't money, nor a well-furnished house, nor clothes that make a man happy, but the possession of a good wife; and it took me ten years to find it out. It took me ten selfish years—years that I had been spending thinking more about myself than anybody else, you know. And all that while I'd got so used to it that I never took any notice of the patience and forbearance and tenderness that was always being shown to me. It's all right, thinks I, and it's me that's master, and I've a right to be served. And that's the case with too many of us: we get married, and are precious proud taking the wife out for a bit; but then come the domestic duties, and mostly a few children, when it's hard work to make both ends meet, and so the poor wife gets lower and lower and lower, till she's a regular slave, while the husband looks on, and never stretches out a hand to save her a bit of trouble.

Well, that's measuring other people's corn by your own bushel, and that's right—that's just what it is: that's my bushel, and allowing for it being a bit battered and knocked about, it's surprising what a correct measure it is, and if ever I use that old measure to try any other man's corn, and I find as it don't do for it, I always feel as if I should like to shake that fellow's hand off, for I know he's a trump and a man worth knowing.

Now, I'm going to tell you how I found it all out, and in finding it all out as I call it, let me tell you I mean principally what a fool I had been for ten long years. I needn't tell you when it was, and Jane there don't care to be too nice about the day—very well, we'll say you do, but never mind now—only it was Christmas-eve, and I come home from work with my hands in my pockets, and a week's wage there too, and when I mounted the stairs and went into our shabby room, there was the wife down in the low rocking-chair, with two of the little ones in her lap, and though her head was partly turned away I could see she was crying, and another time I should have flown at her about it, for I don't mind saying as I was a regular brute to her—not hitting or anything of that sort, you know, but sending hard words such as she's told me since hit harder than blows. But I couldn't fly at her then on account of a strange chap as was there. Shabby, snuffy-looking little fellow, with flue in his hair and pits in his chin, where he couldn't shave into, so that, what with his face not being over well washed, and his old black clothes looking greasy, he didn't seem the sort of visitor as you'd care about having in your place, because, though I came home dirty with my trade, I always set that down as clean dirt, and don't mind it.

"Well, what's for you?" I says, precious gruff.

"Two pun fifteen and ninepence, with costs," he says, bringing out a paper; and then you might have knocked me down with it, for I knew it was for rent. There'd been a bother about it several times, and no wonder, and as I'd promised again and again, and never kept my word, as I should have done, why this was come on me, and there was a man in possession.

There was only one thing to be done, and of course that I does at once; goes over the way to the landlord, and when I got into his room I began to bluster a bit.

"It's a deal too bad," I says.

"Have you brought the money, my man?" he says.

"No, I ain't," I says, "and I thinks—"

"Now, look here, Roberts," he says, quite quietly, and holding up his finger, "You're not the sort of tenant I want. You're no credit to the place. If you had been a decent fellow, struggling against the world, and you owed me twice as much, and I saw you meant to pay, why I'd never have put in the bailiffs; but when I see a man going on as you do, why I say if you've money to waste you can pay your rent. Sorry for your wife, but if you can't pay the money now, there's the door. I'm not going to be annoyed in my own place."

He wasn't a big man, but he took me down twenty pegs in a minute in his cool, easy way, and before I knew where I was I'd backed out, and was going across the street, when I recollects the man sitting there at home, and of a Christmas-eve too, and I slowly went back and sent in a message to landlord, and directly after I stood before him again, and after no end of a hard fight he consented to let a pound stop on, and send the man off if I'd pay down one pound fifteen and ninepence.

Well, I thought a minute, and hesitated, and thought again, and then recollected the dirty, snuffy fellow there, and that settled me, so that I paid down the money, took my receipt, and a note to the man, and directly after I was standing in my own place, with that chap gone, and only threepence left of my six-and-thirty shillings for a Christmas dinner; and now it came upon me hot and strong why it was that I stood there like that, and as I saw it all so plain I set my teeth and brought my fist down upon the table in a way as made the candlestick jump, and sent the children trembling up to their mother.

"It's because nobody ever said to me, 'Sam Roberts, what'll you take to eat?'" And then I banged my fist on the table again, and began walking up and down the room.

Nobody spoke to me, but the wife got the children off quietly to bed, and at last, when I was still striding up and down, I felt her hand on my shoulder, and she whispered quite low like—

"Don't mind it, dear."

"But I do," I said, quite fierce and loud, and the poor thing stole away from me again, and though I didn't look at her, I knew she wasn't able to keep the tears back, and that I'd been the cause again.

I took no notice then though, for something was working in me, and at last I told her to go to bed, and she did, while I sat before the bit of fire in the room and thought it over.

Now don't laugh at me when I tell you that I believe in bells, but I can't help it if you do, for they always seem to speak to me like music does, and if there's ever anything will act on me it's the sound of a peal of bells. It was bitter cold that night, and yet I didn't feel it; the wind howled along the street, and I could now and then hear the great flakes of snow come softly patting at the window, and then the sashes would shake, and the wind rumble in the chimney, while every now and then came the sound of the bells, not bright and joyful, but sad and sobbing and mournful. I knew it was a merry, rejoicing time with every one else. I could not attend to that, for I was gradually getting to see one thing that I kept on fighting against, and that was, what a fool I had been.

Fight against it I did, but it was no use, for as the streets got more quiet, and the wind sunk, the bells rang out clearer and clearer, and seemed to keep telling me of it. Now I knew of it by the threepence in my pocket; now it was by the shabby floor; then the beggarly furniture and the miserable fire; and though I didn't cross the room I had it in my mind's eye, and there it all was written plain enough in my wife's face.

And yet I wouldn't own to it, though the bells seemed to be speaking to me, and rang out plainer and plainer all my waste and carelessness, till all at once they stopped for a minute; when one big bell began to toll slowly, "boom, boom, boom"; and that did it, for the next moment I gave a wild sort of cry, and was down on my knees with my hands over my face, and the big tears, hot and blinding, bursting out from between my fingers. But the tears might blind, they could not hide that, though every one seemed like hot lead. They could not hide what I then saw, for the bell still went on, now swept away in the distance, now coming nearer and nearer, till it filled the room, and made the very place seem to tremble and quiver, as did every nerve in my body.

No; the tears could not hide that scene as the tolling bell brought up, and there I could see the snow upon the ground, and two mourners following a little coffin through the street of a country-town with their footmarks left black in the pathway, as though even they were marks of the funeral. And there, too, was the church, and the grey-haired clergyman meeting us at the gate, and me hard, bitter, and sullen, seeing it all unmoved, and listening to the words as came now to my ears borne upon the bells. There, too, was the little grave, and the earth thrown out all black round it, and every spade-full of earth, too, black, just as though everything was in mourning for the little flower as the bitter winter had nipped. Yes; there it all was, with the poor wife sinking down at last upon her knees beside the open grave, and letting a few of a mother's tears fall silently upon the little plain, white coffin, and me—hard, bitter, and cold.

"Boom, boom, boom"—how it all came back, and how I saw it all now. How plain it all was that I had been a fool and my own enemy, and ready to blame every one but myself for my ill success; and at last muttering "pardon, pardon," I held up my hands, and then started to my feet, for the bells had stopped, and my hands were taken by some one there in the dark, so that I trembled; till I heard my name whispered, and this time I did not turn from the offered comfort.

Just then out rang the bells again, bright, cheerful, and merry; and, though I listened attentively, and tried to make them go with my thoughts, they seemed now quite to have left me to myself.

And then, without thinking of the bitter night, or our poverty, or what we should do for a Christmas dinner, we sat there together wrapped up in one idea, and that was that there was a change come over me, for somehow I felt quite a different man; and, though no word was spoken, we seemed to understand one another, and that was quite enough for us.

All at once I turns to the wife, and I says, "I don't know what's come over me, lass; feelings have got the better of me; I'm almost choking." And then we both started up, for it seemed hot, and close, and heavy in the room.

"Why, it's fire somewhere," I says, and then I turned all over hot and trembling, and the wet stood upon my forehead, for I thought the place below was on fire, and we on the second floor with three children.

I ran to the window and opened it, and just then there was the rattle of a policeman going, and first one voice and then another shouting, "Fire!" while directly after there was a tremendous noise as shook the house from top to bottom, and made the plaster off the ceiling come rattling down on our heads, while the shop-front seemed to be blown out. Then there came another crashing explosion, and that was the jingling noise and falling of window-glass upon the pavement; and then came screaming and crying out, the sounds of people running and kicking at doors, shouting cries for help, and a hundred people outside shrieking, "Fire!"

For a minute I stood with my hands to my head, as though it was all a dream. I felt lost, and could not tell what to do, but the next moment I had two of the children in my arms; and, shouting to the wife, "Slip on a few things!" I tore open the door and darted down the stairs through the heat and smoke to the first-floor, where the rush of flame and smoke almost drove me back; but I knew it was for life, and I dashed down the rest of the way along the passage, and then fell staggering down with my load upon the pavement.

They had us up, though, in a moment, blackened, scorched, half suffocated, and smarting; and then, after casting one look up at our window, where the wife stood with one little one in her arms, I ran towards the blazing passage, but a policeman and two men had hold of me in a moment.

"Hold back, man!" said one of 'em; "it's madness to try it."

"Certain death," says another.

"Yes, if you don't let go!" I roared, feeling as furious as a wild beast at being held back. "Let go; I tell you they'll be burnt to death if I don't save them;" and then I fought with 'em to get away, but they were too strong for me; and, more coming to help, I could do nothing.

"Pray, let me go," I cried at last, quite pitifully, for I could hear shrieks for help from up above, and felt that some one would think I had taken care of myself and left her to perish; and then, what with the shrieks and the thoughts, I felt almost mad, and strove and plunged so, that I got free and dashed at the door where the flames came pouring out.

I believe that I should have rushed in, but at that moment there was another loud explosion, and I seemed to be lifted off my feet, and thrown back into the road, where I lay quite helpless and half-stunned for a few moments. But I soon came to again, just as they were going to carry me through the crowd, and begging of them not to take me away, I got them to let me stop, for the men wanted to see what was going on; for now the flames were mounting up higher and higher, and rushing out of the first-floor windows, while that one under where my poor wife stood shrieking for help was glowing with light, and I knew the fire would burst out there directly.

The gunpowder canisters in the shop as they exploded had all helped to make the fire burn more rapidly, and before the first engine came, the place was blazing furiously, while, instead of trying anything to save her who stood at the window, people did nothing but shriek and scream and wring their hands. I soon saw, unless something was done the fire would get the better of us, while in spite of all I could think of, there seemed no way to save her who stood crying there for the help we could not give—nothing but for her to jump out. I ran about through the crowd here and there, calling to the people to save her, and for the time quite mad and frantic that I could not get at her, when all at once there was a loud shout and cheer, and the people gave way, as along at full speed came the tall fire-escape.

I ran to help drag it along, and in a few moments they had it leaning beneath the window, but it was too short, and I groaned again, for it seemed only brought to raise our hopes, and then dash them down; but the next moment the fly ladder was pulled up by ropes, and before any one could stay me, I tried to get up.

But the escape man was before me, and up and up he went, till there came a fierce burst of flame and smoke right upon him and beat him back, so that he crept down again, till he reached where I was coming up, and then I got past him and past the flames where the escape was quite on fire, and then up to the window where my wife stood clutching the child, and leaned half-fainting from the window.

It was a hard matter to reach to them, but I got one foot upon the sill, dashed out a pane of glass to get a hold of the sash for my hand, and then began to wonder how I could save them, when I heard a cry from below and a regular yell of shrieks as the light escape ladder was burned through and fell to the ground, so that it was only by an effort I saved myself from felling; but I crept inside the room with a horrid sensation upon me, for I felt that our last hour was come, and a frightful one it was.

The wife just turned her horrified face to me once, and then fainted, while I could see but little of what was going on below, on account of the rising flame and smoke, and as to the heat it was awful—so stifling, that I was glad to hold out the heads of them with me, for the smoke came rolling through the door.

I knew that in a few minutes we must be burned to death, and how awful those thoughts were that came upon me is more than I can describe, and yet in spite of all there seemed a calmness, even when I heard a crackling behind me, and saw the flickering light playing through the smoke behind as the flames were creeping into the room.

Just then I heard a shouting below, and some one to the left cried to me. I looked up and found there were two men at the third-floor window of the next house, and one of them shouted:—

"Put her down and try and catch this," and then he began swinging a rope towards me till I got hold of it; and without waiting for instructions made it fast round the wife's waist, helped her out of the window, and held on till they had the rope tight, and shouted to me, when I left go, and saw her go clear of the flame and smoke with such a fearful swing that I felt sure they would let go, and I shrunk back, for I dared not look.

Before a minute was over I heard them shout again, and then I looked out trembling, and caught at the rope again two or three times before I could get it, for it was a hard matter to get it swung far enough. But I had it at last, and pulled in as much as they could spare, so as to tie it round the little child somewhere about the middle, when they saw me make a sign, for I could not shout, I was that choked, and then they hauled in while I kept hold too, so as to keep the little thing from swinging down so fearfully.

It was a good long rope, and even when they had the little one safe there was enough left for me to fasten it with a half hitch round my waist and climb out and hang by the window-sill till they were ready, for the room was burning, and the flames came over me, quite scorching my hands, so that in another few minutes I must have dropped. But the rope tightened, and I left go, swinging through the air right clear of the smoke and flame; and then I felt myself dragged up and in at the window, but I did not see or hear anything more for some little time.

It was a shocking fire, certainly, but it's when people are at the worst that they find out how neighbourly those around could be, for we found them as took us in; and in spite of being so frightened and scorched, after two or three hours' sleep we did not feel so bad but we could put on the things that were lent us, and I can't help thinking that we should have given thanks somewhere else for our escape besides in our bedroom, if it had not been for our burnt-off hair.

And in spite of all loss and care, that was a pleasant Christmas-day we spent, where everybody seemed as if they could not make enough of us; and, at the same time, there was a feeling in my heart that seemed to cheer me and make me look hopefully to the future. For the clothes and furniture that we had lost were none to be so proud of—rather different to what we now have round us, and when I tell the wife so, I get a pleasant smile, for she says there's light behind every cloud.

## Chapter Six.
## Haunted by Spirits.

"But what an out-of-the-way place to get to," I said, after being most cordially received by my old school fellow and his wife, one bitter night after a long ride. "But you really are glad to see me, eh?"

"Now, hold your tongue, do," cried Ned and his wife in a breath. "You won't get away again under a month, so don't think it. But where we are going to put you I don't know," said Ned.

"Oh I can sleep anywhere, chairs, table, anything you like; only make me welcome. Fine old house this seems, but however came you to take it?"

"Got it cheap, my boy. Been shut up for twenty years. It's haunted, and no one will live in it. But I have it full for this Christmas, at all events, and what's more I have some potent spirits in the place too, but they are all corked down tightly, so there is no fear at present. But I say, Lilly," cried Ned, addressing his wife, "why we shall have to go into the haunted room and give him our place."

"That you won't," I said. "I came down here on purpose to take you by surprise, and to beg for a snack of dinner on Christmas-day; and now you are going to give me about the greatest treat possible, a bed in a haunted room. What kind of a ghost is it?"

"You mustn't laugh," said Ned, trying to appear very serious; "for there is not a soul living within ten miles of this place, that would not give you a long account of the horrors of the Red Chamber: of spots of blood upon the bedclothes coming down in a regular rain; noises; clashing of swords; shrieks and groans; skeletons or transparent bodies. Oh, my dear fellow, you needn't grin, for it's all gospel truth about here, and if we did not keep that room screwed up, not a servant would stay in the house."

"Wish I could buy it and take it away," I said.

"I wish you could, indeed," cried Ned, cordially.

Half an hour after Ned and I were busy with screwdriver and candle busy in the large corridors, turning the rusty screws which held a large door at the extreme end of the house. First one and then another was twirled out till nothing held the door but the lock; the key for which Ned Harrington now produced from his pocket—an old, many-warded, rusty key, at least a couple of hundred years old.

"Hold the candle a little lower," said Ned, "here's something in the keyhole," when pulling out his knife, he picked out a quantity of paper, evidently very recently stuffed in. He then inserted the key, and after a good deal of effort it turned, and the lock shot back with a harsh, grating noise. Ned then tried the handle, but the door remained fast; and though he tugged and tugged, it still stuck, till I put one hand to help him, when our united efforts made it come open with a rush, knocking over the candle, and there we were standing upon the portal of the haunted room in the dark.

"I'll fetch a light in a moment out of the hall," said Ned, and he slipped off, while I must confess to a certain feeling of trepidation on being left alone, listening to a moaning, whistling noise, which I knew to be the wind, but which had all the same a most dismal effect upon my nerves, which, in spite of my eagerness to be the inmate of the closed room, began to whisper very strongly that they did not like it at all. But the next minute Ned was beside me with the light, and we entered the gloomy dusty old chamber—a bed-chamber furnished after the fashion of the past century. The great four-post bedstead looked heavy and gloomy, and when we drew back the curtains, I half expected to see a body lying in state, but no, all was very dusty, very gloomy, and soul chilling, but nothing more.

"Come, there's plenty of room for a roaring fire," said Ned, "and I think after all we had better come here ourselves, and let you have our room."

"That you will not," I said, determinedly. "Order them to light a fire, and have some well-aired things put upon that bed, and it will be a clever ghost that wakes me to-night, for I'm as tired as a dog."

"Here, Mary," shouted Ned to one of the maids, "coals and wood here, and a broom."

We waited about, peering here and there at the old toilet-ware and stands, the old chest of drawers and armoire, old chairs and paintings, for all seemed as if the room had been suddenly quitted; while inside a huge cupboard beside the fireplace hung a dusty horseman's cloak, and in the corner were a long thin rapier and a quaint old-fashioned firelock.

"Strikes chilly and damp," said I, snuffing the smell of old boots and fine dust.

"Ah, but we'll soon drive that out," said Ned. "But you'd better give in, my boy. 'Pon my word, I'm ashamed to let you come in here."

"Pooh! nonsense!" I said. "Give me a roaring fire, and that's all I want."

"Ah!" cried Ned. "But what a while that girl is;" and then he stepped out into the passage. "Why, what are you standing there for?" he cried. "Come and light this fire."

"Plee', sir, I dussent," said the maid.

"Here, give me hold," cried Ned, in a pet; "and send your mistress here;" and then he made his appearance with a coal-scuttle, paper, and wood; when between us we soon had a fire alight and roaring up the huge chimney, while the bright flames flickered and danced, and gave quite a cheerful aspect to the place.

"Well," cried Mrs Harrington, who now appeared, "how are you getting on?" but neither Ned's wife nor her sister stood looking, for, in spite of all protestations, dressed as they were, they set to sweeping, dusting, airing linen, bed, mattress, etcetera, we helping to the best of our ability—for no maid, either by threats or persuasion, would enter the place—and at last we made the place look, if not comfortable, at all events less dismal than before we entered. The old blinds came down like so much tinder when touched, while, as to the curtains, the first attempt to draw them brought down such a cloud of dust, that they were left alone, though Mrs Harrington promised that the place should be thoroughly seen to in the morning.

Returning to the drawing-room, the remainder of the evening was most agreeably spent; while the cause of my host and hostess's prolonged absence produced endless comments and anecdotes respecting the Red Chamber—some of them being so encouraging in their nature that Ned Harrington, out of sheer compassion, changed the conversation.

"Well, my boy," said Ned, when the ladies had all retired for the night, "you shan't go to bed till the witching hour is past;" so he kept me chatting over old times, till the clock had gone one—the big old turret-clock, whose notes flew booming away upon the frosty air. "Christmas-eve to-morrow, so we'll have a tramp on the moors after the wild ducks—plenty out here. I say, my boy, I believe this is the original Moated Grange, so don't be alarmed if you hear the mice."

"There's only one thing I care for," I said, "and that is anything in the shape of a practical joke."

"Honour bright! my boy," said Ned; "you need fear nothing of that kind;" and then I was alone in the Haunted Chamber, having locked myself in.

My first proceeding was to give the large fire an extra poke, which sent a flood of light across the room, and the flames gushing up the chimney; my next, to take one of the candles and make a tour of my bedroom, during which I looked under the bed, behind the curtains, and into armoire and cupboard, but discovered nothing. Next thing I tried the

23

windows, through which I could just dimly see the snow-white country, but they were fast and blackened with dirt. The chimney-glass, too, was so injured by damp, that the dim reflection given back was something startling, being more like a bad photograph of life-size than anything else; and at length, having fully made up my mind that I was alone, and that, as far as I could make out, there were neither trap-doors nor secret passages in the wall, I undressed, put out the candles, and plunged into bed.

But I was wrong in what I had said to my host about sleeping, for I never felt more wakeful in my life. I watched the blaze of the fire sink down to a ruddy glow, the glow turn blacker and blacker till at last the fire was all but extinct, while the room was dark as could be. But my eyesight was painfully acute, while my hearing seemed strained to catch the slightest passing sound. The wind roared and rumbled in the great chimney, and swept sighing past the windows; and, though it had a strange, wild sound with it, yet I had heard the wind before, and therefore paid but little heed to its moans.

All at once the fire seemed to fall together with a tinkling sound, a bright flame leaped up, illumining the room for a moment, then becoming extinct, and leaving all in darkness; but there was light for a long enough interval for me to see, or fancy I saw, the cupboard door open and the great horseman's cloak stand out in a weird-like manner before me, as though covering the shoulders of some invisible figure.

I felt warm—then hot—then in a profuse perspiration, but I told myself it was fancy, punched my pillow, and turned over upon the other side to sleep. Now came a long, low, dreary moan, hollow and heartrending, for it seemed like the cry of some one in distress; when I raised myself upon one elbow and listened.

"Old cowl on a chimney," I muttered, letting myself fall back again, now thoroughly determined to sleep, but the moaning continued, the wind whistled and howled, while now came a gentle tap, tap, tapping at my window, as if some one was signalling to be admitted.

"Tap, tap, tap;" still it kept on, as though whoever tapped was fearful of making too much noise; and at length, nerving myself, I slipped out of bed, crossed the room, and found that the closet door was open, but a vigorous poke inside produced nothing but dust and two or three very sharp sneezes. So I fastened the door, and listened. All silent: but the next moment began the tapping upon the dirty window-pane again; and, impelled by a mingled sensation of fear and attraction, I crept closer to the sash, and at length made out the shadow of something tapping at the glass.

"Bah! Bah!" I exclaimed the next moment as I shuffled across the room and back to my bed, "strand of ivy and the wind." But I was not to be at peace yet, for now there came a most unmistakable noise behind the wainscot—louder and louder, as if some one were trying to tear a piece of the woodwork down. The place chosen seemed to be the corner beside the cupboard; and at last, having made up my mind that it was the rats, I dropped off to sleep, and slept soundly till morning, when I heard the cheery voice of my host at the door.

"Oh, all right," he said as I answered; "I only came because the girl knocked, and said that something must be the matter, for she could not make you hear."

On descending to breakfast, I found that I was to undergo a rigorous cross-examination as to what I had seen and heard; but one elderly lady present shook her head ominously, freely giving it as her opinion that it was little better than sacrilege to open the haunted chamber, and finishing a very solemn peroration with the words—

"Stop a bit; they don't walk every night."

This was encouraging, certainly; but in the course of the afternoon I went up to my room, and found that it had been well cleaned out, while many little modern appliances had been added to the dingy furniture, so that it wore quite a brightened appearance. The insides of the windows had been cleaned, and a man was then upon a ladder polishing away at the exterior, when I drew his attention to a number of loose ivy strands, which he cut off.

In the cupboard I found plenty of traces of rats in the shape of long-gnawed-off fragments of wood pushed beneath the skirting-board; while, upon holding my head against the chimney, the groaning of the cowl was plainly to be heard, as it swung round dolefully upon some neighbouring chimney.

A pleasant day was spent, and then, after a cosy evening, I was once more ushered into the chamber of horrors, this time being escorted by the whole of the visitors, the gentlemen affectionately bidding me farewell, but not one seeming disposed to accept my offer of changing rooms. However, Ned and Mrs Harrington both wished me to go to their room, when I of course refused; and once more I was alone.

It was now about half-past twelve and Christmas-morning, a regular storm was hurrying round the house, and a strange feeling of crepitation came upon me when I had extinguished the light; and then on climbing into bed I sat and listened for a while, laid my head upon my pillow, and the next moment, or what seemed the next moment, I was startled by a strange beating sound, and as I became aware of a dim, peculiar light, penetrating the room, I heard a low, muffled voice cry appealingly—

"Your hot water, sir—quarter to eight!" while I could hardly believe my eyes had been closed.

Christmas-day passed as it generally does in the country, that is to say, in a most jovial, sociable way; and after fun, frolic, sport, pastime, forfeit, dance, and cards, I stood once more within the haunted chamber with the strange sensation upon me, that though I had met with nothing so far to alarm me—this night, a night when, of all nights in the year, spirits might be expected to break loose, I was to suffer for my temerity.

As soon as I entered and secured the door, I felt that something was wrong, but I roused up the fire, lit the wax candles upon the dressing-table, and then looked round the room.

Apparently I was alone, but upon opening the big closet door, the great cloak fell down with a ghostly rustle, while a peculiar odour seemed to rise from the heap. The long, thin sword too, fell, with a strange clanging noise as I hastily closed the door, and then setting down the candle tried to compose myself to look at matters in a calm, philosophical manner. But things would not be looked at in that way, and now I began to feel that I was being punished for all, since the next moment I could see the eyes of the large portrait between the windows gleam and roll, now showing the whites, now seeming to pierce me, so intense was their gaze. Then the figure seemed to be slowly coming down from the frame nearer and nearer, till it was close to me, when it slowly receded, and a shade passed over the canvas, so that it was gone.

But for shame and the fear of ridicule, I should have opened the door and cried for aid; in fact, I believe I did rise from the chair and try to reach the door, but some invisible power drew me into a corner of the room, where I leaned panting against the wall to gaze upon a fresh phenomenon. I had brought a chamber candlestick into the room, and after igniting the pair of candles upon the toilet table, placed the flat candlestick between them, and left it alight, but now—no—yes—I rubbed my eyes—there was no mistake.

*There were six candles burning.*

I started, shook myself, muttering that it was deception; but no, there burned six candles, while their flames were big and blurred with a large, ghastly, blue halo round each, that had a strange weird light; and now I tried to recall what I had read in old ghost stories about corpse candles, for I felt that these three must be of that character.

In an agony of fear I tried to run up to the dressing-table to dash the weird lights over, but again the same strange influence guided my steps, so that I curved off to the bed, where I sat down, trembling in every limb—limbs that refused their office—while I gazed upon the candles which now began to float backwards and forwards before me, till I could bear the strange sight no more, and throwing myself back, I buried my face in the bed.

But there was no relief here, for as I threw myself down at full length, the great bedstead gave a crack, a rattle, and a bound, and then in an agony of dread I was clinging to the bedding, for the huge structure began to rise slowly higher—higher—higher—sailing away apparently upon the wings of the wind, and then again sinking lower and lower and lower to interminable depths, so that I involuntarily groaned and closed my eyes. But that was of no avail, for I could feel the great bedstead career, now on one side, now on the other, and ever going onward through space like some vessel upon a vast aerial sea.

The rapid gliding upward, in spite of the dread, seemed attended with somewhat of an exhilarating effect; but the falling was hideous in the extreme—for now it was slowly and gently, but the next moment the speed was fearful, and I lay trembling in expectation of feeling the structure dash upon the ground, while every time I unclosed my eyes I could see the gyrating candles, and turned giddy with confusion.

And now, with one tremendously swift gliding swoop, away we went, faster and faster, more rapidly than swallows upon the wing. Space seemed obliterated; and, by the rushing noise and singing in my ears, I could feel that the bedstead was careering on where the atmosphere was growing more and more attenuated, while soon, from the catching of my breath, I felt sure that we should soon be beyond air altogether. The candles were gone, but there were stars innumerable, past which we sped with inconceivable rapidity, so that their light seemed continued in one long luminous streak, while ever more and more the speed was increasing, till it seemed that we were attached to some mighty cord, and being whirled round and round with frightful velocity, as if at the end of the string; and now I trembled for the moment when the cord should be loosed, and we should fly off into illimitable space, to go on—on—on for ever!

At last it came, and away I went; but now separated from the bedstead, to which I had clung to the last. On—on—on, with something large and undefined in front of me, which I felt that I should strike, though I was powerless to prevent the collision. Nearer—nearer—nearer, but ever darting along like a shooting-star in its course, I was swept on, till, with a fearful crash, I struck what I now found to be the lost bed, and tried to cling to it once more; but, no! I rolled off, and fell slowly and gradually lower—lower, and evidently out of the sphere of the former attraction, so that at last I fell, with only a moderate bump, upon the floor, when, hastily rising, I found all totally dark, and that the bedpost was beside me; when, shudderingly dragging off some of the clothes on to the carpet, I rolled myself in them, and went off into a heavy sleep.

The next morning several of my friends made remarks upon my pale and anxious looks; and soon after breakfast, Ned beckoned me into his study, and begged of me to tell him whether I had been disturbed.

For a few minutes I felt that I could not tell of the horrors of the past night, even though I had vowed to sleep in the haunted room still; but at last I began my recital, and had arrived at the point where the bedstead set sail, when Ned jumped up, crying:

"Why, I thought from your looks that you really had been disturbed. But I say, old boy, I suppose we must look over it, as it's Christmas; but, do you know, judging by my own feelings, I think I'd better make the punch rather less potent to-night."

"Well, really," I said, "I think so too."

"Do you?" said Ned.

"Oh, yes," I said, "for my head aches awfully;" and no wonder, seeing how it had been Haunted by Spirits!

## Chapter Seven.
### On the Down Line.

I couldn't stop indoors, for I couldn't bear to see them all. The children didn't seem to mind it so much, for they ran about and played, and their little hearts were light; but there was some one sitting by the wretched little fire, looking that pale and worn and miserable, that it went quite to one's heart.

Christmas-morning, with the bright sun shining in through the dirty windows, while from everywhere the rays went flashing as they lighted upon the frost, rime, or snow. Such of the blue sky as we could see from our court, was as bright and clear a blue as could be seen out in the country, while the pavement looked dry, and you could hear the snow crunch under the people's feet. But there was no brightness with us, and at last I went out, for I couldn't stop indoors.

Was it my fault? I kept asking myself; had I tried hard enough to get took on again; or ought we to have been more saving when I had a situation? Ah! I asked myself all this again and again as I went out, leaving them at home in a regular state of beggary; for we had come down to the last shilling.

I've always noticed as poor men keep their hands in their pockets; and I did mine that sharp, cold morning, and went sauntering along the streets, wondering what it would all come to, and how we were to manage. There was every one I met looking cheerful and bright; here and there shops a little way open, just as if they were winking at you, because they were so full of all sorts of good things; people were going in and coming out with loaded baskets; while, when I got near the baker's, it was enough to make a hungry man savage to see the stream of people, with their happy, jolly faces, bearing in geese, turkeys, and great fat mottled pieces of beef; and all looking as though there wasn't such a thing as poverty.

Everybody seemed in a hurry, and every face seemed twinkling and bright with the thoughts of good things to come, till at last, from feeling low and miserable, I got to be reckless and savage, and felt as if I should have liked to have had it out with the world there on the spot.

Every one you met in the big streets was like nature that morning—dressed in the best clothes; some bound for church, some out visiting; and do what I would, I couldn't find one face that looked miserable. There were the cabs and carriages rattling along; 'buses loaded; the bells ringing merrily; while there seemed to be a something in the air that made you feel bright in spite of yourself; and after being savage for an hour and a half, I seemed to catch the infection from the people about, and more than once I caught myself going to whistle.

But the thoughts of what I'd left at home made me stop short, with my face all screwed up, and from going to one extreme I got to another; and at last, ready to break down, I found myself sitting on the stone-setting of the railings of one of the West End churches.

Beadle comes out after a bit and has a look at me, as much as to say, "Are you a beggar, or ain't you?" but he never says nothing; and after a bit he goes in again. Policeman comes by beating his white gloves together, and he looks very suspiciously at me, as if he couldn't quite make up his mind; and then he goes on, and says nothing. And there I sat in the cold, feeling nothing but the misery gripping at my heart, and at last, seeing nothing but a pale worn face in a bare room, where a troop of hungry children were wanting bread.

Sounds strange that, and some may think it stretched. But let them climb some of the dirty stairs at the East end, and they can find such sights any day and every day.

No; I could see nothing then, but the place we called home; and I might have sat there till I froze, if all at once something that seemed almost like a vision had not come before me; for as I sat there with my head upon my hands, there came a light touch, and looking up, there stood a little bright-eyed, golden-haired child before me, her beautiful cheeks ruddy with the keen air, while a tiny bright tear was in each eye, as with a pitying look she pushed a penny into my hand; when I was so utterly took aback, that her bright scarlet cloak was some distance off as she tripped along beside a tall stately lady, before I could recover myself.

That did it. It seemed to bear down pride, anger, everything, and taking me so suddenly, I couldn't bear it, but there in that open street my head went down again upon my hands, and in the hopeless misery of my heart I cried like a child.

But only for a minute, when I jumped up and hurried along the street, to catch one more sight of the bright pitying little angel; but she was gone, and at last, making sure that she had gone into one of the houses, I walked slowly back to the churchyard.

When I got there the people were beginning to come out of the big church: carriages were drawing up; from out of the open doors there came the rolling sound of the organ; and as I stood there against the railings, watching the happy-looking crowd, it seemed to me that I must be a sort of impostor, for to see how folks were dressed there couldn't be such a thing as misery in the world.

All at once I started, and took hold of the railing, for I heard a voice that put me in mind of the time when I was started from the Great Central line. Just in front of me, and coming towards a carriage that a lad held open, were a lady and gentleman dressed tip-top, and he was laughing and chatting to her. But I only just saw that she was very handsome, for I was watching the gentleman's eyes—bright, piercing blue eyes, such as you seldom see; and in a regular state of muddle in my own mind, and wondering about where those eyes had come across me before, I leaned forward right in the way, staring fixed-like at him.

"Stand back, my good fellow," he says, and then, just as the lady lightly stepped into the carriage, he stops short, fixes those eyes of his on to mine, and then, with his hand playing with his big brown moustache, he burst out laughing, when I knew him in a moment. It *was* him; and as I thought of the misery of the past year that he had caused, something seemed to rise up in me, and for a moment I felt as if I could have knocked him down. But the clenching of my fist made me feel that penny, and that brought up another face, when turning dejected once more, I turned aside, saying—

"Ah! it's fun for you, but pretty nigh death for me;" but before I'd got two steps off, he had his hand on my shabby blackened moleskin jacket, and he says—

"Gently, my friend, I must introduce you;" and before I knew what he was about, he had me at the door of the carriage, and he says—"Look, Marian, here's our honest charioteer, the Vulcan who drove us down to Moreton;" and then he whispered something that made the lady smile, and a bright colour come all over her handsome face. "Do you drive the mail now?" he says, turning to me.

"*Never* touched a handle since, sir," I says. "They had me afore the board two mornings after, and discharged me." And then the thoughts of it all seemed too much for me, and I turned husky and choky, and couldn't speak for a minute, when I says, with a sort of gulp:—

"Can't help it, sir; I've been werry hard drove since—wife—children—" and then I choked again as I shunted off what I was saying.

"Stand back a bit," says the gentleman to his servant, and then, in so kind and gentle a way, he says to me—"Why, my poor fellow, I wouldn't have had this happen on any account;" and then I saw a tear or two in his lady's beautiful eyes, and they both stopped talking to me a good quarter of an hour, free as could be, telling me that they had me to thank for much happiness, as theirs was a runaway match. And at last, when they drove off, nodding and smiling at me, I had the gentleman's card, so as to call on him next morning, when he said his father, being a railway director, I should be took on the line at once; and, what was more to the purpose then, there were five sovereigns in my hand.

I didn't know what to do, whether to laugh or cry; and I'm sure I must have looked like a madman as I tore through the streets, and rushed upstairs into our room, when the first thing I did was to scrape up every bit of coal at the bottom of the cupboard and put it a-top of the fire.

"Lay the cloth, my lass," I says, seizing a dish; "and, Lord bless you, look alive!" The children stared, and then laughed and clapped their hands, while I rushed out to the cook's shop in the lane, looking like a wolf.

There was a roast goose just up, and cissing away in the big pewter dish all amongst the gravy, with the stuffing a smelling that rich, it was enough to drive you mad.

Just as I slipped into the door, the waiter—red-nosed chap—with a dirty white wisp of a handkercher round his neck, looking like a seedy undertaker—the waiter says: "Two goose—apple sauce—and taters;" and the master sticks his fork into the buzzum, and makes a cut as sent the stuffing all out of a gush.

"Hold hard," I says, "that's mine;" and ketching hold of one leg, before he knew what I was up to, it was on my dish. "Now then, ladle on that gravy," I says, "and let's have the setrers;" and saying that, I dabs a sovrin down on the edge of the pewter.

I think they were going to send out for a policeman, but the sight of that little bit of metal settled it, and five minutes after I was carrying the change—not much of it neither— the goose under a cover, and the waiter following behind with a tray, with vegetables, sauce, and aside the great wedge of pudding, a pot of half-and-half.

When the waiter had gone out of the room, and the little ones were hooraying and tapping with their knives, I got to the top of the table, the wife went to the bottom, and I began to say grace, when our eyes met, she ran to me, and then for a good ten minutes she was a sobbing in my arms; while I—there; that's private, and I think I've confessed enough.

There; I don't care whose it was, or where it was, all I know is this, that there wasn't such a dinner eaten or enjoyed anywhere that day throughout the length and breadth of our old country; and though sometimes it was hard to see where I stuck the fork, or cut with the knife, I was smiling all the time. As for the wife, she would keep breaking down till I shouted at her, when she went at it and helped me keep the young ones going; and at last of all I'd have taken a shilling for what was left of the goose, and whoever bought it wouldn't have been the best off in the bargain.

The very next week I was took on the London, Highshare, and Ploughshare railway, and that through the gent who got me discharged from the Great Central, which happened this way.

The Christmas-Eve afore what I've told you was one of those yaller, smoky, foggy times, when trains are all later than they should be, even worse than might be expected at Christmas-time. The lamps were burning in the booking offices all day, while the steam hung like a cloud in the roof of the terminus. I was sitting in the engine-shed on our horse—steam-horse you know—waiting to run the mail down to the north, when Ben Davis, my stoker, says:

"There they goes again, 'bang, bang,' I wonder what it's cost the company to-day in fog signals;" and then as I didn't say nothing, he says, "Ah! this is just such a night as it was four years agone, when poor Tom Harris was cut up the night afore the pitch in,"—smash you know. "Poor Tom; he knowed it was a-comin' to that, and he told me all about it; for I stoked him."

Just then time was up, and all hot and hissing, I runs out to the switches, and comes back on to the down line, where we were coupled on to the train, when Ben goes on: "Poor chap; he'd been outer sorts for some time, and I do think he took more than he should; but one way and another, he was horribly low-spirited, and would quite upset you with the way he'd talk. The last night as I stoked him, he got telling me his reg'lar tale, about a run down he had, and one as he had never forgotten about, being on full swing in a terribly dark foggy night, he heard a whistle, and looking back he could see a train coming on at an awful rate just behind him, when of course he put on more steam. But that didn't seem no good; for coming round the curve, he could see the train closing up fast; and at last, when half mad with fear, and ready to jump off, he saw that the train was on the up line, and the next minute it was alongside his; and there they two were racing abreast of each other; when he slackened, the other slackened, and when he did t'other, they did t'other. Same length train; same size engine; same lights; and fire door open like his; so that he could see the driver's face; and he says, says he, 'I nearly dropped; for it was me as was driving that 'tother train.' On they goes together into the tunnel, and out they goes together. When he looked back, there was all the carriages lit up, and all just as if it was his own train; but whistling at the short stations when he did, and keeping an exactly same pace. It was like being in a cloud, the fog was so heavy; while the steam from both funnels mixed together.

"It was Christmas-eve, just like this; and yet cold as it was, he said, poor chap, the water dripped from his face as they rushed on. He knew it couldn't last long, for there'd be an up-train directly, and then there must be a fearful smash; but yet something seemed to tell him as there wouldn't; and watching as they went by station after station, he stood trembling at his post. All at once he could see the up-train coming; and then he put on a spurt so as to be ahead when the smash came; but that was no use, for the train kept aside his, and then all at once there was a shriek, and a rush, and the up-train was right behind; while along side his, there was that same engine just in the same place, and him a-driving it. Poor Tom used to make me creep when he told that tale, and he didn't live long arter; for one night there was something wrong in front of our engine, when he wouldn't wait till we stopped, but got along as we were going, and when I was expecting him to come back, and looked—for I'd been putting on more coal—there was some blood splashed all about the screen, and when I stopped and run back, there was poor Tom lying all to bits in the six foot. And they do say as he's been seen by some of the chaps a running a ghost engine along the line at express rate, sometimes one line, and sometimes the other; and when he meets another train, there's a whistle and shriek, and he's gone."

"That's werry pretty," I says. "I'd have that put in a book, if I was you;" and just then there was a bit of door banging, the second bell rang, the guard's whistle chirruped, and then with a scream we started, the steam puffing out of the funnel in round white balls, and slowly spreading overhead till it came faster, and hanging over us like a plume of white feathers, it streamed back over the train.

Such a night: thick as thick; and every now and then it was "bang, bang" as we went over the fog signals, and had to pull up and go very slowly, so that we were a good ten minutes going the first half-mile; and then past the first short station we went very slowly.

Thirty-five miles down was our first stoppage, where we took in water, and then another forty took us to Moreton, which was our next stoppage. By degrees we got on faster and faster, but the darkness was something terrible; while the signal lights at the short stations were almost useless, for I couldn't see them till we were close up, so being already very late through its being Christmas-time I pushed her along, trusting to the line being all clear.

"Ah!" says Ben all at once, "we're jest a-coming to the spot where poor Tom was cut up. Poor old chap," he says; "and it was just here as he first saw that train running by his side."

Now, of course, I knew well enough that it was all gammon; but Ben talked so serious that it give me quite a shiver, and as we came suddenly upon the lights of a station, and raced through, my heart gave a jump, for it almost seemed as if a train was aside us; and even after passing the station, I looked out, for there was the train lights reflected on the fog on each side; but directly after I laughed at myself.

"It was just about here as he must have gone down," says Ben to me—shouting in my ear, for we were going fast; "and they do say as sometimes he mounts an engine and—*Yah-h-h!*" cried the poor fellow, falling down upon his hands and knees; while regularly took aback, I shrunk trembling up in the corner of the screen, and there stopped staring at a horrible looking figure, as seemed to start all at once into the light just as if he'd rose out of the coals. And then he came right up to me, for poor Ben had fainted.

As we were staring at one another I could see as the figure was buttoned up in an oilskin coat, while a close fur cap covered its head, and a handkercher was round the lower part of the face, so that I could see nothing but a pair of fierce bright eyes; and there it stood with one hand holding the side of the screen.

As long as I kept quiet it never moved; but directly I tried to get to my place it motioned me back. At last, half-desperate, I faced it; for a bit of thinking told me it must be a man, though Ben's story had a bit upset me.

"Here's Richford close here," I shouts, "where we stops;" but in a moment I saw the barrel of a pistol flashing in the light of the fire, and then I shrunk back again into the corner. If he would only have turned his back for a moment I should have pinned him, but he only glanced round once, when Ben shuffled back into the far corner of the tender; and there we were five minutes after rushing through Richford at full speed.

"Now," he says, leaning down to me, "rouse up, and push on faster; and don't you dare to stop till we get to Moreton:" and when a man says this to you with a pistol in his hand, why, what else can you do but mind.

"Now," thinks I, "this is a pretty go;" and then I kicks up Ben to come and stoke; but he wouldn't move, and what wanted doing I had to do myself; and so we raced on, for he made me put on more steam, seeing through my dodge in a moment, when I slackened instead; and on we went, with the night seeming to grow darker every moment. But it was race on, past station after station like a flash; and, one way and another, I began to grow excited. The guard had been letting go at the gong, but of course I could take no notice; no doubt, too, he had screwed down his break, but that seemed to make very little difference, with the metals in such a greasy state with the heavy frosty mist; and we raced along at such a rate as I've never been at since.

More than once, I made sure we should be crash into the tail of some goods-train; but though we passed several coming up, nothing was in our way, and at last, after the wildest ride I ever had, we began to get near Moreton, just as the water was beginning to get low. "And now," he says, fiercely, "draw up just this side of the station;" and I nodded: but, for all that, I meant to have run right in, but he was too quick for me, and screwed down the brake so that we stopped a good fifty yards short of the platform, when he leaped down, and I was going to follow, but a rough voice said, "Stand back," and I could see some one in front of me; while, by the lights of the train, I just saw a carriage next the tender opened, and some one hurried off to where a couple of lights were shining; and I could hear horses stamping; and then—it all didn't take a minute—there was the trampling of hoofs and the rolling of wheels, and the man who stopped me from getting down was gone.

"Get up," I says to Ben, as we run into the station; "it warn't a ghost:" but Ben seemed anything but sure on that point. While, as we finished our journey that night, I put that and that together, and made out as this chap, who must have been a plucky fellow, got from the next carriage on to the tender while we were crawling through the fog just outside London; and all to prevent stopping at Richford, where, no doubt, somebody had telegraphed for him to be taken; while, though the message would perhaps be repeated to Moreton, it was not sure to be so, and his dodge of stopping short where a conveyance was in waiting made that all right.

I drove the up-mail next day to town; but that was my last on the Great Central, for, when summoned before the Board, it was pay off, and go; and that, too, without a character.

### Chapter Eight.
### Preparing for Christmas.

"You want to go to sleep? Well you shall directly, but I want to say just a word about next week and Christmas-Day."

"Well say away," I said very drowsily.

"Well, dear," said Mrs Scribe, "You see mamma's coming."

"Sorry to hear it," I said in an undertone.

"For shame," said Mrs S. "How can you talk in that way, when you know what interest she takes in you, and how she praises all you write. No, now, it isn't gammon, as you so politely call it. Well, and if she did say you always introduced 'the wife,' or 'the missus,' so often, what then? You would not have her flatter you, and say what she didn't mean, would you now, dear?"

I couldn't help it, for the wind was easterly and I was very tired, so I only said, "Bother!" But there, I dare not commit to paper all that was said to me upon the subject. A word or two will suffice upon a matter familiar to every Benedict.

"Ah, sir," said Mrs S, "you did not say 'bother' after that walk when we gathered cowslips, and I gave you leave to speak to mamma. What did you say then?"

"Too long ago to recollect," I said.

"No it is not, sir. You said—"

"There, for goodness sake, don't be casting all one's follies in one's teeth," I exclaimed.

"Well then, just listen quietly to what I was going to say about mamma coming."

"Go on then."

"Now don't be a cross old goose, and—"

"Gander," I suggested.

"Now don't be so stupid and tiresome, dear, but just listen. Now, Mrs Parabola's furniture is going to be sold to-morrow, and you'd better go and pick up a few things."

"Pick up," I said, "why they won't let you have anything unless you pay for it."

"Dear me, how exceedingly witty," said Mrs S. "Have you quite finished, sir?"

I felt scorched, so held my tongue, and submitted to the scolding.

"Now I see that Jane has completely ruined that dinner-service: the vegetable-dish covers are all broken but one, and that has no handle; the soup tureen has a great piece out of the side; there are only five soup plates left, while as to the dinner plates, they are that cracked and chipped, and—"

"If you want a new service, why don't you say so, and not go dodging about and beating the bush in that way?" I exclaimed viciously.

"Then you know, dear," continued Mrs S, without noticing my remark, "we want some more glass, and I'd get one of those nice wool mattresses Mrs Parabola was so proud of, and we must have a fresh carpet in the dining-room, for ours is perfectly disgraceful. What? people come to see us and not our carpets? Well I suppose they do, but we need not disgrace them by making believe to be so poor. And let's see, there's a very pretty china tea-service that I certainly would get, dear, and a few of those damask table-cloths and napkins."

"'Those damask table-cloths and napkins?'" I said. "Why, how the dickens do you know anything about them?"

"Why, I went to see, of course, and the auctioneer's men were very civil and let us go over the house."

"Humph," I said. "Anything else you would like?" When if she did not keep on talk, talk, talk for a good hour about the odds and ends, as she called them, that it would be advantageous to buy.

Now, it so happened that when I married I thought I had properly furnished my house; but year after year I have gone on finding out that this was a complete mistake, while now, at the end of some thirteen years, it seems to me to be as far from perfect as ever. But here, in this case, as Mrs Scribe's mamma was coming down to spend Christmas, I could of course say nothing, so after faithfully promising that I would visit Mrs Parabola's during the three days' sale, I was allowed to go to sleep.

"Going to the sale, Retort?" I said the next day to a friend.

"Well, no," was the stammered reply; "I never buy at sales."

"Never mind, walk there with me." Mr Retort consented, and we strolled on together to where a gaily-patterned hearthrug hung out of a window, bearing one of the auctioneer's bills. Men were hanging about with porters' knots, and mostly wearing head coverings composed of Brussels carpet; Abram was there, Isaac was there, Jacob was there, and the whole of the twelve patriarchs, all looking hook-nosed, unctuous, unsoaped, and evidently revelling in the idea of what a glorious "knock out" there would be after the sale. The dining-room was set apart for selling purposes; the long table stood, with all the leaves in, while its telescopic principle was so put to it that in places it was quite out of focus, and the leaves did not meet. The "elegantly-designed genuine Turkey carpet" was ingeniously folded, so that all the worn parts were hidden, and the brighter and unworn portions prominently spread out upon the long table. The scroll fender stood upon the chimney-piece, the plated-ware upon the sideboard, while ranged along the walls were the bureaus and wardrobes out of the bedrooms; at which innovation, or rather intrusion, the large portraits upon the walls gazed down most ferociously.

"Porter, sir?" said a man, touching his carpet-cap to Retort.

"No, thank you, my man," said my friend, politely, "I never take beer."

"No, sir, I mean to carry home what you buy," said the man.

"Oh, dear me, no," said Retort, "I never purchase at sales."

The man thrust a ribald tongue into his long lank cheek, while, at the same moment I was earnestly examining the aforesaid Turkey carpet, and wondering whether it would be an improvement upon the one in our own room, when a man, whose name must have been Isaacs or Moss, insinuatingly offered me a catalogue.

"Thank you," I said: "I have one."

"Shouldn't recommend it, sir," said the new-comer. "The drawing-room carpet would just suit you, for it by rights should have been laid in a dining-room."

"Thanks," I said, "but don't let me detain you."

No detention in the least. Mr Isaacs was a broker, and for the usual trifling commission he could secure anything in the sale for me at a considerable reduction in the price I should have to give.

"For you see," said Mr Isaacs, see-sawing the edge of a leaf of the catalogue between two of his excessively dirty teeth, "if you attempt to bid for yourself the brokers will consider that you are taking the bread out of their mouths, and combine against you, and run things up. Couldn't secure a thing yourself, I assure you, sir."

"Isn't this a public auction?" I said, in what was meant to be a dignified way.

"Oh, yes, of course," said Mr Isaacs; "but you see, sir, these sort of things are always managed for gentlemen by brokers. Gentlemen never bid for themselves."

I left Mr Isaacs under the impression that I was not a gentleman, since I fully intended to bid for myself, and steadfastly refused to pay attention to the various eligible lots he kept introducing to my notice as I passed from room to room of the mansion, gradually getting better filled with visitors bound on bargain-seeking errands.

"Why, you'll pay dear enough for what you buy, depend upon it," said Retort. "What with brokers and buyers, I don't see much chance for you."

"Perhaps not, but look here," I said. "This is how I manage: I get, say in a corner, where I can just see the auctioneer's face, and then taking care not to make much movement or to do anything that will take the enemy's attention, I give him a quiet nod for my bid each time, while seeing that I am a buyer, he always looks out for my nods. Don't you see?"

"Just so," said Retort, "a capital plan, no doubt."

The sale began, and having obtained a pretty good place, I bid for several little things. Two or three times over I saw that the brokering clique were running them up, but by a judicious bit of management I let them run on, and then left my friends with the last bid, so that they were quite satisfied and let me bid and buy as I liked.

I had secured, as the day wore on, several undoubted bargains, amongst which was some of the damask linen which had taken Mrs Scribe's fancy; but the room was insufferably hot and stuffy, and evidently too much for poor Retort, who disappeared.

At length the dining-room Turkey carpet came on, and in spite of various shabby parts, I made up my mind to have it for divers reasons, among which I might enumerate its probably going for a song; secondly, durability; thirdly, its eminent respectability, for no one could find fault with a dining-room covered by a Turkey carpet.

"Five pun'," said one of the brokers, after the auctioneer's introductory remarks.

I nodded.

"Five ten—five ten—six—six ten—seven—seven ten—eight ten—nine ten. Nine ten," said the auctioneer, drawing bid after bid from different parts of the room, while, forgetting my nodding system in the excitement of the moment, I stood confessed. Now I had set ten pounds down in my own mind as the price I would go to, and was rather surprised to find how quickly it had reached to "nine ten," as the auctioneer termed it. However, seeing that the carpet was pretty good, and my room large, I thought I would go a little farther, for I must confess to feeling a little spite against the party of Jews who now seemed to be running me up again. So on went the bidding again, till it had reached to fourteen pounds.

"Let the gentleman have it," said Mr Isaacs, with a grin. But, no, "fifteen pounds" was bid from somewhere else—evidently by a confederate.

"Sixteen," I formed with my mouth.

"Seventeen bid," cried the hammer-man.

"I will have it," I muttered, "in spite of the scoundrels, for it would cost twenty for a good Brussels, and there's no wear in them."

"Going at seventeen—seventeen—*sev-en-teen*—*sev-en-teen*. Going at seven-*teen*. 'Eighteen.' I thank you, sir. Eighteen—eighteen—eighteen. Nineteen is bid," said the auctioneer, while the Jews grinned and chuckled.

"Not half its vally yet, sir," cried Mr Isaacs. "Don't give it away, sir. Orter make fifty pun', at the least."

"Thou villainous Shylock," I muttered to myself, "but I can afford a few pounds sooner than be beaten."

"This splendid Turkey carpet, fit for any nobleman's mansion, now stands at nineteen pounds," cried the man in the rostrum. "Say another pound for you, sir!"

I nodded.

"Twenty pounds—twenty—twenty—guineas—twenty-one pound is offered. It's against you, sir, at twenty-one pounds."

I nodded again.

"Twenty-two pounds," cried the auctioneer. "Twenty-two pounds. Any advance upon twenty-two pounds," he continued, amid much chuckling, when, as there was no further reply to the challenges, I became the fortunate owner of the carpet at double its worth.

"Name," cried the auctioneer, and then catching my eye, he nodded, and went on with the next lot.

"I'll keep out of sight again, I think," I muttered, and returned to my corner, feeling very hot and bristly, as I determined to reopen the knocking-out discussion in the morning papers, for it was evident that I was the victim of a conspiracy.

But I was warm in temper as well as body, and therefore determined not to be driven away, so I purchased an elegant set of card and occasional tables at about double their value; gave six pounds ten for the damaged dinner-service; seven pounds for the china; five guineas for a wool mattress, and found myself at last bidding twelve shillings an ounce for some of the plate.

The Jews seemed frantic with delight, but I knew all the while it was only to conceal their anger and annoyance; and, though I kept carefully out of sight, I knew the bolts and shafts of their coarse allusions were being directed at me, while their hidden confederate on the opposite side of the room bid furiously. Once or twice I felt disposed to leave off, and let the high-priced lots be knocked down to the Israelitish villain. "But no," I said, "I'll have what I want in spite of them, and cunning as they are;" for the rascals kept sending their chaff flying at their confederate as well.

"What a good job Retort has gone!" I muttered; "I shall never have the face to tell anyone what I have given." And now, as it was fast getting dusk, and our Jewish friends were beginning to be sportive and indulge in such little freaks of fancy as bonneting the porters, and accidentally causing articles of furniture to fall against their fellows, all of which tended to make the confusion worse than before, I left the auctioneer hurrying through the last of that day's lots, and made the best of my way out; when, to my surprise, I found Retort in the hall.

"Ah, well met!" I exclaimed, hurriedly following his example; and thrusting my pencilled catalogue into my pocket, feeling very desirous not to talk of the day's purchases until a little softened down by dinner and a glass or two of sherry. However, Retort did not seem at all disposed to speak upon the subject; and, after a little pressing, the touchy bachelor consented to dine with me and take pot luck.

But pot luck that day was nothing to be grumbled at, for Mrs Scribe had exerted herself to have everything snug, as she afterwards told me, in consequence of my having been "a good boy," and undertaken to get the few things she wanted before mamma came down. So pot luck that day consisted of some well-made ox-tail soup—not at all burnt—caught, as our queen of the kitchen terms it—a nice flakey bit of crimped cod with oysters; boiled fowls and tongue; two species of kickshaws; Stilton and celery. The bottled ale was good, the sherry pleasant, and Mrs S amiability itself; so that by degrees the creature comforts acted like anodyne or unguent to my raw temper; and when my smiling partner left us over our wine, I leaped out of my chair, opened the door, and earned the smile tendered for my acceptance.

"Hem!" said Retort, as soon as we were alone.

"Come, fill your glass, Tom," I said; "that's a capital glass of wine, even if it isn't one of your wonderful vintages. I call that Pantheon Port—fit drink for all the gods—ruby Ambrosia."

"Hum," said Retort very superciliously—"Gilbey's, eh?"

"Now, I do call that shabby," I said, "to sneer at a fellow because he frankly offers you a cheap glass, and isn't above owning to it. Now, if you had dined with old Blunkarn, he'd have given you a worse glass, and vowed it was '20 port."

"But how did you get on at the sale?" said Retort hastily, so as to change the subject.

"Rascally!" I exclaimed, firing up. "Those confounded Jews!"

"Wasn't it scandalous," said Retort.

"The most iniquitous affair I ever saw!" I exclaimed.

"The scoundrels ought to be indicted for conspiracy," said my friend.

"*I'll* show them up, my boy," I said. "I'll send columns to the papers if they'll only put them in."

"Ah, do," said my companion. "Now, you see, I bid for a thing or two."

"You," I said; "why, what for? Bachelor in lodgings?"

"Well—er—er—yes," said Retort, stammering, "er—er at present, you know—at present."

"Why, you don't mean to say—" I burst out.

"Hush, my dear fellow! don't speak so loud."

"That you've proposed to Miss Visite?"

"Well—er—yes, my dear sir, I have," simpered the great booby.

"Then I congratulate you," I exclaimed. "Here, Nelly," I said, running towards the door.

"No, no, no—don't, don't, there's a good fellow," cried Retort, dragging me back towards the table; "don't call Mrs Scribe. Let me break it to her gently some other time. I'd rather do it myself."

"Just as you like," I said, good-humouredly; and then I toasted the future Mrs Retort's most honoured name.

"Well," continued Retort, drawing forth his catalogue, "I was telling you that I bid for a few lots, but those fellows run them up so, that I couldn't get a thing."

"Yes, it was too bad," I muttered, fumbling in my pocket for my catalogue, to find that I had left it in the coat I had taken off.

"Here, Emily," I said, when the maiden answered the bell, "fetch that catalogue out of my coat-pocket in the dressing-room. Don't show it to any one else. Bring it straight here;" for I was rather alarmed lest Mrs Scribe should see the figures made beside the lots I had secured.

Emily soon returned, and then, with a somewhat darkened brow, I began to refer to the different items.

"What did you bid for, Tom?" I said to my friend, who was poring over the list, evidently deep in for furnishing. "But I never thought of your getting married, old chap; though I did half fancy that you were sweet after Miss V."

"Why, you don't suppose I should have wasted a day at a sale if I had not wanted things, do you?"

"Never gave it a thought," said I. "And so you didn't buy anything after all?"

"No," said Retort. "Did you?"

"Well—er—er—um, ye-e-es; a few things—a few."

"Things went dear, though, didn't they?"

"Well, yes, on the whole, they did. But what did you bid for?"

"Oh, I thought that Turkey carpet would just suit us; and as you were going in for the drawing-room Brussels, why, I bid for it; but those Israelitish villains run it up to twenty-two pounds."

I was so out of breath for a moment that I couldn't speak.

"Then," continued my dear friend, "I wanted those card and occasional tables, but couldn't get them; they bought the dinner-service, too, at six ten, and the china for seven pounds. Then I took a strong fancy to that wool mattress, but of course I wasn't going to give five guineas for it. It certainly was a beautifully soft and thick one, but one could buy it new for the money, or less."

"Did you bid for any of the plate?" I gasped in husky tones.

"Well, 'pon my word, old chap, I'm half ashamed to own it, but I really was stupid enough to go as far as eleven and sixpence an ounce for it—which is an absurd price, you know. But there, thank goodness! I've escaped, for I haven't bought a single lot."

I did not speak for quite five minutes, for the simple reason that I could not. What was I to do, or what was I to say? I wanted to call him names, and take him by the collar to shake him till his teeth chattered. But who could so treat a guest?

"Let's go up and have some tea," I said at last, very hoarsely; and then, recovering myself, I stopped him, for I felt sure he would begin talking upstairs, while Mrs Scribe, on the subject being broached, would ask—what as yet she had not had opportunity for—what I had secured.

"Stop a minute, Tom," I said. "Don't say a word about the sale upstairs."

He looked at me strangely, and kept his counsel as well as mine—and not a single word has since passed our lips; but in after days, when dining at our house in company with his wife, I have seen his eyes wander from the Turkey carpet to the dinner-service, and again, in the drawing-room, from the occasional tables to the china tea-cups and saucers; and then he has glanced darkly at me, with the look of a found-out conspirator, and I have looked darkly at him. But, no, not even to the wife of my bosom have I ever unburdened myself respecting the prices I paid for the new acquisitions to our furnishing department. While as to that five-guinea wool mattress, I could almost swear that, whoever stuffed it, stuffed in the miserable sheep's trotters and bones, for whenever by chance we have slept in the visitors' room, upon airing principles, I have always felt lumps right through the feather bed.

"No, my love, the price has nothing to do with you," I said, while being cross-questioned. "You have the things, so you ought to be satisfied."

"So I am, and it's very good of you," said Mrs Scribe; "and now you'll be good, too, and not tease mamma—now, won't you!"

"All right."

"And I say, dear."

"Well!" (from under the counterpane).

"Don't, now—same as you did last time—don't ask poor mamma how long she means to stay."

"All right," (very muffled in tone).

"No, dear, it isn't all right if you ask her such a thing. It looks as if you meant that you wanted to get rid of her again."

"So I do," (this time so smothered that it was audible only to self).

"Good-night, dear."

"Goonight."

"What a nice, comfortable, pleasant-feeling, long-napped carpet, George. I do like a Turkey carpet above all things; it is so warm and aristocratic-looking, and then, too, so durable. Now, I'm sure, my dear, I am right in saying that you picked it up a bargain at a sale."

"Yes, that he did, mamma dear," said Mrs Scribe; "but he won't tell me what he gave for it. Do tease him till he tells you."

"Now, how much was it, sir?"

"Another slice of turkey, Mrs Cubus?"

"Well, really, my dear, I don't think—er—er—well, it really is a delicious turkey. Oh! half that, George. And why don't you say mamma? Yes, just the least bit of stuffing, and—er—a chestnut or two. That's quite enough gravy, thank you. Now, what did you give for the carpet?"

"Oh," I said, "it's Christmas-time, so I shall make a riddle of it. Guess."

"Well, let me see," said Mrs S's Mamma. "You gave—what shall I say? About eighteen feet square, isn't it?"

"Very good—that's it exact."

"Well, then, my dear, as you bought it a bargain, I should say you gave five pounds for it—or say guineas—but, no, I'll say pounds."

"Capital!" I said, with the most amiable smile I ever had upon my countenance; "I did give five pounds for it."

"*Plus seventeen*," I whispered into my waistcoat.

"What, dear?"

"Merry Christmas to you," I said, bowing over my glass of sherry.

And that was my last bargain-hunt.

## Chapter Nine.
## The Ice-Breaking.

Down by the woods in the rocky valley,
Where the babbling waves of the river sally,
  Where the pure source gushes
  And the wild fount rushes,
  There's the sound of the roar
  That is heard on the shore,
Where the tumbling billows the chalk cliffs bore;
  For down from each hill
  With resistless will,

The floods are fast pouring their waters so chill,
And the West has risen with a cry and a shout,
Dash'd at the North to the Ice-king's rout;
   Then off and away,
   For the livelong day
Has rush'd through the woodlands - no longer gay,
   Splitting the branches;
   While avalanches
   Of melting snow
   Bend the pine-boughs low,
And the earth with the spoil of the warfare strow.


   And now once again
   Comes the pitiless rain,
Pouring its torrents from black clouds amain;
Till the river is swollen and bursting its bounds,
And its muttering wrath sweeps in ominous sounds
   On the wintry breeze,
   Louder and louder by rising degrees.

The Ice-king is routed - his reign is past,
And the frost-bound river is rending fast;
And the West wind sweeps with a mournful sough,
And the flood tears through with the force of a plough.
   Splitting and rending,
   The ice unbending,
   As with mighty burrow,
   It carves out a furrow
   Of churning wreck;
   While, as if at its beck,
   The foam-capped streams
   Loose the Ice-king's beams,
And each crystal fragment, with wild weird gleams,
   Now sinks - now rises,
   As each stream still prises,
Till the loosen'd river in fury rolls
Away through the valley; while icy scrolls
Are swept from the bank, where the snow lay heavy,
And snow-drift and ice joins the West's rude levy;
   Which at barrier scouts,
   At each rock mound shouts;
Sweeping along towards the land of the plain,
Tingeing the waters with many a stain;
Foaming along in an eddying sweep,
And gliding in speed where the flood ploughs deep,
Rooting the reeds from their hold on the bank,
And widening its track where the marsh lies dank.


   Away tears the river
   With an earthquake's speed,
   Over the snow-cover'd lowland mead,
   Laughing aloud at each reckless deed,
   As the stricken farmers the ruin heed,
   Whirling along on its bosom the reed

    And the sharp, jagg'd ice and the harmless bead,
    With the unchained course of a wild-born steed,
Till the hills where it passes quiver.

Away and away, and still onward away,
And there's ruin and havoc in lowland this day;
    For the waters brown
    In their rage tear down,
Menacing shipping and threatening the town;
    They've beat down the weir,
    And dash'd at each pier,
And swept o'er the bank to the widespread mere,
    Whose icy sheet,
    As though torn by heat,
Has fallen in fragments where torrents meet;
    While now for the bridge,
    There's an icy ridge
    On the river's breast,
    Swept along by the West,
Whose might shall the strong beams and deep piles wrest,
    Till the bridge goes down,
    By the flooded town,
Where the lowing kine and the penn'd flocks drown.

    But the damm'd stream rages,
    For naught assuages
    Its thirst for ruin;
    And again undoing
    The toil of years,
It hurries along till the rocks it wears.

And now there's a crash and a mighty rattle
As a stalwart mound gives the river battle;
    And soon engaging,
    The waves leap raging,
    Where the mound is gash'd,
    By the churn'd ice dash'd,
    While from out of the dam,
    With the force of a ram,
    Comes each huge, strong beam,
    On the breast of the stream,
    With the speed of an arrow,
    Where the banks are narrow;
    But the rocky face
    Stays the furied race,
As round it the waters in madness enlace;
    Lashing and tearing
    With rage unsparing,
    To beat down the stay
    In the deadly fray;
And then, for more ruin, to hurry away;
    But the hill stouthearted
    The water has parted,
    And away in a sever'd stream they tear
    Like famish'd lions fresh from their lair,

Devouring, destroying, and bearing away
Each barrier, bank, or each timber'd stay;
Till they slacken their race by the sandy verge
Of the parent sea, whose wild, restless surge
   Lashes the shore.
Towards her breast leap the rivers in eager guise,
Lost in the billows that hurrying rise
To welcome the treasures they pour.

## Chapter Ten.
## A Horror of Horrors.

"Very, very glad to see you, my boy," said my friend Broxby, as I reached his house quite late on Christmas-eve, when he introduced me to his wife, a most amiable woman of an extremely pleasing countenance; to Major and Mrs Major Carruthers, a very pimply-faced gentleman, with a languishing wife troubled with an obliquity of vision, which worried me greatly that evening from her eye seeming to be gazing upon me, while its owner wore a perpetual smile upon her lip. Mrs Major Carruthers' brother was also there, a young man, like myself, of a poetic turn, and troubled with headaches, besides several others, ladies and gentlemen, who occupied divers relative distances in connection with my friend Broxby and his charming wife.

"Why you're as nervous and bashful as ever, my boy," said Broxby, in his rough, good-natured way, and I tried to laugh it off, particularly as it was said before so many people in the well-lit drawing-room; but even before the fearful shock my nerves received I always was of a terribly nervous temperament, a temperament which makes me extremely susceptible.

As I am now forty I have given up all hopes of ever getting the better of it, even as I have felt compelled to give up the expectation of whiskers, curling hair, and—well no, not yet, for, as the poet says, "We may be happy yet," and some fond, loving breast may yet throb for me in the future. I may add that my hair is fair, my face slightly freckled, and that I have a slight lisp, but it is so slight that you do not notice it when you get used to me.

After a long, cold ride down by train to Ancaster, and a six miles' ride in Broxby's dog-cart from the station, where I was met by his groom, the well-lit drawing-room seemed so cheering and comfortable, and as I grew a little more at home I began to be glad that I had left my chambers to their fate for the time, and come down to bask awhile in the light of so many lustrous orbs.

I was just feeling somewhat confused from the fact of Mrs Major Carruthers having rested her eye upon me and smiled sweetly, when as a matter of course I felt bound to do either one thing or the other, look angry and suppose that she was laughing at me, or smile sympathetically in return. I did the latter, when, as I said before, I became confused to see that Major Carruthers was frowning fiercely at me, while his face looked quite currant-dumplingified from the fierce hue assumed by his pimples. But just at that moment a servant announced something to my host, who came forward, slapped me on the shoulder, and I followed him out of the room into his study, where a small table was spread expressly for my delectation.

"You see we dined two hours ago, Augustus, so I'm going to chat and have a glass of sherry with you while you freshen up. I thought it would be more snug for you here in my study, so cut away."

I must confess to having felt hungry, and I directly commenced the meal, while my friend chatted pleasantly about the party I had met in the drawing-room.

"Why, we must find you a wife, one of those fair maidens, my boy. A good, strong-minded, lovable woman would be the making of you. Good people, those Carruthers, only the Major is so fearfully jealous of his wife—simple, quiet, good-hearted soul as ever breathed. And oh, by the bye, I have to apologise to you for something really unavoidable. I would not trouble you if I could help myself, but I can't. You see the Major is a first cousin of my wife's, and we always ask them to our little gatherings, while it so happened that Mrs Major's brother was staying with them, when, as it was either bring him or stay away themselves, Laura, my wife you know, thoughtlessly said 'Bring him,' never stopping to think that every bed in the house was engaged. What to do I could not think, nor where to put him, till at last I said to myself why Gus Littleboy will help me out of the difficulty, and therefore, my lad, for two nights only I have to go down on my inhospitable marrowbones and ask you to sleep double. We've put you in the blue room, where there's an old four-poster that is first cousin to the great bed of Ware, so that you can lie almost a quarter of a mile from each other, more or less you know, so you won't mind, will you old fellow, just to oblige us you know?"

Of course I promised not to mind, and a great deal more, but still I did mind it very much, for I omitted to say that, er—that er—I am extremely modest, and the fact of having a gentleman in the same room was most painful to my feelings.

We soon after joined the party in the drawing-room; and, feeling somewhat refreshed, I tried to make myself agreeable, as it was Christmas-time, and people are expected to come out a little. So I brought out two or three conjuring tricks that I had purchased in town, and Broxby showed them off while I tried to play one or two tricks with cards; but, somehow or another, when Mrs Major Carruthers drew a card, I had forgotten the trick, and she had to draw another card which she dropped; and, when it was on the carpet, we both stooped together to pick it up; and you've no idea how confusing it was, for we knocked our heads together, when I distinctly heard some one go "Phut" in precisely the same way as a turkey-cock will when strutting; when, to my intense dismay, I again found that the Major was scowling at me fiercely.

"Then I should go to bed if I were you, Timothy," I heard Mrs Major say soon after; and, on looking across the room, I saw that she was talking to her brother, but her eye was upon me, and she was smiling, so that I felt perfectly horrified, and looked carefully round at the Major; but he was playing cards, and did not see me.

So Mr T Peters left the room, and Broxby did all he could to amuse his visitors, till the ladies, one and all, declared they must retire, when the gentlemen drew round the fire; and a bright little kettle having been set upon the hob and a tray of glasses placed upon the table, my friend brewed what he called a night-cap, a portion of which I left four of them discussing when Broxby rang for a candlestick, and told the maid to show me the bedroom.

"Did you have my portmanteau taken up?" I said to the maid.

"Yes, sir."

"And carpet-bag?"

"Yes, sir."

"And writing-case?"

"Oh yes, sir; all there—that's the door, sir; you'll find everything well-aired, and a nice fire;" and then the maiden tripped off and disappeared at the back. But I had left my skin rug in the hall; and, as it was so excessively cold, I went down the broad staircase once more, and fetched it; returned to the bedroom door, opened it to make sure I was right—not a doubt of it: nice fire—the great four-post bedstead with the great blue hangings. No; they were green, and I was about to start back, only a heavy breath from the bed told me that I was right; and, besides, I recollected that blue always looked green by candle-light; and this was the case, too, with the paper I observed.

"Most extraordinary people that Major and his wife," I thought; and then I wound up my watch, laid it upon the chimney-piece, carefully locked and bolted the door, and then, drawing a chair up to the fire, sat down to give my feet a good warm. The room was most comfortably furnished, and the chair soft and well stuffed; when, what with the heat of the fire, the cold wind during my ride, and, perhaps, partly owing to the night-cap I had partaken of, I fell into a sort of doze, and then the doze deepened into a sleep, in which I dreamed that the Major had called me out for endeavouring to elope with his wife, when it was that strange eye of hers which had run away with me, while her set of false teeth were in full chase behind to seize me like some rabid dog.

The horror became so great at last that I started from my sleep, kicking the fender as I did so, when the fire-irons clattered loudly.

"What's that?" cried a familiar voice, which sounded rather softly, as if from beneath the clothes.

"Only the fire-irons, my dear sir," I said, blandly—"I kicked them." The next moment an exclamation made me turn sharply round; when, horror of horrors! there was a set of teeth upon the dressing-table, and from between the curtains of the bed Mrs Major's eyes fixing me in the most horrifying way.

"Monster!" cried a cracked voice, which sent me sprawling up against the wash-stand, whose fittings clattered loudly; while at one and the same moment I heard the voice of the Major talking, and the loud, hearty laugh of Broxby upon the stairs.

I was melting away fast when more of Mrs Major appeared through the curtains; in fact, the whole of her head, night-cap, papers and all, and the cracked voice shrieked—

"Monster, there's help at hand!—Alfred, Alfred, help! help!" and then the head disappeared; when I heard from inside the curtains a choking, stifling noise; and then came a succession of shrieks for aid.

"For pity's sake, silence, madam!" I cried, running to the door; but the next moment I ran back.

"Open this door, here!—open!" roared the Major, kicking and thundering, so that the panels cracked. "Matilda, my angel, I am here."

"Don't, don't; pray don't scream, ma'am," I implored.

"Oh! oh! oh! help, help, help! murder!" shrieked Mrs Major.

"Here, hi! oh! villain! A man's voice! Break in the door; smash it off the hinges. I am here, Matilda, I am here. Broxby, what is this?" roared the Major; and then the door cracked and groaned beneath the blows thundered upon it.

"Oh! oh! oh!" shrieked Mrs Major.

"What shall I do?" I muttered, wringing my hands and trembling like a leaf. I ran to the bed to implore Mrs Major to be still, but she only shrieked the louder. I ran to the door, but fled again on hearing the thunderings and roarings of the Major, who beat frantically, louder and louder.

"Sir, sir," I cried, "it's a mistake."

"Oh! villain," he shrieked. "Here, here, a poker; my pistols. Broxby, there'll be murder done."

"Madam, oh! madam," I cried, in agony, "have pity, and hear me."

"Oh! oh! oh! help! help!" shrieked the wretched woman; when I heard the door going crack, crack; the panel was smashed in, and the sounds of the hubbub of voices entered the room, wherein I could detect that of the Major, more like a wild beast than anything, when, dashing to the window, I pushed back the fastener, threw up the sash, and crept out, lowered myself down till I hung by my hands, when, with my last look, I saw an arm reaching through the broken panel, the bolt slipped, the key turned, and a rush of people into the room; when, losing my hold, I fell crash into a tree, and then from branch to branch to the ground, where I lay, half-stunned, upon the cold snow.

"There he is," shouted a voice from above me, whose effect was like electricity to my shattered frame, for I leaped up, and gaining the pathway, fled to the road, and then on towards the station, only pausing once to listen for the sounds of pursuit and to tie my handkerchief round my head to screen it from the icy breeze. I ran till I was breathless, and then walked, but only to run again, and this I kept on till I had passed the six miles between Broxby's Beat and Ancaster, where I arrived just before the night mail came in, at a quarter to four.

One of the porters was very civil, and, supposing that my hat had been blown off and lost, sold me a very dirty old greasy cap for five shillings, and then I once more felt safe as I leaned back in a carriage, and felt that we were going towards London at the rate of forty miles an hour. But I did not feel thoroughly safe until I had gained entrance, in the cold dark morning, to my chambers by means of my latchkey, and having barricaded the door, tried to forget my sorrows in sleep, but I could not, while, as my laundress supposed that I should be away for a week, everything was in a most deplorable state, in consequence of the old woman meaning to have a good clean up on Boxing-day.

I did not go out for a week, for I had to take precautions for my health's sake, putting my feet in hot water, and taking gruel for the bad cold I caught; but for that, and the nervous shock, I was not hurt, though my clothes were much torn. It was about eight days after that a letter arrived while I was at breakfast, bearing the Ancaster post-mark, directed to me in Broxby's familiar hand; but I had read it twice, with disgust portrayed on every lineament, before I perceived that my late friend had evidently written to his brother and to me at the same sitting, when, by some hazard, the letters had been cross-played and put in the wrong envelopes, for the abominable epistle was as follows:—

"Dear Dick,—You should have come down. Such a spree. My ribs are sore yet with laughing, and I shall never get over it. I sent old Gus Littleboy an invite. Poor fool, but no harm in him except blundering. The Major was here; quite a houseful, in fact. Gus was to sleep with Tim Peters, and got somehow into the Major's room while he was down with me finishing the toddy. Murder, my boy. Oh! you should have been here to hear the screaming, and seen the Major stamp and go on. He kicked the panel in, when poor Gus fled by the window, and has not sent for his traps yet. For goodness sake contrive for the Major to meet him at your place when I'm up next week. It will be splitting, and of course I can't manage it now.

"Yours affectionately,
"Joe Broxby."

I need scarcely tell a discerning public that I refused the invitation sent me by Mr Richard Broxby, of Bedford Square, when it arrived the next week; while when, some months after, I encountered the Major and his wife upon the platform of the Great Nosham, Somesham, and Podmorton Railway, I turned all of a cold perspiration, for my nerves will never recover the shock.

## Chapter Eleven.
### Cabby at Christmas.

Rather cold outside here, sir; but of course, if you like riding on the box best, why it's nothing to me, and I'm glad of your company. Come on. "Ony a bob's worth, Tommy," says that chap as drove Mr Pickwick, him as set the old gent and his friends down as spies. The poor chap must have had a bad day, you see, and got a bit raspy; and I've known the time as I've felt raspy, too, and ready to say, "Ony a bob's worth, Tommy." You see ours is a trade as fluctuates a wonderful sight, and the public's got it into their heads as we're always a-going to take 'em in somehow or other; so jest like that American gal in the story, "Don't," says Public. "Don't what?" says we. "Don't overcharge," says Public. "Well, we wasn't a-over-charging," says we. "No, but aint you going to?" says Public. Puts it into our heads, and makes us charge extra through being so suspicious. You see we're poor men, but not such a bad sort, considering. Public servants we are, badged and numbered, bound to do work by fixed rule and charge, so what I say is that you should treat us accordingly. "Civil and pleasant," says you—"Civil and pleasant," says we. "Drawn swords," says you—"Drawn swords," says we. Peace or war, which you likes, and the Beak for umpire. There's a werry good sorter clay underneath some of our weskets, if you only takes and moulds it the right way, when you'll find all go as easy as can be; but make us ill-tempered and hot, why of course we turns brittle and cracks; while, you know, if you goes the other way too far, and moistens our clay too much, why—Well, human natur's only human natur, is it? and of course the clay gets soft and sticky, and a nuisance. Keep half-way, you know, and then you're all right, and will find us decent working, when you moulds us up and brings out a model cabby.

You see you calls them black fellows men and brothers, but I'm blest if I think some people thinks as we are; for, instead of brothers, they treat us as if we was werry distant relations indeed, and then sets to and fights it out with us for every sixpence we earns. Don't believe a word we say, they don't, and as to thinking we're honest—bless your heart no, not they! "Oh, they're a bad lot, kebmen," says Mrs John Bull, and she says as the straw's musty, the lining fusty, and the seat's dusty, and then grumbles at the horse, and blows up the driver and flings dirt at him.

"You rascal—you scoundrel! I'll summons you; I'll put you on the treadmill; I'll have the distance measured; I'll—I'll write to the *Times* and have your rascality exposed. Drive me to Bow Street—no to Great Marlbro' Street—or—there—no, take your fare, but mind I've taken your number, and I'll introduce the subject in the House this very night."

"I'll—I'll—I'll," I says to myself. "Nice ile yours 'ud be to grease the wheels of Life with." And that was Mr MP, that was; for it was over a mile as he rode. And only think of wanting to put a Hansom driver off with sixpence. Then, again, I drives a gent to the rail, and his missus with him, and when he gets out he sorter sneaks a shillin' into my hand, and then's going to shuffle off, when "Wot's this here for?" I says.

"Your fare, my man," he says, werry mildly.

"Hayten-pence more," I says.

"Sixpence a mile, my good man," he says, "and Mogg's guide says that—"

"Mogg's guide doesn't say that kebs is to be made carriers' waggons on for nothing," I says; and then the porters laughed, and he gives me the difference of the half-crown; and only nat'ral, for I'll tell you what there was. First there was three boxes—heavy ones—on the roof; two carpet-bags and a portmanty on the seat aside me; a parrot's cage, a cap-box, a gun-case, and a whole bundle o' fishing-rods, and umbrellys, and things on the front seat; and him and his missus on the back. And arter the loading up and loading down, and what not, I don't think as it was so werry dear. I sarved him out, though, for I took and bit every blessed bit o' silver, making believe as I didn't think 'em good, and stood grumbling there till the porters had got all the things in, and Master Generous had put hisself outer sight.

You see, sir, it ain't us as has all the queer pints; there's some as I knows on, if they was brought down to kebbing, 'stead of being swells, they'd be a jolly sight worse than we.

Didn't know Tom Sizer, I s'pose? No, you wouldn't know him, I dare say. Out an out driver, he was, poor chap. But what was the use on it to him? Just because he was clever with the reins, and could do a'most anything with any old knacker of a 'oss, the guv'nor sets him up the shabbiest of any man as went outer the yard. There he was, poor chap, with the wust 'oss and the wust keb, and then being only a seedy-looking cove hisself, why he turned out werry rough. But that didn't matter; Tom allus managed to keep upsides with the guv'nor, and was never behind. Being a quiet sorter driver, yer see, he'd got some old ladies as was regular customers, and one way and another he made it up. And it was always the guv'nor's artfulness, you know: he had old 'osses and a old keb or two, and if he'd sent some men out with 'em they'd ha' brought back a'most nothing.

A regular sharp, teasing winter came on; rain, and freeze, and blow; and then our pore old Tom he got dreadful shaky at last, and his cough teased him awful, so none of us was surprised when we found one day as he warn't come to the yard; nor we warn't surprised next day when he didn't come; nor yet when a whole week passed away and his keb stood under the shed, and his 'oss kep in the stable, for they was such bad 'uns none of our chaps'd have anything to do with 'em; and more'n once I see the guv'nor stand with his hat half-raised in one hand, and scratting his head with t'other, as he looked at the old worn keb, as much as to say, "I shall never make anything outer that any more."

Christmas arternoon comes, and I thinks as I'll go and have a look at Tom. So I tidies up a bit, puts on a white choker, and ties it coachman's fashion, and fixes it with a horse-shoe pin, as my missus give me when we was courting. Then I brushes my hat up, and was just going off, when the missus says, "Wot d'yer want yer whip for?" she says. "Wot do I want my whip for?" I says, and then I stops short, and goes and stands it up in the corner by the drawers, for it didn't seem nat'ral to go out without one's whip, and it ain't often as we goes out walking, I can tell you.

Well, I toddles along, and gets to the place at last, where Tommy held out: tall house it was, just aside Awery Row, and opposite to a mews; werry pleasant lookout in summer-time, for the coachmen's wives as lived over the stables was fond of their flowers and birds; but even in winter time there was allus a bit o' life going on: chaps cleaning first-class 'osses, or washing carriages, or starting off fresh and smart to drive out shopping or in the park. Fine, clean-legged, stepping 'osses, and bright warnished carriages and coachmen in livery; and all right up to the mark, you knew.

So I goes on upstairs, for I knowed the way to his room, along of having had supper with him one night—mussels and a pot of stout we had—so I didn't ring three times like a stranger, but walks up one pair, two pair, three pair stairs, and then I stops short, for the door was ajar, and I could see a gentleman's back, and hear talking; so I says to myself, "That's the doctor," I says, and I sets down on the top stair to get my wind, and then I turns quite chilly to hear poor old Tom's voice, so altered and pipy I didn't know what to make of it, as he says.

"There, sir, don't stand no more; set down. Not that chair, 'cos the leg's broke. Try t'other one. Well," he says, "I takes this as werry kind of you to come and see a poor fellow as is outer sorts and laid up—laid up! Ah! it's pretty well knacker's cart and Jack Straw's castle with me. The missus there's been cleaning and a-tidying up, and doing the best she could; but, in course, with me in it, the bed can't be turned up, and so the place can't look werry decent. I do take it as werry kind of a gent like you climbing up three pairs o' stairs o' purpose to come and see me—it quite cheers me up. Not as I wants for visitors, for I has the 'spensary doctor, and there's four sorter journeymen preachers comes a-wherretin' me; till, as soon as I sees one on 'em coming in all in black, I thinks it's the undertaker hisself. The doctor came half an hour ago—two hours, was it? ah, well, I've been asleep, I s'pose; and then time goes. He's left me a lot more physic and stuff, but I ain't taken it, and I ain't a-going to; for what's the use o' greasing the keb wheels when the tires is off and the spokes is all loose and rattling, and a'most ready to tumble out. 'Tain't no use whatsomever, whether they've been good ones or bad ones. It's all up; and you may wheel the keb werry gently through the yard under the shed, and leave it there, and wot odds; there's fresh 'uns a-coming out every day with all the noo improvements, so what's the use o' troubling about one as is worn out and out. There ain't no use in trying to patch when all the woodwork's worm-eaten, while the lining's clean gone; what with bad usage and bad weather; and, as to the windys, they ain't broke, but they're grown heavy and dull, and I can't see through 'em; and you'll soon see the blinds pulled down over 'em, never to come up no more—never no more!"

Then there come a stoppage, for the pore chap's cough give it him awful, so as it was terrible to listen, and I'd ha' slipped away, ony I felt as I should like to have just a word with my poor old mate again.

"There," he says, "I've got my wind again; you see it's up hill, and this cough shakes a fellow awful. Never mind, though; I hope there's rest up a-top for even a poor fellow like me; and, do you know," he says, quite softly, "I begins to want to get there, though it does grit me to think as I can't take Polly on the box with me; but that's a hard thing to understand—that about life, and death, and 'ternity—for ever, and ever, and ever. That's what the youngest parson as comes talks to me about. Nice fellow he is; I like him, for he seems to want to light one's lamps up a bit and clear the road—seems fond of one like, and eager to give one a shove outer the block. But there; I ain't lived to six-and-sixty year without having my own thoughts about religion and that sort of thing. I know as we're all bad enough, and I s'pose a-top of the hill there it will all be reckoned against one, and kep' account on, good and bad. As I sez to Polly, after that chap had been here as is so fond of hearing hisself speak, and allus calls me 'my friend;' 'Polly,' I sez, 'it's no manner of use; I ain't a-going to turn king's evidence and try to shirk out of it that way: what I've done wrong will go to the bad, and what I've done right I hope will go to the good, while I'm sure no poor fellow could be more sorry than me for what's amiss.' When we goes afore Him as judges up there, sir, it will all be made light, and there won't be no feeling as justice ain't done. There won't be no big fellows in gowns and wigs a-trying to swear a chap's soul away—making a whole sarmon out of a word, and finding out things as was never before thought on at all. I've been before 'em, and examined and cross-examined, and twisted about till you don't know what your a-saying of. And so, when I thinks of all this lying still in the night, listening to the rumbling of the kebs—kebs as I shall never drive no more; why, I feels comfortable and better like; don't seem to see as it's so werry serious, as my number's been took, and I'm summoned; 'Done my dooty,' I says, 'and kep' home together as well as I could; and it would ha' been all the same if I'd ha' been born a dook, I must ha' come to it same as I'm a-coming now.' Of course I should ha' had a finer funeral; but there, lots of fellows as I knows on the rank, chaps as is Foresters, they'll drive behind me with their windy-blines down, and a little bit o' crape bow on the ends o' their whips; they'll smoke it at night in their pipes, and take it werry much to 'art when they thinks on it, and puts their blines right again—but mine won't open no more now."

"Nigher I gets to the top of the hill," he says, "slower I goes; but slow and sure I'm a-making way, and shall be there some time: not to-day, p'raps, nor yet to-morrow, but some time afore long, for I knows well enough how my number's been took, and my license is about gone. Well, sir, I drove a cab thirty year, and it was never took away afore; and so I ain't a-going to complain."

"Going, sir?" he says: "Then I'll take it as a favour, sir, if you'll just see that young genelman—the parson as I likes, and ast him to come. He left his card on the chimbley there for me to send for him when I felt to want him, and he seems to be the real doctor for my complaint. I was to send if I wanted him before he came again, and I'd rather not see them others too. That first one helps me on a bit, and somehow, I seem to want to be a-top of the hill now, and he's first-class company for a pore chap on a dark road. Nothing like a real friend when you're in trouble, and he seems one as will help."

"Good bye, sir," he says, werry softly. "The warnish is all rubbed off, and the paint chipped and showing white and worn; the bottom's a-falling out, and the head's going fast; so once more, sir, good bye, for the old keb'll be broke up afore you comes again. Good bye, sir; you'll tell him to come here, as told of mercy and hope."

And then some one stepped softly by me, and went down the creaking stairs, and I got ready to go in; but, not feeling in a bit of a hurry, for there was something seemed to stick in my throat, and I knew I shouldn't be able to speak like a man when I got into the room, so I stops outside a bit longer; and then, when I made sure as it was all right with me once more, I steps softly in, and then stops short, when I turned worse than ever; for there, kneeling down by his bed, was poor Mrs Sizer sobbing, oh, so bitterly! and then I thought of how he said he'd like to take her on the box with him. And there, you'll laugh, I know, at calling it a beautiful sight to see them pore, plain, weather-and-time-worn people taking like a last farewell of one another; and it was no good; I daren't speak, but slowly and softly backed out, thinking about the years them two had been together working up hill, up hill always; and then it didn't seem so strange that, when one of these old folks dies, the other goes into the long, deep sleep, to be with him. And then a-going down the stairs softly and slowly, I says to myself, "there's a deal o' rough crust and hard stuff caked over us, but a pore man's heart's made of the real same material as God made those of better folks of;" and Lord bless you, sir! use him well, and you'll find the way to the heart of a cabby.

Poor Tom! he was a-top of the hill nex' day, and I never saw him again. But he was a good sort, was Tom. Thanky sir, much obliged; merry Christmas to you!

## Chapter Twelve.
### Drat the Cats.

Dumb animals would be all very well, no doubt, and I don't suppose I should have much objection to keeping one, but then where are you going to get 'em? That's what I want to know; I never come across anything dumber yet than old Job Cross's donkey, while that would shout sometimes awful, and rouse up the whole neighbourhood. No; I've got no faith in keeping dogs and cats, and birds and things in a house, and sets them all down as nuisances—sets my face against 'em regular, and so would any man who had been bothered as I have with cats.

Pussy—pussy—pussy—pussy; puss—puss—puss. Oh, yes, it's all very fine. They're pretty creatures, ain't they? sleek and smooth, and furry and clean, and they'll come and rub up against you, and all so affectionate. Bother! why, they never do it unless they want to be fed, or rubbed, or warmed in the nice warm glow of the fire, or in somebody's lap. Why, see what savage little brutes they are to one another, and how they can spit and claw, and swear and growl, while their fur's all set up, their tail swelled out like a fox's, and their eyes round and bright enough to frighten you. No; I know what cats are—pretty dears. Who licks the top of the butter all over, and laps up the milk—eats my bloaters, steals mutton bones off the table, pretending to be asleep till you leave the room for a moment, when she's up on the table and tearing away like a savage at your dinner or supper?

"Poor thing; it was only because it was hungry," says my wife. Perhaps it was, but then I didn't approve of it: so I gave the poor thing away.

Now, I daresay, most men's wives have got some failings in them. I mean—ain't quite perfect. You see mine ain't, and though, I daresay, she's no worse than other women, yet, she has got one of the most tiresome, aggravating, worrying ways with her that any one could come across. I don't care whether its spring, summer, autumn, or winter, or whether it's all on 'em, or none on 'em, it's allus the same, and she's no sooner got her head on the pillow, than she's off like a top—sound as can be. 'Taint no good to speak—not a bit—you may just as well spare your breath, and almost the worst of it is, she mends wrong way, and gets sleepier and sleepier the longer she lives. But that's only "almost the worst" on it; not *the* worst of it, for the worst of it is, that she will be so aggravating, and won't own to it. Say she can't help it; well, then, why don't she own it, and tell me so—not go sticking out, as she'd only jest shet her eyes, and was as wide awake as I was.

Now, I'll jest give you a sample. We live in a part where there's cats enough to make the fortunes of five hundred millions o' Dick Whittingtons. The place is alive with 'em; scratching up your bits of gardens; sneaking in at your back doors, and stealing; making Hyde Parks and Kensington Gardens of the tops o' your wash-houses and tiles of your roof; and howling—howling—why, no mortal pusson would believe how them cats can howl. They seem to give the whole o' their minds to it, and try it one against another, to see who's got the loudest voice, and setting up such a concert as makes the old women cry, "Drat the cats." But that ain't no good: they don't mind being dratted, not a bit of it; and if you go out into the back garden, and shy bricks, why, they only swear at you—awful.

Well, you see, we live in a very catty part, and it seems to me as if the beasts warn't fed enough, and do it out of spite, for no sooner does it get dark, than out they come, tunes their pipes, and then you can hear 'em. No matter where you are, back or front, there they are, a-going it, like hooroar, till I'm blest if it ain't half enough to drive you mad. Why, there's one old black Tom, as you can hear a mile off, and I wouldn't bet as you couldn't hear him two, for he's got a werry peculiar voice of his own. I think it's what musical people calls a tenner, though it might be a hundreder for the noise it makes.

He's an artful old brute, though, is that Tom; and I've tried to come round him scores of times, but it ain't no use, for he won't believe in me. I've taken out saucers of milk and bits of fish, all got ready on purpose for my gentleman, but do you think he'd come? No, thank you. And as soon as ever he ketches sight of me, he shunts, he does, and goes off like an express train in front of a runaway engine.

But I was going to tell you about my wife. Now, nex' Monday's a fortni't since I come home werry tired and worn out—for porter's work at a big terminus at Christmas ain't easy, I can tell you; while, when we are off night dootey, it's only natural as one should like a quiet night's rest, which ain't much to ask for, now is it, even if a man does only get a pound a week, and a sixpence now and then, as swells make a mistake, and give you through not having read the notice up on the walls about instant dismissal, and all that? Well, tired out regularly, and ready to sleep through anything a'most, I goes to bed, and as I lays down I thinks to myself—

You may howl away, my beauties, to-night, for I can sleep through anything.

And really I thought I could, but I suppose it was through having a hyster barrel on my mind, that I couldn't go off directly—for there was one missing, and a fish hamper, both on 'em. No doubt, having been stolen by some one in the crowd on the platform; while I got the blame; and I put it to you, now, could a railway porter, having a pound a week, and Sunday dooty in his turn, have his eyes every wheres at once?

So I didn't go to sleep right off, but some one else did, and there, just outside the window, if one o' them cats didn't begin.

"Wow-w-w, wow-w-w, wow-w-w, meyow-w-w," and all such a pretty tune, finished off with a long low swear at the end.

I stood it for ten minutes good, turning first one side, and then another, pulling the clothes over my ear, and at last ramming my head right under, with my fingers stuck in my ears, but there, Lor' bless you, that was no good, for I'll warrant the song of one of them pretty, soft, furry nightingales to go through anything, and at last I finds that I was only smothering myself for nowt, and I puts my head out of the clothes again, and give a great sigh.

"Me-ow-ow-ow," says my friend on the tiles.

"Hear that, Polly?" I says.

No answer.

"Me-ow-ow-ow-ow-ow-ow," says my friend outside.

"Hear that, Polly?" I says, for there warn't no fun in putting up with all the noise yourself, when there was some one else in the room to take half share. "Polly," I says, giving her a nudge, "hear that?"

"Eh!" she says; "what say?"

"Hear that?" I says.

"Yes," she says; "what?"

"Why, you were asleep," I says.

"That I'm sure I warn't," she says.

"Well, then, did you hear that?" I says.

"Yes; what was it?" she says.

"What was it?" I says. "There; go to sleep again," I says; for I felt quite rusty to think anybody else could sleep through such a row, while I couldn't.

"Meyow—meyow—wow—wow-w-w-w," goes the music again.

"Two on 'em," I says, as I lay listening, and there it went on getting louder and louder every moment, both sides and over the way, and up and down the street, till I'm blest if I could stand it any longer.

"Oh, you beauties," I says; "if I only had a gun." And then I lay there, listening and wondering whether I mightn't just as well get up and have a pipe; and at last of all, because I couldn't stand it any longer, I gets up, goes to the window, opens it softly, and says—

"Ssh!"

Lor' bless you! you might just as well have said nothing, for there they were a-going it all round to that degree, that it was something awful, and I stood there half dressed, and leaning out of the window, wondering what was best to be done. There was no mistake about it; there they were, cats of all sorts and sizes, and of all kinds of voices—some was very shrill, some very hoarse, and some round and deep-toned, and meller. Now and then some one would open a winder, and cry, "Ssh," same as I did, but as soon as they smelt what a sharp frost it was, they shut them down again, and at last I did the same, and made up my mind as I crept into bed again, as I'd go where there was no cats.

Yes, that was a capital idea, that was—to move to a place where there was no cats, and on the strength of that determination, I went off fast asleep.

Next morning over my breakfast, I got thinking, and come to the conclusion, that I'd cut myself out a bit of a job. Where was I to get a little house or lodgings where there was no cats, for were not the happy, domestic creatures everywhere? No; that was of no use, but I warn't going to stand having my rest broken night after night in that way; so I mounted a trap, for I'd made up my mind, that out of revenge, I'd have a full-sized railway rug lined with scarlet cloth, while the rug itself should be of *fur*.

First night I sets my trap, I baited it with a bit of herring. Goes next morning and found the herring had been dragged out at the side, and the trap warn't sprung. Sets it next night, baited with two sprats; goes next morning to find 'em gone, but no pussy. And so I went on, week after week, till I got tired out, and tried poison, which hit the wrong game, and killed our neighbour's tarrier dog. Then I thought I'd try an air-gun, but somehow or another there was a fault in that gun, for it wouldn't shoot straight, and I never hit one of the nuisances. A regular powder-and-shot gun I couldn't try, because it would have spoken so loud, that all the neighbours would have heard and known who was killing the cats.

Last of all, one moonlight night I was down at the bottom of our garden, when I happens to look up towards the back door, and see a long-tailed tortoise-shell beauty sneaking into the kitchen.

"All right, my pretty one," I says, quietly. "You'll do for the middle of the rug," and then stealing softly up, I got to the door, slips in, and had it to in a moment, and then getting hold of the copper-stick and lid, just like a sword and shield, I goes forward to the attack.

No mistake, there was Mrs Puss glaring at me like a small tiger, and as I advanced, she made a rush by me, but there was no escape that way, and then I shut the kitchen-door.

Bang—crash went the crockery, for as I made a hit at the brute, she flew on to the dresser, and along one of the shelves, sending jugs and plates down helter-skelter on the floor, where they smashed to bits.

"All down to your credit, my beauty," I says, and I made another hit at her, when "whoosh," spitting and swearing, she was up on the chimney-piece in a jiffey, and down came the candlesticks, while Polly puts her head in at the door, and then, seeing what was the matter, bangs the door to, and keeps on shouting to me to drive the thing out. But talking was one thing, and acting another, for you never did see such a beast; she was here, there, and everywhere in the same moment; and though I kept hitting at her with the copper-stick, I could hit anything else but her, as you'd have said, if you'd seen me fetch the vegetable-dish and cover off the dresser with a smash, and then seen the copper lid split in two, when I shied it at her.

Why, she flew about to that degree, that I got frightened of her, for at last she came at me, tore at my legs, and then was over my shoulder in an instant, while feeling quite scared, I just saw her dash up the chimney, and she was gone.

"But you won't stop there, my lady," I says, and I was right, for next moment the brute came scrambling down, and we went at it again: she cutting about, and me hitting at her till I got savage, for I never touched her once. Now I hit the table; now it was something off the dresser; now she'd dodge behind the saucepans and kettles, on the black pot-board under the dresser; and now there'd be such a clatter and rattle, that Polly gave quite a scream, for she was wide enough awake then, I can tell you; but the jolly a bit could I touch that precious cat; and at last she stood in one corner of the kitchen, and I stood in the other looking at her, with her tail like a bottle-brush, her fur all up, and her back set up like an arch, and then I thought I'd try coaxing.

"Pussy, pussy, pussy," I says, but she only swore and spit at me.

"Poor pussy; come then," I says; but she wouldn't come near me, and then I turned so savage that I threw the copper-stick at her, but only hit the tea-tray as stood on a little side-table.

"Bang, clang, jangle," down it come on to the floor, and then there was a rush, and a smash, and a scream from Polly; and I stood skretching my head, and looking at the broken kitchen-window—for the beauty had shot right through it when the tea-tray fell down, and now there was nothing to do but pick up the pieces, and go and ask the glazier to come and put in the broken square.

"Oh, what a kitchen," says Polly, as she came in, and really it did look a bit upset, and then seeing as she was put out, and going to make a fuss, I says—

"Bad job; ain't it, my gal; but it warn't me; *it was the cats!*"

"Drat the cats!" says Polly; and she looked so scornful and cross, that I give up all thoughts on the instant of ever getting a skin rug; but if there is any one mortal thing as I do hate, it's a cat.

### Chapter Thirteen.
### An Australian Christmas.

No snow, no frosts, no bare trees, but in the daytime glowing, sultry heat, and of a night soft, balmy, dewy, moonlit hours, and yet it was Christmas-time, and the whole of the past day I had been picturing to myself the cold, sharp, bracing weather at home, with the busy shops and the merry Christmas faces, and now on that 24th of December I was dreaming away of the old home, fourteen thousand miles away; going over again the sad hearts with which we come away, and how we gazed till our eyes swam at the fast fading shores; recalling every sigh and sorrowful thought, when all at once there seemed to be a feeling of horror come over me, and I started up on the heath bed and looked about. But all was still; close beside me lay Abel Franks, my mate and companion, sleeping heavily; the moon was shining through the little window right upon the two dogs stretched before the fireplace, and made it light enough for me to see that everything was in its place. There were the skin rugs on the floor, the rough bench, stool, and table; the guns, rods, nets, and oars of our boat; the shelf with its pile of birds' skins, the brightest hued which fell to our guns; skins of opossum and kangaroo hung against the wall; the burnt-out lamp on the table, with the fragments of our supper, all just as we had left them, while as the surest sign that nothing had disturbed me the dogs were curled up quite motionless, when their quick ears would have heard a step in an instant.

I lay down again and listened attentively for a few minutes, and once heard faintly the howl of a wild dog, but that was all, and there in the stillness of night, in that far-off Australian wild, I was slowly dozing off when I again started up and this time Abel was up too staring at me.

"What is it, Harry?" he cried, as at the same instant I asked him a similar question, and then up leaped both dogs, set up the rough hair round their necks, and ran to the door growling fiercely. The moment after came the cracking of sticks, a rustling through the bushes, and a heavy body fell up against the door, making the rough woodwork creak.

Living as we did in a hut of our own making, furnished by ourselves, our own cooks and managers, we studied dress and toilets but very little; our custom was to throw ourselves down upon our skin-covered bed of heath, so that upon this occasion we were both instantly upon our feet, and, seizing our guns, stood in readiness for action, if defence were needed, for in the days of Australia's early settlements, before the bursting forth of the gold fever, many were the raids made by the savage, and the worse than savage bushranger, escaped "hand," or convict, sent over from the mother country as a part of the dregs of her population, to settle in the infant colonies.

To open the door seemed the first thing, but we naturally hesitated, for that meant giving perhaps an enemy admission to our fortress, for the noise at the door might have been but a ruse to get the better of our caution. A heavy groan, however, decided us, and as I stood with my double gun ready cocked, and a couple of ready patched bullets rammed hastily down upon the charges of duck-shot, Abel cautiously undid the fastenings, and the two dogs, no mean aids at such a time, stood ready for a spring.

There was something startling and oppressive there in the stillness of the great wild, quite two miles as we were from the nearest station, and now roused from slumber in so strange a way; but there was no time for thought, for grasping his long knife in one hand, with the other my companion sharply opened the door, and as he did so a figure fell into his arms. The moonbeams, which streamed in at the open door, gave enough light to show us that we had nothing to fear from the new-comer, who lay before us groaning, while the dogs darted out after a momentary pause by his side, and began scouring about the open.

"Shut the door—quick—quick," groaned the man, "they're tracking me."

We quickly acted upon his advice, and then, carefully covering the window and door with rugs, obtained a light and began to examine our visitor. And a ghastly spectacle he presented: a gash on his forehead was bleeding profusely, covering his face with blood; his shirt was torn and dragged half off, while one arm lay doubled under him in a strange unnatural position, as if it were broken.

"Why it's Jepson," cried Abel in a whisper, and as he spoke the wounded man started, opened his eyes and stared wildly, but closed them again, groaning heavily.

We lifted the poor fellow on to our bed, all the while listening for the warning we expected momentarily to hear from our dogs, for without explanation we knew well enough what had happened, namely, a night attack upon the little station of our neighbour, Mr Anderson, whose shepherd had made his escape to us.

Abel was, like me, all in a tremble, for we knew not yet what was the extent of the disaster, and though we neither of us spoke, we knew each other's thoughts; and our trembling was not from fear for ourselves, but for what might be the fate of Mary Anderson, the blue-eyed Scottish girl, whose presence lent a charm to this far-off wild.

Hastily binding up the poor fellow's head, I looked at and laid in an easier position his arm, which was also bleeding, having evidently been broken by a ball from gun or revolver. A few drops of rum poured between his teeth revived him, and he was able to answer our questions.

"Rangers, sir—six of 'em. They've burnt the place down, shot the master and young Harry, and gone off with Miss Mary and the servant gal. I was tracking them, but they were too much for me; two of them hung back and caught me from behind. I did all I could, and then ran on here."

The exertion of saying this was too much for him, and he fainted away, while half mad with grief and horror, Abel and I stood gazing at one another.

It was evident that the villains would not molest us, for they probably only followed poor Jepson for a short distance, and then hurried after their companions. If they had been in pursuit we should have known of their presence before this from the dogs, which now came whining and scratching at the door for admittance.

We did all we could for the shepherd, and then, following Abel's example, I drew the shot charge from my gun, replaced the bullets, buckled on an ammunition pouch, and then reloaded and primed my revolver. Seeing these preparations going on, the dogs immediately became uneasy and eager to be off, and though our quarry was to be far different to any to which they were accustomed, it would have been a strong, daring man that could have successfully combatted our four-footed allies.

Our preparations were soon made, and then, after placing the spirit and water beside the wounded man, we started off for Anderson's Creek through the dense tea-scrub, for in our then excited state we made for the shortest cut. The moon was fast sinking towards a heavy bank of clouds, but she gave us light for best part of our journey, while the remainder was made plain for us by the glowing house and farm buildings in our front.

I couldn't help it—when I saw the wreck of that house where I had spent so many happy hours, and shudderingly thought of poor Mary, dragged off by the bloodthirsty villains, I stopped short and gave vent to a bitter groan.

This roused Abel, who cried savagely to me to come on; for, faithful and true friends in everything else, there was one rock upon which we split, and that was our admiration for Mary Anderson. He was maddened himself, and scarcely knew how to contain his feelings, but the idea of me grieving for her at such a time seemed to exasperate him, and he almost yelled out—

"Don't be a woman, Fred; come on, or we shall be too late."

"Too late!" Too late for what? A shudder ran through me as I asked myself the question, and taking no notice of Abel's angry manner, I was at his side in an instant, and we dashed on though the bushes.

Just as we got up to the rough fence Abel stumbled and fell over something, and on recovering himself he stooped and raised the head of a man. The ruddy flames shone full upon his countenance, and we saw that it was Harry, one of Mr Anderson's men. He was quite dead, for the side of his head was battered in. Abel softly laid down the poor fellow's head, and then we went cautiously round the building, with guns cocked and ready, in case the villains might be lurking about, though we knew enough of such catastrophes to feel assured that directly they had secured all the plunder and ammunition they could carry off they would decamp.

The greater part of the buildings were blazing. The house was nearly level with the ground, but the men's shed and the wool store still blazed furiously, and on getting round to the back we both raised our pieces to fire, but dropped them again directly, for just in front, squatting round some glowing embers, were a party of black fellows, whom we might have taken for the perpetrators of this foul outrage, had we not known of their peaceable, inoffensive conduct.

In another instant they were running up to us, and a tall fellow, evidently their leader, suddenly threw himself into position, with his long, slender spear held horizontally, as if for throwing, and with the point aimed directly at my breast. Even in the midst of my trouble and anxiety I could not help thinking what an effect such a salute would have upon a stranger, for the unerring aim with which these untutored men can throw a spear is something surprising. But in another instant the spear end touched the ground, and the party closed round us, chattering and begging, and earnest in their efforts to make us aware that they had not been the guilty parties.

"Mine no fire," said the leader. "No black fellow kill."

"No, no," I said; "but who was it?"

"Dat Sam, Sooty Sam," said the savage, holding up six fingers, and pointing towards the bush.

I nodded, and shuddered, for I knew but too well the character of the mulatto convict known as Sooty Sam.

"You give me tickpence, mine shar," cried the fellow.

Money was an article I seldom carried then, unless bound for the nearest settlement for stores, but I happened to have a fourpenny piece in my tobacco pouch, and I gave it to him.

"Dat not tickpence, dat fourpenny," shouted the fellow, indignantly, for constant communion with the settlers had induced a strong desire for the coins that would procure rum or whisky.

A display of my empty pocket, however, satisfied my black ally, and leading us towards one of the sheep pens, he coolly pointed out the body of Mr Anderson, shot through the head, and lying just as he had fallen.

We soon learned from the blacks which way the men had fled, and tried to induce them to go with us to track the marauders, but without avail, night work being their special abomination, and nothing short of a fire like the present sufficing to draw them from their resting-place. We knew that our proper course was to rouse the neighbours at the nearest stations, but in our impatience to pursue the scoundrels prudence and management were forgotten. Unable to gain the assistance of the blacks, we determined to commence the pursuit alone with our dogs, after promising the fellows "much rum" if they would rouse the neighbouring settlers, who, we knew, would soon be on our trail; but in spite of the direction being pointed out, we found, to our disappointment, that the darkness would prove an enemy, and that we must wait for daylight, and reluctantly turned back.

All at once a ray of hope shot through my breast; just before me was old Gyp, my favourite dog, a great half-bred sheep and wolf hound, who was growling and snarling over a heap of what looked like sail cloth, but which inspection showed to be a tattered duck frock, filthily dirty, and stained with blood, evidently having been cut off by some wounded man.

Old Gyp was licking the bloody part, and growling angrily, and on my speaking to him, and encouraging him, he yelped and whined; and then, setting his nose to the ground, ran a few yards, looked back, yelped again, and then would have set off full speed along the trail, had I not called him back and tied a piece of tar band to his neck, holding the other end in my hand.

Abel's eyes glittered as he saw the great powerful beast strain to be off, and then, without a word, we set off at a trot, and leaving the glowing fire behind, plunged into the darkness before us.

We reckoned that the villains had about two hours start, but encumbered, as we knew they must be, with booty, and the two women, we felt sure that, even with the horses they had doubtless taken, they could not have retreated at a very great rate; why, though we both felt that it was like plunging into the lion's jaws, and that most likely one, if not both of us, would lose our lives in the impending struggle, there was not a thought in either of our breasts that savoured of fear, for the desire to overtake the villains was intense.

But it was a fearful task. The darkness was now terrible, and the eager beast struggled on, irrespective of bush or thorn, while every now and then some thick tuft in the track would trip me up. Abel had a hard task to keep up with me. But before daylight matters grew better, for we were in the wood, where there was scarcely any undergrowth, and when day broke we were threading our way through the sombre forest, where the tree trunks were all around, apparently endless, and so similar that only the sagacious beast before us, or a native, could have found a way through.

Now and then we could catch a glimpse of a star or two, but directly after the clouds seemed to close up again, and we stumbled on till a faint light announced the coming day, which found us blackened, torn, and bleeding, but as feverishly eager for the fray as ever.

As for track, that was invisible to us, excepting now and then, where the print of a horse's hoof showed in a moist place, and told us that the faithful beast with us was worthy of the trust placed in him. Now we were out in the open, then making our way again through the tea-scrub, and then skirting a ravine beside the range of rugged, bleak rocks, standing out bold and barren, while the ravine, now here and there green, where a pool of water remained, or a tiny rivulet trickled along where we saw a rushing river in the rainy season.

If one's heart could have been at rest how beautiful was the scene around, tree, bush, flower, and rugged mossy stone, where the track wound in and out, now down into the deep ravine, now crossing the little bright rill which sometimes trickled beneath the grass, and again appeared, leaping from rock to rock. Birds everywhere flitting and climbing about the trees, or hanging in places, like flowers of gorgeous hues.

But there was no peace for us, and we strode on till from the early freshness of the morning we were panting through the heat of the day, heat so oppressive that it grew unbearable, and but for the errand of life and death upon which we were engaged, we should have rested until the sun was again low down in the horizon.

Sooner or later we felt sure that we should come upon some traces of the marauders, and we were not disappointed, for, all at once, the dog gave a whining bark, and began snuffing about in the grass, where lay a bottle evidently but lately cast aside. Then on again, panting, with parched lips and tongue: any doubts that we had formerly had respecting the dog's ability to trace the marauders being now fully put to flight.

And now the track led us right down into the deep ravine, where the sides rose seventy or eighty feet high on either side, at times almost perpendicular; but in spite of the roughness of the path, the coolness was most grateful as we struggled on beneath the shade.

I was at times so faint that I could gladly have rested, but the thought of those on before acted as a spur to my flagging energies, and I pressed on. Abel seemed to know no fatigue, and when he was in front, holding the dog, I had hard work to keep up with him, while I could hear him muttering to himself angrily as he pressed on.

All at once we pulled short up, startled by the threatening aspect that had come over the heavens. It was evident that a storm was coming on; and knowing, as we did, the character of the rain in the region we were in, the thought crossed both our minds, what would the ravine be if a storm came. But the dragging of the dog roused us, and again we pressed on, feeling convinced that we must be close upon the scoundrels; and indeed we were so close that, at the next turning, we came in sight of them—six, with two horses, two of the fellows being mounted, and with one of the women before him.

No sooner were we in sight than the dog bayed loudly; the two mounted men dashed on, while the other four posted themselves to oppose our further passage. There was no turning to the right or left, for the rugged banks effectually opposed all exit, in some parts completely overhanging the glen, and, outnumbered as we were, ours was but an awkward position. However, in the excitement of the moment, fear seemed to have fled, and holding the dog back, we hurried forward to where the fellows stood, taking advantage of every screen which presented itself as we advanced, for we knew how much mercy we had to expect as soon as we came within shot.

Fortunately for us, the huge blocks of quartz lying about afforded ample shelter, and we darted from place to place, each minute getting nearer and nearer. All at once, as I made a run forward to a mass in my front, there was a sharp reverberating crack, and I heard a bullet whistle by my ears, but the next moment I was in safety, and then Abel rushed to my side, but he was not so fortunate, for, as he crossed the open, two shots were fired, one of which grazed his shoulder and just drew blood.

It was now a matter of regular Indian warfare, and we knew well enough that if we dashed forward we must be shot down before we could get hand-to-hand with the ruffians, so Abel took one side of the rock, and I the other, to try and get a return shot at our enemies. It was a mass some fifty feet in length, and when I reached the end I heard Abel fire, and directly after, he fired again, emptying his second barrel, when there was a reply of three shots.

I was hopeful that, hearing two shots, the fellows would think we were both together, and taking advantage of some low bushes, I crawled right to the side of the ravine, and then screening myself behind a buttress, found that I could climb up a few feet to where there was a ledge, which I soon reached, and was then some twenty feet above the bottom, well screened by some bushes; and, to my intense satisfaction, I found, upon creeping to the edge and thrusting my double-barrel between the leaves, I had a good sight at two of the miscreants, whose heads and shoulders were just visible.

As I looked, Abel gave two more shots from his gun, and I saw the chips fly from the rock a little farther off, and then the two men I had not seen before rose up and delivered their fire—dropping down again directly—and evidently with some effect, for I heard a dismal howl, which told of the dog being struck. Directly after, one of the fellows in sight began to crawl forward, evidently intending to take us in the flank; but he had been outwitted, and with the barrel of my gun trembling as I took aim, I fired, and he lay motionless.

In an instant his companion turned in my direction, evidently saw the puff of smoke, and raised his gun towards where I was; but he was too late, I already had him well covered, and I fired again, when the poor wretch gave a wild shriek, sprang into the air, and then fell out of sight amongst the bushes.

I was so horrified that I lay there trembling, so that I could scarcely reload. The perspiration ran off my forehead, and my teeth quite chattered, but it was but for a few moments, for I recalled the scene of the past night, and then remembered what must be the fate of the prisoners were they not rescued. I felt that it was but life for life, and with another shot I might myself be weltering in my blood. The next moment I was cautiously peering out again to get another aim, and now my hand was quite steady. I could see the place where one of the men had shown to get a shot at Abel, but nothing of him was visible, so I crawled a little more forward, when in a moment there was a sharp pang in my left arm, so acute that I could not refrain from crying out, as I started up on one knee; and then I fell again, for, as I heard a second shot, my cap was struck from my head, and I saw that one of the men had changed his position, and was a little higher up the valley, leaning forward to see the result of his aim. But he was too eager, for the next moment there was a shot from Abel and the fellow rolled over, and lay full in my view, quivering and clutching at the ground, tearing up tufts of grass, and gnashing his teeth frightfully. Then came a run and a rush, and I saw the last of the four rush up the ravine, running zigzag, but I got a sight at him, in spite of my pain, and Abel fired too, though apparently without effect; and then the sky seemed to turn black, and the rocks around to swim, and I saw no more till I found Abel leaning over me, dropping some spirit between my lips from his flask.

"There, old fellow," he said, grimly, as he bound up my arm. "Can you walk?"

I nodded; and seeming to gather strength each moment, I followed him down into the ravine, where we found that two of the men were quite dead, while the other was in a dying state, but he struck at us savagely with his knife whenever we tried to approach.

I saw Abel's hand playing angrily with the butt of his revolver, and but for me I believe he would have shot the fellow as he lay, but I hurried him on, and we cautiously proceeded for about a hundred yards, but this time without our dog to track, for the poor brute was lying bleeding to death, shot through the lungs.

All at once there was a shot from a little gully on our right, when Abel threw up his arms and let fell his gun, which exploded as it fell, and then the poor fellow staggered, and went down upon his face.

I did not stop to think that the next bullet might find its billet in my heart, but dashed forward towards the spot from whence the shot had been fired, and directly after I was face to face with an enemy. He was sitting with his back supported by a block of stone, and his gun across his knees, glaring at me with a look of the bitterest hate, and a moment's reflection would have told me that he was wounded unto the death, but in the anger and heat of the moment there was no pausing for thought, and the next moment both barrels of my gun, held pistol-wise, were discharged into his breast.

I ran back to Abel, and raised his head, but with a sickening, deathly feeling, I again let it fall, for the expression of his wild and staring eyes told too well how true had been the aim—the last sting of the dying viper; and when I somewhat recovered, it was to cover the body with fragments of stone, to keep off the birds, and then, weak and faint, I struggled on after the two mounted men.

But a change had now come over the scene; the wind tore furiously overhead, while where I was toiling along it was a perfect calm. Then came the rain—a few big drops, then a cessation; then again a loud and furious howling of the wind; then a calm; while, piled up in huge, lurid, black masses, the clouds seemed to shut out the light of day, save when they were rent asunder by some jagged flash of lightning of a vivid violet hue. Ever and anon there was a glare of light playing behind the clouds, lighting them up in the most glorious way, so that the rolling massy-looking vapours were displayed in all their grandeur, while along the edges, quivering and darting, there was an incessant tremulous light of every brilliant sunset hue. Now came the thunder in a mighty diapason, rolling along the ravine, and seeming as if the sound split and crumbled upon the bare summits of the range of mountains, while fragments of the giant peal were scattered, and came hurrying along the ravine. Then, again, burst after burst of huge, bellowing, metallic peals rumbling hollow and deafening as though discharged from some vast cannon mouth. Blackness again, as if it were night; till in a few seconds came again a blinding flash, displaying the wild aspect of the glen, but only to leave it darker than before; and now again a few drops of rain, pattering upon the dry ground, and splashing from the surface of the lichen-covered rocks, then a sharp fall as of a thunder shower, and I crept beneath the shelter of an overhanging rock, while I hastily covered the lock of my gun, and tried to load it with my one uninjured hand, when again came the lightning playing down the ravine, then black darkness and bellowing, deafening thunder, and then down came the rain—not pouring—not streaming, but in one huge cataract of hissing and foaming waters, as though, indeed, the heavens were opened and the fountains of the great deep broken up. It was as though to have stood beneath it for a moment would have been to be beaten down and swept helplessly away by the waters bubbling and foaming at my feet.

But how refreshing and cooling it seemed as I bathed my fevered brow and moistened the handkerchief hastily bound round my bleeding arm; while, though stopped from continuing my pursuit, I knew that it was impossible for the fugitives to proceed, and I waited anxiously for the cessation of the storm.

Once there came a lull, but only for a few moments, while the brilliant rose-coloured and violet lightning played around, when down came the rain again, more violently than ever, as though it would never cease. The ravine had been turned into a little river, once again towards which, winding in and out amidst the huge blocks of rock, hundreds of watercourses were hurrying. Now it was black darkness, and nothing visible, and the next moment again flaming swords appeared to cut through the rain, and light up the ravine with every rainbow tint; and still came that deafening mighty rushing sound of the waters, as though I were standing upon the spray-wet rock beneath Niagara.

I was standing where a weather-stained mass jutted out from the rocky side and protected me from the heavy fall, but from every jagged and time-worn point around the water streamed down as it leaped and plunged from the mountain side into the ravine. At some early epoch in the world's history, the earth must have divided in some awful internal throe, and then imperfectly closing, have left this long rift forming a watercourse in the rainy season, but in the dry-time merely a stony bed, with here and there a pool. Save where the rains had washed away, and masses of rock had fallen, the sides showed how once they had been torn asunder, and displayed prominence and indentation at every bend.

All at once the rain ceased, as if in obedience to an omnipotent command, the black clouds passed over, and the sun shone down into the ravine. But what a sight met my gaze. Already up to my knees, and teeming along with awful velocity, was a mighty clay-stoned river, eddying, foaming, and sweeping round the rock-strewn bed, and bearing with it leaf, branch, and trunk; bushes and masses of grass torn from the gully sides; while large pieces of rock were being moved from their places, or tottered where they stood.

I stood waiting for the waters to subside, for where I stood it was impossible to scale the rocks, even for an active man, while in my crippled state, I could not have climbed a foot. But they did not seem to subside at first; and I fancied that they perceptibly rose, till I called to mind that I had altered my position a little. But now there was no doubt about it; the waters were rising fast, and I trembled as I thought of being swept away, and my helplessness to cope with the rushing stream; while, again, it was horrid to be prisoned there, while the poor girl I sought to rescue was perhaps being borne farther and farther away. Then came a grim smile as I thought of the vengeance which had overtaken four of the miscreants, and then I shuddered as I thought of the cost at which it had been purchased—poor Abel now perhaps swept from his stony resting-place and borne far away towards the sea.

But now it was time to think of self and life, for the water was rising fast, and as I stood hesitating and watching for a place of safety, and to which I could wade, heard above the present rushing of the waters, came a hideous hollow-sounding roar, and gazing with affrighted eyes, I saw as it were a tall wave rushing down the ravine, making the water in its path foam and roar as, like some large cylinder, it rolled over and over, sweeping all before it, and the next moment I was caught, torn from my feeble hold on the rock, and hurried along, buffeting the strangling waters.

Those were horrible moments: now I was beneath, now above, now dashed half-stunned and senseless against some mass of rock, now thrust down and held beneath the rushing stream by the branches of some torn-up tree. It was impossible to swim, while even in the stillest water such an effort would have been hard to a wounded man. A few despairing thoughts crowded through my brain as I feebly buffeted the waves, and struggled for a few more draughts of the fresh air of heaven, and then after grasping and catching at twigs, branches, and masses of floating turf, I was dashed against a mass of rock, to which I tried to cling. There was a cleft in it wherein I thrust my fingers, and then tried to hold on by my teeth on the soft crumbling stone. At first the little projection broke off, filling my mouth with pieces of grit, but despairingly I again hung on by my teeth, and this time hope seemed to dawn again within my breast, for I thought if I could hold on for awhile, the waters must subside. But as the thought animated me, there came a fiercer rush than ever, I felt the mass of rock totter, roll over, and I gave a wild despairing cry, as I was again swept away faster and faster, while the horrid dread of death gave place to a strange lulling sensation as I closed my eyes.

Once more I was aroused by a violent blow, and as my arm was raised mechanically to grasp, I passed it over the trunk of a large floating tree, and holding on for dear life, I was hurried down with the foaming waters.

The hard battle for breath past, fear came again, and I looked despairingly from left to right for rescue from my perilous position, but everywhere ruin and desolation, while the din of the rushing waters was frightful. Everywhere the sides of the ravine seemed to be crumbling down, and masses of earth and rock were undermined and fell with a terrible splash into the stream, growing more furious every moment, while, wherever the gorge narrowed, the turbulence was awful.

Dashed against masses of drift wood, and bruised against the summits of the projecting rocks, I was faint and despairing, when all at once the roots of the tree I was in caught against a massive stone, the trunk swung round, and I found myself brought up by the side of the gorge, where the branches of a tree hung down; and rousing my last strength I clutched them, and drew myself up, till I could rest my knees upon the floating tree; then I nearly over-balanced myself as the trunk rolled about, but getting hold of a stouter branch I again drew myself up, so that I stood, and then as the trunk again broke loose and floated away, I got one foot upon the rocky side, and hung suspended over the stream, whose waves seemed to leap angrily, to beat me down.

To an uninjured man a slight effort would have been sufficient to place him in safety, but a strange fear seemed to creep over me, as I felt that in a few moments I must fall from my hold, and be swept away. But once more the desire for life came again to renew my strength, and slowly and painfully I got hold for my other foot, and then crawled to a rift, where a little stream of water was rushing down from the table-land above, when by dint of again battling with the blinding water, falling from weakness again and again, I managed to reach the top, crawl beyond the reach of the stream, and then fell exhausted, where I could gaze down upon the raging torrent.

The pain from my wounded arm roused me at last from a half-drowsy, fainting state, and then I eagerly drank from the spirit-flask in my pocket. I then loosened the handkerchief round my wound, and remembering that my task was yet unperformed, I examined my powder, which was fortunately dry, and after carefully wiping, reloaded my revolver, which was safe in my belt, but my gun was lost when I was swept away. The sun was now setting, and I tried to make my plans for the future, but a sense of confusion and dizziness seemed to rob me of all power of action, and at last I threaded my way amongst the trees slowly and painfully, keeping close to the great gully, and listening to the hurrying waters; now shuddering as I thought of the past—now stopping short to think of the possibility of those I was I was in search of being yet in between the walls of the rift, when the storm came, and then I trembled for their fate. But all seemed troubled and confused as I stumbled along, trying to recover my lost ground, for I must have been swept back a mile, though what I could have done to save those I sought from their peril would have been but little. The last I remember then is kneeling down to try and make out some object borne along by the stream, surging along in the darkness below me, for all seemed wild and blank, till I was again hastening with Abel through the wood, guided by the burning farmstead, and watching the black demon-like figures flitting about. Then I could feel the dog tug tug at the string as we tracked the bushrangers, and I listened to his low whimpering cry. Then again came the fight in the gully, and I saw again the agonies of the man I shot, as he griped and clutched with talon-like fingers at the earth; and then came the horrible crashing, rushing voice of the mighty stream, as it raged along, sweeping all before it in its headlong passage. Now, again I was stifling and strangling, grasping and clutching at everything I touched, and then I seemed to be borne under, and all was darkness.

The sun was high in the heavens when I awoke from my stupor-like sleep, with my head throbbing, and gazed at the brilliant blue sky above me, trying to recall the past. I was in pain, and could not raise my arm; there was a delicious cool breeze fanning my cheek, while bright, fresh, and pure, all around seemed grateful to the senses; but as I lay there was a strange trembling vibration of the ground beneath me, and I wondered as with it came a tremendous roar—a rushing noise.

All at once thought came again with a flash, and I shuddered as I recalled the past, and thought of having slept so many hours. Then I sat up and saw that I had fallen within a few feet of the precipice where the stream rushed along still fiercely and impetuously, but with the swift fierceness of a deep and mighty current.

I might well tremble as I gazed upon that huge current—a torrent which had risen fifty feet in a few hours, sweeping all before it, and I trembled again as I thought of those I sought. I rose to my feet and tottered for a few paces, but was soon fain to sit down beneath a tree, and there in the great wild I stayed, faint and weary, hour after hour, listless and but little troubled, as I sat within sound of the rushing waters.

It was towards night when all at once I roused up and stared around me, for it seemed that I heard voices. I listened and all was silent; but again the sound came, again heard above the roaring of the torrent, and then I tried to give the well-known call of the Australian woods, when to my inexpressible joy it was answered, and five minutes after I was surrounded by a party, half squatters, half blacks, who had been upon the track for the murderers of Mr Anderson.

I learned afterwards that the blacks had followed our trail till the storm was coming, when they immediately hurried back, and the whole party had a very narrow escape, but though they had struck the gully again and again, they had seen no traces of those they sought, and but for my hearing them, they would have passed me on their return.

They turned back once more upon learning my history; and, guided by the blacks, kept as close to the brink of the rift as was possible; while, after refreshment and rest, I struggled on with them, hoping against hope that the two poor girls might yet be alive. I knew that if they had escaped they could not be far off; and so the sequel proved.

The search was about concluded; and, sick at heart, I listened to the talked-of return.

"Poor things! they must have been swept away," said one of the squatters, when he started, and ran towards the gully edge, for a long, wild cry for help arose apparently from beneath our feet.

One of the blacks then let himself over the edge, and climbed down, to return directly after with the announcement that Miss Anderson was below.

A rope of handkerchiefs and straps was soon improvised, with which the black again descended; and in a few minutes the poor, fainting girl was drawn up from the shelf of rock upon which she had been for hours resting; and, after regaining her strength somewhat, she related how that, when the storm set in, the men had hurriedly dismounted; and, securing their horses at the bottom, climbed with the two poor girls to the shelf where she was found—a place well sheltered by the overhanging rock; and, of course, at the same time thoroughly hidden from those who passed above.

Then came a time of horror, for they could climb no higher; and slowly they had seen the water swell and rise till it came nearer and nearer; and at last, giddy with fright, the poor servant had slipped from her hold into the fierce stream. The men hesitated for a moment, but directly after let themselves down, and swam boldly after her. Soon after there came a shout, and then one or two strange, gurgling cries, which chilled the hearer's blood, and then all was silent save the rushing of the river, till voices were heard overhead when her cry for help brought salvation.

Times have altered since then, and I often look with pride at the wife who shares my home in the wilderness; and now, years after, in spite of the changes that have taken place, and the safety of person and property in the colony, Mary never hears an unusual noise by night without tremblingly grasping my arm, and listening eagerly, while she recalls the horrors of the deep gully.

## Chapter Fourteen.
## Gnashing of Teeth.

Hush! Be silent! Let this be to you as if whispered under the seal of confession, for it is of the secret, secret. Never let it be known to a soul, or body, let it never even be said aloud, lest some vagrant wind should bear it away, and it become known to the vulgar herd.

Hush, listen! Keep it secret. I am a man who has known sorrow and deep affliction. My heart has been broken—broken? no, hammered to pieces—powdered, till there cannot be a fragment left that has not dissolved away amidst my tears. And how was this, say you? Why, because I loved her. I knew it not at first, but it came upon me imperceptibly, like the pale dawn upon the daisy mead, growing brighter each moment until the sun riseth, and all is one glowing scene of beauty. It was all sunshine then, and earth was brighter day by day in my kindling eye. A new life seemed bursting forth within me. I found charms, where all before was dreary. I slept—but to dream of my beloved image, and awoke but to muse upon her perfections. She was a doctor's little daughter, but the taint of medicine was never upon her, and to love her was a new-born hope. Yes, I dared to hope—presumptuous wretch that I was; but by that which casts the shadow of Wilkie Collins, I will name "No Name." Yes, I hoped that my ardent passion was returned—that is to say that not mine, but another ardent passion was given in exchange. Had not she smiled upon me? and had not her hand rested in mine for an instant, squeezed it, and then gently glided away, while I was bursting with the desire to press my lips upon it? I dared not be too sanguine, but yet hope whispered me that I was loved—that she would be all my own—mine—far off perhaps in the future might the realisation of my wishes be, but I could wait. I was still young, eighteen in a month, and what were a few years, when so peerless a queen awaited me?

Time slipped rapidly by, though I counted the minutes ere I could cull and lay the choicest of flowerets before her—flowers bought with money at Covent Garden Market—flowers received with smiles, while some bud would be culled and placed amidst the ebon ringlets that wantoned around her alabastrine neck. The light of gratitude would beam from those tender dark eyes when some book, poem, or musical trifle that I had sought was presented with a stammered excuse for daring to bring them beneath her queen-like notice. Her coral lips would part, and display the pearly treasures beneath, when I would shrink back timid and fearful lest I should be guilty of a theft and steal a treasure from the coral bow.

I loved her—madly loved her. I paced the square by night to gaze upon her lamp-lit casement—content with gazing upon the blind alone, but enraptured if the shadow of her fairy form was cast upon that blind; misery-stricken if, warned off by the policeman, I had to leave the square, smarting under the knowledge that I was watched. But still I kept long vigils by the house lest evil should befall her, and I not be there to ward it off. But nothing happened: the house did not catch fire; burglars never assailed it; no ruffians ever attempted abduction; and the two mysterious figures who entered by the front door at two o'clock on the Tuesday night, were her father and brother; while the dark man who went down the area was only the policeman. But those were agonies until I knew the truth, and was sweetly rallied for my anxiety. But though no prodigies of valour were ever performed by me, they were there ready in my bosom—a bosom which burned to shed its last drop in her defence.

Months flew by, and then in the balcony one night I told my love of my anxieties, my troubles, my cares, and then, in the intoxication of the moment I saw not that we stood plainly out against the illuminated window, for I only knew that her blushing face was hidden upon my shoulder as I clasped her to my breast and reiterated my vows of love. And she? Ah! she would be mine—mine for ever; and she whispered those words as a ribald street boy sung out "Lul-liety."

Oh, life of blisses! Oh, hours of too-brief happiness! Why passed away—why gone—gone for ever? The moments were too bright to endure, and a cloud crossed the sun of my young and ardent love, raining tears—tears of agony upon my earthly paradise. Doubt, suspicion, hope, fear, all swept across my trusting spirit ere I would give entrance to that fearful brain-enslaving jealousy—maddening jealousy. Oh, but it was a hard battle, for I could not believe her false, even though the evidence was clear as the noon-day sun. The current of my life was changed, and from an open trusting soul I became a spy. I dogged her footsteps, coward that I was, for I dared not upbraid her. But the villain who had robbed me of my peace, for him was reserved the corked-up bottle of my wrath, ready for pouring upon his devoted head. I felt that I could rend him limb from limb, and tear out his false, deceitful heart. I had three times seen him leave the house, and knew him at once as a rival. I hated him with ten thousand-fold fury, but still I must be just. Of noble mien, of polished exterior he was fitted by nature to gain the heart of a weak woman; and even as I passed him I fancied that I could trace a smile of triumph beneath his black moustache. For yes, he passed me almost upon the steps of the house, and then entering a well-appointed brougham, he was driven off.

For days I watched for this demon in black, with his dark eyes, lustrous hair and whiskers, and glistening teeth, for he was, in my sight, a dark tempter, but he did not return. But I saw something which set my brain almost on fire. She left the house morning after morning, and my heart whispered that it was to keep assignations with the treacherous villain.

But I did not upbraid her; I was cheerful and sarcastic in her presence, while she grew strained and strange. And I, knowing that my manner had produced the change, laughed a loud, long, harsh laugh, and left the house with a dramatic scowl upon my brow, and at last, after days of watching, I followed her with the sensation of a hand clutching and compressing my heart. My temples throbbed, my brain swam, and as I hurried along I stumbled against the passers-by.

At last I staggered so heavily against a man that an altercation ensued, a crowd collected, and when I escaped, the cab that I had been tracking was gone.

Oh, the tortures I suffered! oh, the agonies of my mind! but impotent as I felt, what could I do, but wait hours until I saw her return, and then with closely-drawn veil hurry into the house, where I dared not trust myself to follow, for I felt, oh! so bad—so dreadfully bad, I didn't know what to do.

I returned to my abode where I offended my father, upset my mamma, and quarrelled viciously with my poor saintly sisters. And oh! what a night I passed! In the morning when gazing in the mirror, I started with affright from the wretch who met my gaze.

"Take some medicine, Alfy," exclaimed mamma, when she saw that I turned with disgust from my breakfast.

Kind, well-meant words, but what medicine would ease my sorely-distressed mind. But no, I could not eat; and though hours too soon, I could contain myself no longer, but hurried off, engaged a cab, driven by a tiger, who afterwards preyed fearfully upon my pocket, and then had the vehicle posted, where, unseen, I could watch the door of her habitation. The hours passed slowly away as I sat gnawing my fingers, and comparing the present tempest of the heart with the past bliss.

"Go, ungrateful!" I exclaimed aloud.

"Where, sir?" said the cabman; coming to the door and touching his hat.

"No where;" I exclaimed, "stay here."

"Certainly sir, only I thought you shouted."

At length the wretch slept upon his box, whilst I, wretch that I was, envied the poor fellow, and longed for peace and rest from the burning, maddening, torturing pain I suffered. Then I started, for I saw her page come from the house, and in a short space of time return with a cab.

She, false girl, was evidently waiting in the hall—yes, ready now for an assignation, though I had been kept an hour at a time when about to take her to horticultural fête or opera—and directly after and still more closely veiled, she tripped lightly over the pavement and entered the vehicle.

My driver was already well tutored, but he was asleep.

"Follow that cab!" I cried, hurriedly, as I poked at the somnolent wretch with my cane.

"Aw right;" he exclaimed; till I savagely thrust at his ear, when he roused up with a start, jerked the reins, and began to follow the wrong cab.

"No! no!" I shrieked, excitedly; "the other street. That! that! The one turning the corner."

"Then why didn't yer say so at first;" growled the ruffian, blaming me for his own neglect; when on jangled the wretched vehicle closely behind that containing the false one, whilst I pressed and stifled down the feelings battling for escape. Then I endeavoured to arrest the desire to stay her in the street, and prevent the meeting my instinct told me was to take place; for I was determined to confront them, and then cast her off in his vile presence, ere in the far-off Antipodean South I fled, to seek forgetfulness or a grave.

The cabs stopped, and then I saw her enter the door of a noble-looking mansion, where she was evidently expected. What could I do? In my impotence I sat for a while madly raging in my cab, for, gifted with a strong imagination, I could, in fancy, see all that was taking place: soft glances, clasped hands, the arm of the foreign-count-looking fiend around her waist, her head resting upon his shoulder, and then eyes meeting eyes, and her face buried in that hideous black beard. Oh! it was too much; and I sprang out of my cab, ran up the steps, tore at the bell, and then, as if by magic, the door was opened, when, guided by instinct, I pushed by the servant, and hurried up the drawing-room stairs. Unheeding the shout of the liveried menial, I paused for a moment undetermined before three doors, when, hearing low muttered sounds, I opened the one right before me, and entered.

Will time ever erase the agony of that moment from my memory? Shall I ever again know that state of happy rest—those peaceful hours, ere I gazed upon thy false, false face? Oh, Eva! Alas! no. My heart still answers No!

I glided like an avenging serpent into the room, so silently that they heard me not, and then for a moment I was spell-bound with agony, for there was almost what I had pictured. With her bonnet thrown off, her long dark hair hanging over the back of the fauteuil in which she reclined, and her eyes raised towards his, was the false one. While he, the blight and crusher of my life, leant over her, caressing her cheek, and bending nearer and nearer, and nearer still—but I could bear no more: my eyes seemed blinded with fury, and to be starting out of their sockets; my brain burned; and with one wild, hoarse cry of "Fiend," Nemesis-like I launched myself upon him.

In a moment, with a cry of dread, he wrenched himself round and confronted me with his ashen face, but with a wild "Ha! ha!" I had him by the throat, and we wrestled here and there, tumbling the rich furniture in every direction, till, with almost superhuman strength, I dashed his head through the pier-glass behind him.

There was a fearful crash, and the wretched woman shrieked aloud; but I was deaf to her cries as she implored me to spare him. I laughed again madly, and still held to the struggling wretch, till, half strangled and in despair, he dashed something in my face, when, as it fell shattering to the floor, I started back and held my enemy at arm's length.

Aghast I gazed upon Eva, but she covered her face with her hands, and tried to swoon, as she sank in a heap upon the floor. But I had seen all—all in that horribly-distorted mouth. A fearful light had flashed across my brain, and, as servants came hurrying into the room, I thrust my enemy from me, and parting the people at the door, darted down the stairs and fled for my life.

Forgetful of the waiting cab, I was tearing along the pave, when the driver, fearful for his fare, galloped his wretched knacker after me, and then I staggered in, and sunk back amongst the hard cushions, ready almost to heap the dirty straw from beneath my feet upon my wretched head, but still I could hear the sympathising words of the cabby as he closed the door.

"Pore chap, it must ha' been a scrauntch."

For he knew where I had been—where I had seen all—all in that fearful moment—the gnashing teeth which lay at my feet, the man's face, Eva's distorted, mumbling mouth; and I had fled, never to see her more—never to know rest for the aching misery within my heart. Alas! I had seen all, and oh! cabby, faithful charioteer, 'twas indeed an awful scrauntch, for my fancied rival was Michael Angelo Raphael, the Dentist.

It is only fair to state, on behalf of the young gentleman from whom the above emanated, that he really seemed very bad indeed; in fact, desperate. But as he could eat very heartily, and evidently used a great deal of pomatum, his case is hopeful.

### Chapter Fifteen.
### The Monarch of the Mould.

 Sing, poet divine
 Of your sparkling wine
Of Catawba, the luscious nectar;
 While my humbler lays
 Shall rise in praise
Of a king on whose fame I'll hector.

 But your lips don't shoot,
 For my king's but fruit,
And your brows don't frown with scorning;
 For if to an end
 Came my noble friend,
The nation would go into mourning.

 'Tis that fruit of earth
 That the West gave birth,
Introduced to our good Queen Bessy;
 For its glorious savour
 Has a sweeter flavour
Than an epicure's *entrée* messy.

 Potato, potato,
 My heart's elate, oh!
When you smile on my table brightly;
 With an epidermis
 That, so far from firm is
That it cracks when I grasp you tightly.

 For a roast, bake, boil,
 Stew or fry in oil,
No fruit can be called thy equal;
 For carrot or turnip
 Might him or her nip,
And cause an unpleasant sequel.

  But thou, free from guile,
   Indigestion - bile—
Brought home to thy charge were never;
   For thy soft white meal
   Is the dinner leal
Of Great Britain's sons for ever.

   To say the least,
   For a Christmas feast,
'Twould be quite an act of folly,
   And far less shirky
   To leave goose or turkey,
Than a bowl of potatoes jolly.

   Why, the old king's friend
   Sir Loin to attend,
Would surely ne'er brown if he knew it;
   And the very ale
   Turn beadless - pale,
While the beef turn'd cold in its suet.

   The firmest friend
   Mother earth could send
To her children when pots were minus;
   Of a pan not the ghost,
   But they still could roast
The old king whereon still we dine us.


   By disease tried sore—
   May it come no more!
For what should we do without him?
   For Jamaica yam
   Is a sorry flam,
And an artichoke - There, pray scout him!

   Or who'd think nice
   Soppy plain-boil'd rice,
Or parsnips or chestnuts toasted?
   Earth has no fruit
   As a substitute
For the 'tater plain-boil'd or roasted.

   So waxy and prime
   In the summer-time,
When new, with your lamb and gravy,
   And your young sweet peas,
   Devour'd with ease—
Of that you may make "affidavy."

   Or in autumn glowing
   To crown the sowing,
I love to gaze on the furrows
   And ridges tumid
   Where moistly humid
The jolly old nubbly burrows.

O vegetable!
  Long as we're able
Our gardens shall smile with your flower;
  As in long straight rows
  This old friend grows
So humbly where others tower.

  A cabbage to cut
  Is all right, but
Where is its strength and stamina?
  Though right with ham on
  Your table, or gammon,
At best 'tis a watery gammoner,


  You may go if you list,
  Where you like 'tis miss'd
Before any *entrée* or other
  Grand preparation
  Of a French cook's nation,
And naught can the great want smother.

  Feast on, grandee!
  From your board I'll flee
To my honest old friend in his jacket;
  For 'twill sit but light,
  Though you may feel tight
If you too indiscreetly attack it.

  And, glorious thought!
  It can be bought—
This gem of whose wealth I've boasted—
  For a bronze to be got,
  In our streets "all hot,"
Half cooked by steam and half roasted.

  Who wouldn't be poor
  (Not I, I'm sure),
To enjoy such a feast for a copper?
  Split open - butter'd—
  Oh, joy ne'er utter'd!
And pepper'd - and - "what a whopper?"

  Just look at the steam,
  At the can's bright gleam,
And look at the vendor cheery;
  And hark to his cry,
  Now low, now high,
Speaking feasts for the traveller weary.


  Go pick yourself,
  And spend your pelf,
Three pound for twopence - they ask it—
  With eyes full winking;

And while you're thinking,
The scale's tipp'd into your basket.

And you who'd wive,
Pray, just look alive,
And before you declare each feeling,
Watch your little mouse
On her way through the house,
And catch her potato peeling.

You know of the cheese,
And Pimlico's ease,
When he pick'd out a wife by the paring;
But a better plan
For an every-day man—
Though an innovation most daring—

Is to watch the play
Of the knife, and the way
That the coat of potato's falling;
Just look out for waste,
And beware of haste,
For thrift's not the meanest calling.

Kidney, regent, fluke,
Fit for earl or duke,
Or a banquet for Queen Victoria;
Own'd I but lyre,
I'd never tire,
Of singing to thy praise a "Gloria."

May you mealy wax,
Never tried by tax,
Ever free from *Aphis vastator*.
Of fruits the king,
Its praise we'll sing,
Potent, pot-boy, "potater!"

## Chapter Sixteen.
## Spun Yarn.

Uncle Joe came and spent Christmas with us last year; a fine, dry, mahogany-visaged old man-o'-war's-man as ever hitched up his trousers, and called it, "hauling in slack."

"Forty-five years' boy and man, I've been a sailor," he'd say; "rated AB, I am; and AB I hope to keep till I'm sewed up in my hammock and sent overboard; for none of your rotting in harbour for me, thanky."

Uncle Joe ran away to sea when quite a boy, and he had served enough years in the Royal Navy to have been an admiral, but what with our scheme of promotion, and some want of ability on the old fellow's part, he was a first-rate able seaman, but he never got a step farther. One can always picture him in his blue trousers and loose guernsey, with its wide turn-down collar, his cap set right back on his head, and the name of his ship on the band, in gilt letters, while his big clasp-knife hung by the white lanyard round his waist. Clean, neat, and active, the sinewy old chap came rolling in after my father; neck open, eyes bright, and face shining and good-humoured.

"Cold, cold, cold," said my father, entering the room where we were clustered round the fire. "Freezes sharp; and, bless my heart, there's a great ball of snow sticking to my boot," saying which, the old gentleman, who had just been round the farmyard for the last time that night, went back into the passage and rubbed off the snow, while Uncle Joe, chuckling and laughing, walked up to the fireplace and scraped his shoes on the front bar, so that the pieces of hard snow began sputtering and cissing as they fell in the fire.

"Cold?" said Uncle Joe, filling his pipe, and then shutting his brass tobacco-box with a snap; "Cold? 'taint cold a bit, no more nor that's hot," and then, stooping down, he thrust a finger and thumb in between the bottom bars, caught hold of a piece of glowing coal and laid it upon the bowl of his pipe, which means soon ignited the tobacco within. "My hands are hard enough for anything," he growled, taking the place made for him beside the fire, when he tucked his cap beneath the chair, and then took one leg upon his knee, and nursed it as he smoked for awhile in silence.

"Now, come, Christmas-night," cried my father, "and you're all as quiet as so many mice. What's it to be, Joe—the old thing?"

"Well, yes," growled my uncle; "I won't say no to a tot o' grog," and then he smoked on abstractedly, while my father mixed for the wanderer whom he had not seen for five years.

"Wish to goodness I'd brought a hammock," said my uncle, at last. "I did try whether I couldn't lash the curtains together last night, but they're too weak."

"I should think so, indeed," exclaimed my mother. "That chintz, too. How can you be so foolish, Joe?"

My uncle smoked on, apparently thinking with great disgust of the comfortably-furnished bedroom in which he had to sleep, as compared with the main-deck of his frigate.

"But 'taint cold," he all at once burst out.

"Three or four degrees of frost, at all events," said my father.

"Pooh; what's that?" said my uncle. "That's hot weather, that is. How should you like to sleep where yours and your mate's breath all turns into a fall of snow, and comes tumbling on to you? How should you like to nibble your rum as if it was sugar-candy, and never touch nothing of iron for fear of burning your fingers like, and leaving all the skin behind? This ain't cold."

"Here, draw round close," cried my father; "throw on another log or two, and Uncle Joe will spin you a yarn."

The fire was replenished, and as the many-hued flames leaped and danced, and the sparks flew up the chimney, every face was lit up with the golden glow. The wind roared round the house, and sung in the chimney, but the red curtains were closely-drawn, the table was well spread with those creature comforts so oft seen at the genial season, and closing tightly in—chair against chair—we all watched for the next opening of Uncle Joe's oracular lips. And we had not long to wait; for, taking his pipe out of his mouth, he began to point with the stem, describe circles, and flourish it oratorically, as he once more exclaimed—

"'Taint cold; not a bit! How should you like to spend Christmas up close aside the North Pole?"

No one answering with anything further than a shiver, the old tar went on:—

"I can't spin yarns, I can't, for I allus gets things in a tangle and can't find the ends again, but I'll tell you about going up after Sir John Franklin."

"Hear, hear!" said my father, and Uncle Joe tasted his grog, and then winked very solemnly at my father, as much as to say "That's it exact."

"Little more rum?" hinted my father. Uncle Joe winked with his other eye and shook his head and went on:—

"You see, ours was a strong-built ship, fitted out on purpose for the North seas, and what we had to do was to go right up as far nor'ard as we could get, and leave depots of preserved meats, and spirits, and blankets, and pemmican, and all sorts of necessaries, at different places where it was likely that the party might reach; and to mark these spots we had to build up cairns of stones, so that they might be seen. Well, we'd got as far as our captain thought it prudent to go, for we were back'ard in the year, in consequence of the ice having been very late before it broke up that year, and hindering us a good deal; and now that we had landed all as was necessary, and built up the last cairn, the captain says to the officers, he says, 'We'll go back now, or we shall be shut in for the winter.'

"'Twasn't so late in the autumn, and no doubt you were having nice warm weather, but things began looking precious winterly round about us. Great icebergs were floating about, and fogs would hang round them. Snowstorms would come on, with snow with such sharp edges that it would seem a'most to cut your ears off. The shrouds and clews and sheets would be all stiff and covered with ice, while, as to the sails, they were like so much board, and it got to be tough work up aloft.

"'Cold this here,' I says to a shipmet. 'Pooh,' he says, 'this ain't nothing yet.' Nor more it warn't nothing at all; and there we were going along as well as we could, with double lookouts, and plenty of need for them to use their eyes, for we might have been crash on to an iceberg ten times over. Captain used to shake his head and look serious, and enough to make him, with all his responsibility, and all of us looking up to him to take care of us; and last of all we seemed to be right in the thick of it, with the ice-pack all around, and ice and snow, ice and snow everywhere, and us just gently sailing along a narrow open channel of blue water, sometimes going east, sometimes west, just as it happened. Sometimes a little more wind would spring up, and the pack opened a bit, and made fresh channels, so that we got on; then the wind would drop, and the loose ice close round us, so that we hardly moved, and at last one morning when I turns out, we were froze in.

"But not hard stuck, you know; for we soon had that ice broken, and got hauling along by fixing ice-anchors, and then pulling at the cable; but our captain only did it by way of duty, and trying to the very last to get free; for his orders were not to winter up there if he could help it. But there we were next morning tighter in than ever, with the ship creaking and groaning at the pressure upon her ribs, and the ice tightening her up more and more, till at last if she weren't lifted right up ever so many foot, and hung over all on one side, so as we had cables and anchors out into the ice to make sure as she didn't capsize. But there was no capsize in her; and there she sat, all on the careen, just as if she was mounting a big wave; and so she was, only it was solid.

"Days went by, and the sun got lower and lower, and the weather colder and colder. Sometimes we'd see flocks of birds going south, then a herd or two of deer, and once or twice we saw a bear, but they fought very shy of us; and, last of all, the captain seeing that we must make the best of our winter quarters, set us to work unbending sails, striking masts, and lowering spars on deck, and then the stuff was had up, and the deck regularly roofed in, so as to make a snug house of the ship. Stoves were rigged, snow hauled up round the hull, steps made up to the side, and one way or another all looked so jolly, that I began to reckon on spending my Christmas out in the polar regions. Then, too, extra clothes were sarved out, and gloves, and masks, and fur caps; and one way and another we got to make such stuffed mummies of ourselves, that a rare lot of joking went on.

"'Wait a bit,' says my mate, 'it'll be colder yet;' and so it was, colder and colder, till I couldn't have believed it possible that it could be a bit worse. But it could, though; for, before the winter was over, there's been times when if a man went outside the vessel the cold would have cut him down dead almost in a moment, and he not able to help himself. Why, as I told you, down on the main-deck, the breath used to turn into a reg'lar fall of snow, and everything would freeze hard in spite of the roaring fires we kept up; and only think of it, just at this time it was always dark, for the sun had gone lower and lower, till at last he had not risen at all, and it was one long, dreary night, with every star seeming to shoot bright icy arrows at you to cut you down.

"The captain used to do all he could to cheer us up, and keep the horrors off; for you know they will come out there when you're all in the dark and half froze, and wondering whether you'll see home any more. Sometimes it would be exercise, sometimes a bit of a play, or skylarking. Then one officer or another would read, and we'd have have some music or yarn-spinning, and altogether we were very sociable; and so matters went on till it got to be Christmas-day."

In whose honour Uncle Joe treated himself to a hearty libation from his steaming tumbler.

"—Christmas-day," said my uncle, "and *pro*ceedings were made for a grand spread, in honour of the old day and them as we'd left behind us.

"Well, the officers made themselves very sociable, and the grog went round. Some chaps danced, others smoked, and one way and another things went on jolly; but though the little stoves roared till they got red-hot, yet there was a regular fog down between decks, while the captain said that it was about the coldest day we had had yet.

"Towards night it seemed to come on awful all at once, and first one and then another chap began shivering and twisting up his shoulders, and then I saw the captain, who was down, give a sharp look round, and then slip on deck, where I heard him shout out.

"A dozen of us scrambled up on the covered-in deck, feeling cut in two with the icy wind that came down, and then we found as the door out of the bulwarks, and fitted in at the side, had been left open by some one—a door you know that just about this time used to mostly have a man aside it, and when our chaps went to the little ice-observatory it used to be banged to after 'em directly; while if it had been left open but one night, I daresay some on us wouldn't have woke up any more.

"'Who's gone out?' cries the captain, and then the men begins looking from one to the other, but no one answered.

"'Where's Joe Perry,' shouts out some one in front of me. 'It's Joe Perry as is gone.'

"'You're a—something,' I was going to say, but I was that vexed I didn't say it; but, forgetting all about the officers, I gives my gentleman such a cuff on the ear, as sent him staggering; when instead of being angry, I saw the Cap bite his lip, and no end of chaps began sniggering.

"'But where's Bill Barker,' I says, looking round, for I remembered seeing Bill go up the companion ladder about ten minutes before.

"'Pass the word for William Barker,' says the captain, and they passed it, but there was no answer, and then we knew that Bill must have slipped out against orders, thinking he wouldn't be missed, while the chaps were keeping up Christmas, and forgetting that we should feel the cold from the door he was obliged to leave open, so as to get in again.

"'Foolish fellow,' cried the captain, stamping about the deck. 'Volunteers there, who'll fetch him in? These five will do,' he says, and in a few minutes the first luff with five men, were all ready in their fur coats and boots, and masks over their faces, or I oughter say, our faces, for I was one of 'em. And yet you say it's cold here now. Pooh! Why, we were no sooner outside in that bright starlight, with the northern lights hanging ahead of us, much like a rainbow, than it was as if your breath was taken away, and the wind cutting right through and through you, stiffening your joints, tingling powerfully in your nose, and seeming to make you numbed and stupid.

"'Double,' shouts the luff, and keeping our eyes about us, we began to trot along the snowy path towards the little observatory. But he wasn't there. Then we ran a little one way, then another, and all keeping together as well as we could for the rough ice we were going over. But there was nothing to be seen anywhere on that side of the ship, so we trotted round to the other side, always keeping a sharp look out for our poor mate, and hoping after all that he would be all right; but going by my own feelings, I could not help feeling sure that if he had come out without the same things on as we had, it would go hard with him.

"'Here look!' some one shouted in a thick muffly voice, but we were all looking now towards where a couple of bears were coming slowly towards us, while quite plain between us lay on the white snow, the body of poor Bill Barker.

"'Back to the ship,' shouted the first luff, and we were soon once more a-top of the steps and inside, but you needn't think we were going to leave our shipmet in that way, for the next minute saw us going back at the double, but this time well armed.

"As soon as we were within shot, the first luff kneels down, and taking aim, fired his double rifle right and left at the two great brutes that stood growling over poor Bill Barker.

"'Stand firm, men,' he says, then 'prepare to charge.' And then we five stood with our guns and bayonets ready for the brutes as began to come down upon us, while the luff got behind us, and began to load. You see he wouldn't let us fire on account of poor Bill, and I s'pose he had more trust in his own gun than in ours, for he kept on fumbling away in the cold till he was loaded, which was when the brutes were only about a dozen yards off, when he drops on one knee aside me, and taking a good long aim fired when one brute was only five or six yards off—both barrels right into him, and rolled him over and over, just as he would have done a rabbit. But the next moment it was helter-skelter, and hooraying, for t'other bear was down on us with a rush, taking no more notice of our bayonets than if they had been so many toothpicks, and downing two of our chaps like nine-pins.

"'Be firm, men,' shouts the luff, and we three ran at the great brute that stood growling over our two mates, and I don't know about what t'others did, but at one and the same moment, I drove the bayonet up to the gun muzzle right in the bear's flank, and fired as well. Then it seemed that the gun was wrenched out of my hand, and I saw the great brute rear up above me, fetch me a pat with one of its paws, when I caught a glimpse of the luff and heard the sharp ring of his rifle again, and then I seemed to be smothered, for the great beast fell right upon me.

"I don't know how long it was before they got help from the ship, and the great brute dragged off me; but I know that the next thing I remember is being carried into the ship through the doorway, and hearing some one say, that Bill Barker was frozen stiff and cold. But I soon came to, and excepting the bruises, there was nothing worse the matter than a broken rib, which I soon got the better of. But poor Bill was dead and frozen hard when they got him aboard, with his gun tight fixed in his hand, so that they could not get it away for some time; for though the poor chap knew all the orders well enough about going out without proper preparations, like many more of us, he couldn't believe as the frost would have such power—power enough to cut him down before he'd walked a couple hundred yards, for it was something awful that night, though the little brawny chaps that live in those parts, seem to bear it very well.

"Freeze! why this is nothing: them two bears were masses of ice next morning when they hauled 'em on board, while everything we cut, had to be thawed first before the stove-fires. But then we had plenty of provisions, and I don't think I once saw the grog get down so low, as in this here glass of mine—here present."

My father took the hint, and replenished the old sailor's glass.

## Chapter Seventeen.
### Asher's Last Hour.

"Now, once for all," said Asher Skurge, "if I don't get my bit o' rent by to-morrow at four o'clock, out you goes, bag and baggage, Christmas-eve or no Christmas-eve. If you can't afford to pay rent, you'd best go in the house, and let them pay as will." And Asher girded up his loins, and left Widow Bond and her children in their bare cottage, to moan over their bitter fate.

And then came Christmas-eve and four o'clock, and no money; and, what was better, no Asher Skurge to turn out Widow Bond, "bag and baggage," not a very difficult task, for there was not much of it. The cottage was well-furnished before Frank Bond's ship was lost at sea, and the widow had to live by needlework, which, in her case, meant starving, although she found two or three friends in the village who were very sorry for her, or at all events said they were, which answered the same purpose.

However, four o'clock grew near—came—passed—and no Asher. It was not very dark, for there was snow—bright, glittering snow upon the ground; but it gradually grew darker and darker, and with the deepening gloom, Mrs Bond's spirits rose, for she felt that, leaving heart out of the question, old Skurge, the parish clerk, dare not turn her out that night on account of his own character. Five o'clock came, and then six, and still no Asher; and Widow Bond reasonably thought that something must be keeping him.

Mrs Bond was right—something was keeping the clerk, and that something was the prettiest, yellow-haired, violet-eyed maiden that ever turned out not to be a dreadful heroine given to breaking up, and then pounding, the whole of the ten commandments in a way that would have staggered Moses himself. No; Amy Frith, the rector's daughter, was not a wicked heroine, and now that she was busy giving the finishing touches to the altar-screen, and pricking her little fingers with holly till they bled, she would not let the old man go because young Harry Thornton, her father's pupil, was there. And Amy knew that so sure as old Skurge took himself off, the young man would begin making love, which, though it may be crowned in a church, ought not to be made in the same place.

The young man fumed and fretted; and the old man coughed and groaned and told of his rheumatics; but it was of no use; the maiden pitied them both, and would have set them at liberty on her own terms, but remained inexorable in other respects till the clock chimed half-past six, when the candles were extinguished, the dim old church left to its repose, and the late occupants took their departure to the rectory, and the long low cottage fifty yards from the church gates.

"No; it couldn't be done at any price—turn the woman out on such a night; the whole place would be up in arms; but he would go and see if there was any money for him;" and so Asher Skurge partook of his frugal tea by his very frugal fire, a fire which seemed to make him colder, for it was so small that the wintry winds, which came pelting in at keyhole and cranny, all hooted, and teased, and laughed at it, and rushed, and danced, and flitted round, so that they made a terrible commotion all about Asher's chair, and gave him far more cause to complain of rheumatics than he had before.

So Asher buttoned himself up, body and soul too; he buttoned his soul up so tight that there was not space for the smallest, tiniest shade of a glance or a ray of good feeling to peep out; and then he sallied forth out into the night-wind, with his nose as sharp and blue as if it had been made of steel; and, as he hurried along, it split the frosty wind right up, like the prow of a boat does water, and the sharp wind was thus split into two sharper winds, which went screeching behind him, to cut up the last remains of anything left growing.

He was a keen man was Asher; as keen a man as ever said "Amen" after a prayer and didn't mean it. Ill-natured folks said he only seemed in his element on Commination-day, when, after all the Curseds, he rolled out the Amens with the greatest of gusto, and as if he really did mean it, while the rector would quite shiver—but then the wind generally is easterly at commination time, in the cold spring. He used to boast that he had neither chick nor child, did Asher; and here again people would say it was a blessing, for one Skurge was enough in a village; and that it was a further blessing that his was a slow race. He was a cold-blooded old rascal; but for all that he was warm, inasmuch as he had well feathered his nest, and might by this time have been churchwarden; but he preferred being clerk, to the very great disgust of Parson Frith, who would gladly have been rid of him long enough before.

It did seem too bad to go worrying a poor widow for rent on a Christmas-eve; but nothing was too bad for Asher, who soon made the poor woman's heart leap, and then sink with despair.

Old Skurge was soon back in his own room, and the wind at last blew so very cold that he indulged in the extravagance of an extra shovel of coals, and a small chump of wood, and then he drew his pipe from the corner and began to smoke, filling the bowl out of a small white gallipot containing a mixture, half tobacco, half herbs, which he found most economical; for it did not merely spin out the tobacco, but no dropper-in ever cared about having a pipe of "Skurge's particular," as it was named in the village.

Then, after smoking a bit, Asher seemed moved to proceed to further extravagance, in consequence of its being Christmas-eve; so he laid down his pipe, rubbed his ear, and then plunged his hand into his pocket and brought out a small key. The small key opened a small cupboard, wherein hung upon nails some half-dozen larger keys, one of which was taken down and used to open a larger cupboard, from which Asher Skurge brought forth a well-corked and tied-down bottle.

A cunning, inhospitable old rascal, bringing out his hidden treasures to bib on a winter's night alone. What was it in the old black bottle? Curaçoa, maraschino, cherry brandy, genuine hollands, potent rum, cognac? Hush! was it smuggled-up remains, or an odd bottle of sacramental wine? No, it was none of these; but it poured forth clear, bright, and amber-hued, with a creaming foam on the top; and—"blob;" what was that? a swollen raisin, and the grains that slipped to the bottom were rice.

Then what could the liquid be? The old man sipped it and tried to look gratified, and sipped again, and took a long breath, and said "ha!" as he set down the glass, and proceeded to fish out the raisin and bits of rice, which he threw on the fire, and disgusted it to that extent that it spat and sputtered; after which he let the glass stand again for a long time before he attempted another taste, for the liquid was very small, very sour beer, six months in bottle. Another year, perhaps, might have improved its quality; but one thing was certain, and that was, that it could be no worse.

But Asher Skurge was not going to show that he did not appreciate the sour beverage, for he considered himself quite bacchanalian; and, after one loud gust of wind, he poked his fire so recklessly that the poor thing turned faint, and nearly became extinct, but was at length tickled and coaxed into burning.

"Nine of 'em," said Asher, as the old Dutch clock in the corner gave warning of its intention to strike shortly; a chirping, jarring sound, as much as to say "stand clear or you'll be hit;" and just then the clerk stopped short, put down his pipe again, and rubbed the side of his nose uneasily; got up and looked closer at the clock; went to the window and moved the blind to get a peep out, and then came back to the fire and sat rubbing his hands.

"Never knew such a thing before in my life," said Asher. "Never once forgot it before. And just at a time, too, when I'm comfortable. All that confounded woman's fault for not paying her rent. Running after her when I'd my own business to attend to." In fact, the old clerk had been so put out of his regular course that night, what with church decorations and hunting up Widow Bond, that he had quite forgotten to wind up the clock, the old church time-keeper that he had never let run down once for twenty years.

It was a rough job though upon such a night, just as he was so comfortable, and enjoying his beer and tobacco in so jovial a manner. He looked in his almanac to make sure this was the right evening, and that he had not worked his ideas into a knot; but, no; his ideas were all straight and in good order, and this was the night for winding up.

Couldn't he leave it till the morning?

Couldn't he forget all about it?

Couldn't he wait half an hour?

Couldn't he—couldn't he?—No; he couldn't; for habits that have been grown into, can't be cast off in a moment. They may be shabby, and they may be bad habits; they may hang in rags about the wearer, but for all that it takes some time to get rid of them; and if Asher Skurge had not wound up the clock upon this particular night, he would have been unable to sleep in his bed, he would have had the weights upon his chest, the lines hanging round his neck, and the pendulum vibrating within an inch of his nose, while the hands pointed at him, and called attention to his neglect.

No; once a week had Asher Skurge wound up that clock; and, "will he, nill he," it seemed he must go this night and perform his old duty. But he did wait more than half an hour, and then how he did snap, and snarl, and worry the air—the cold air of the room. He might have been taken for a wiry terrier showing his teeth with impotent rage while worried by the attacks of a flea legion; but there was nothing for it, and he got up and tied his comforter three times round his neck; brought the horn lantern out of the cupboard, and then tried to illumine the scrap of candle at the bottom. But there was no illumination in that candle. To begin with, it was only a fag-end—one where the cotton did not reach the end of the grease, and to make matters worse, it had been extinguished in that popular manner—snuffing out with wet fingers. Consequently the candle end spit, spat, and sputtered; sent off little fatty scintillations, and then went out. Lit again, it went through the same process, and upon repeating this twice, Asher grew wroth, seized the offending morsel, and dashed it into the fire, where it flared up and seemed to rejoice in the warmth, whilst its indignant owner wiped his fingers in his scant hair, and then lit a fresh piece, closed the lanthorn, and opened the door for a start.

Talk about Will-o'-the-Wisps and hobgoblins, why Asher looked quite the equal of any ugly monstrosity of the imagination, as he went crunching and grumbling along the snowy path on his way to the belfry-door. The wind was colder than ever, while in spite of the howling din, it was bright and clear overhead, and the stars seemed not merely to twinkle, but quiver and dance.

Asher's journey was but a short one, and mostly along the narrow side path which led amongst the tombstones and wooden tablets; but he cared no more for tombstones, and night walks in churchyards, than he did for walks in the meadows; so on he went, "crunch, crunch," on the frozen snow, never pausing to admire the beautiful old church in its

Christmas mantle, but growling and grumbling, and if it had been any other man we might have said swearing, till he reached the door in the tower and fumbled in the big key.

"Scraun-n-n-n-tch" went the old wards as the rusty key turned in the rusty lock; and "Crea-ee-ee-ak" went the great door upon its old hinges; and then setting down his lanthorn, Asher tried to shut the door again to keep out the bitter wind. But the door would not shut, but seemed as if something was pushing it back against him; and it was not until after two or three vigorous thrusts, that the old man stopped to scratch his head, and took up his lanthorn and examined the hinges; when, sure enough, there was something which prevented the door closing, for there was a great bone stuck in the crack, and it was so squeezed and jammed in that it took a great deal of getting out. But when it was got out, Asher threw it savagely away, for he minded not a bone or two when there was quite a heap in the corner behind him; so he threw it savagely away, and gave the door a bang which made the old tower jar, and the light in his lanthorn quiver, while just then there was a rattling noise, and something round came rolling up to him and stopped up against his feet so that the old man gave quite a start.

"Bah!" exclaimed Asher directly after, for he made no more account of a skull than the grave-digger in Hamlet. "Bah?" he exclaimed; and he gave the skull a fierce kick to send it back to the heap from whence it had rolled. But just then Asher gave a leap—a most nimble one, too, for so old a man; for the skull seemed to have seized him by the foot, and stuck tightly to his heavy boot, which he had driven through the thin bone, and half buried in the internal cavity.

"Why, what the—?" What Asher would have said remains unknown, for he stopped short just as a mighty rush of wind smote the door, howled through the bottom of the tower, and nearly extinguished the horn-protected candle. The old man did not say any more, but kicked and kicked at the skull till it was loosened, when it flew off, and up against the stone wall with a sharp crack, and then down upon the floor; while Asher seized his lanthorn, and, troubled with an unusual feeling of trepidation, began to ascend the ricketty old oak ladder which led up to the floor where the bell-ringers had been that night pulling a few changes out of the five bells.

Asher Skurge crossed the floor, threading his way amongst the ropes, and then began to mount the next ladder; for there was no spiral staircase here. Up the ricketty, loose rounds, and then rising like a stage ghost through a trap-door, the clerk stood at length in the second floor amongst the ropes, which passed through to the bells above; and here, shut up in a gigantic cupboard, was the great clock whose announcements of the flight of time floated over vale and lea.

As the clerk drew near, all at once there began a whizzing, whirring noise, which drowned the "tic-tac; tic-tac" of the pendulum; and then loud and clear—too loud and too clear—sounded the great bell-hammer within, announcing that it was eleven o'clock.

"Ah!" growled Asher, as soon as the clock had struck; "nice time for my job!" and then he pulled out another key, and prepared to open the great clock cupboard.

"Hallo?" said Asher, "what now?" and he started back a step, for there was a tiny head and shoulders poked out of the keyhole, and two bright, glittering little eyes seemed to gaze at the clerk for a moment, and then popped in again.

Asher Skurge felt himself to be too old a bird to be caught with that sort of chaff—he only believed in four spirits, did Asher; and, after gin, rum, brandy, and whisky had been named, the speaker would have got to the end of Asher's spiritual tether. So he put down his lanthorn and the key beside it; rubbed his eyes, lifted his hat, and scratched his head; and then began to warm himself by beating his hands against his breast.

"Gammon!" muttered Asher, taking up lanthorn and key, and going towards the cupboard again. "Gammon!" he exclaimed aloud, and was about to put the key in the hole, when out popped the tiny head again, and remained looking at the astonished clerk, who stopped short and opened his mouth widely.

"It's the strong ale," said Asher; and he made a poke at the keyhole with the key, when "bang, crash;" the door flew open and struck him in the face, knocked him down and his lanthorn out; and of course, you'll say, "there he lay in the dark!"

Not a bit of it. There lay Asher Skurge, certainly; but not in the dark; for shining out from the middle of the clock was a bright, glowing light, which filled the place, and made the bell-ropes shine as if made of gold. There was the great clock with all its works; but high and low, everywhere, it was covered with tiny figures similar to the one which gazed out of the keyhole, and all busily at work: there were dozens clinging to the pendulum and swinging backwards and forwards upon the great bob, while a score at each side gave it a push every time it swung within reach; dozens more were sliding down the long shaft to reach those upon the bob; while the weights seemed quite alive with the busy little fellows toiling and straining to push them down. Astride of the spindles; climbing up the cogs as though they were steps; clinging in, out, and about every wheel; and all, as it were, bent upon the same object—forcing on the clock—hurry and bustle—bustle and hurry—up and down—down and up—climbing, crawling, and leaping in the golden light were the tiny figures pushing on the wheels.

Asher Skurge sat up with his hair lifting on his head, but a staunch and obstinate man was he, and he wouldn't believe it a bit, and told himself in learned language it was a delusion; but for all that, he was very uncomfortable, and felt about for the old horn spectacles he had left in the room at home.

"I don't care; it's all gammon!" exclaimed the clerk; "and if I was to say, 'crafts and assaults of the devil, Good Lord, deliver us,' they'd all vanish."

"No, they wouldn't, Asher!" said a small voice close at his ear.

"Eh?" said Asher, starting.

"No, they wouldn't, Asher," said the voice again; "not till they've kept the clock going till your time's up. You wanted it to run down, but we didn't."

Asher stared about him, and then saw that the tiny figure which first gazed at him from the keyhole was now squatted, nursing its knees, upon his lanthorn, and gazing fixedly at him.

"They wouldn't vanish, Asher," said the tiny figure; "and here they come."

As it finished speaking, the little spirits came trooping towards Asher, and dragged out of his pocket a small key, which opened a padlock, and loosened a chain, and set at liberty the key of the great timepiece; for Asher was determined that no other hands should touch *his* clock, as he called it; but now he saw a couple of score of little figures seize the key, fit it in the hole, and then toil at it till they turned it round and round, and wound up first one and then the other weight.

"How much longer?" cried the little spirit upon the lanthorn.

"One hour," cried all the other spirits in chorus; and the two words seemed to ring in Asher's ears, and then go buzzing round the place, and even up and amongst the bells, so that there was a sort of dumb pealing echo of the words.

"'One hour,'" cried Asher, at length; "what's 'one hour'?"

"One hour more for you," said the little spirit, staring unwinkingly, with its little diamond eyes fixed upon Asher, while its mite of a chin rested upon its little bare knees.

"What do you mean," said Asher, fiercely, "with your one more hour?" and then he tried to get up, but could not, for he found that a number of the little figures had busily tied him with the bell-ropes; and there he was fast, hand and foot.

"What do I mean?" said the little figure; "lie still, and I'll tell you, Asher. I mean that your time's nearly up, and that you have now only fifty-six minutes left."

"It must be the strong ale," muttered Asher, turning hot all over, after vainly trying to loosen his bands. "It must be the strong ale; but I think, perhaps, I'll let Mrs Bond stay another week."

"Ha! ha! ha! she's all right. You see you didn't make a will, Asher."

"How do you know?" cried the old man, now growing quite alarmed. "Who says I didn't make a will?"

"I do," said the little figure. "But don't waste time, man. Only fifty minutes; and time's precious."

"But who are you?" cried Asher, excitedly.

"Me?" said the little thing. "Oh, I'm only a second, like those climbing about the clock; and I'm the last one in your hour. There's one beat off by the pendulum every moment. Don't you see fresh ones keep going down?"

"No!" growled Asher, savagely, "I don't." But he did though, for all that, though he would not own to it. There they were, clinging to the great round ball of the pendulum, and one dropping off at every beat, while fresh ones kept gliding down the long shaft into their places. What became of the others he could not tell, for, as they fell off, they seemed to dissolve in the glow which lit up the old clock's works.

It was of no use to struggle, for the efforts only made the ropes cut into his wrists and legs; and if it had not been that the rope which went round his neck was the part covered with worsted to save the ringers' hands, it seemed to him that he would have been strangled. He was horribly frightened, but he would not own to it, and, in spite of the fierce cold, he felt wet with perspiration.

"How slow the time goes," said the little figure. "I want to be off. You're about ready, I suppose."

"No I'm not," cried Asher furiously, "I've no end to do."

"Turn out Widow Bond for one thing," said the figure with a mocking leer. "Never mind about that. Only forty-five more minutes now."

"What a horrible dream," cried Asher in agony.

"'Tisn't a dream," said the little figure. "You pinch your leg and try now, or stop, I will," and in a moment the tiny fellow leaped down and nipped the clerk's leg so vigorously that he shrieked with pain.

"Don't feel like a dream, does it?" said the spirit.

"Don't think it does," said Asher, "at least I never dreamed so loud before that I know of."

"No, I shouldn't think you did, but you won't dream any more," said the little spirit.

"You don't mean that?" said Asher in a pitiful voice.

"I shouldn't have said it if I had not," said the spirit. "Do you suppose we speak falsely?"

"Oh, I don't know," groaned Asher. "But, I say, let me go this time."

"Thirty-five minutes," said the little spirit; "only thirty-five minutes more, and then my work's done, and yours too."

Asher groaned again, and then gave a furious struggle, which only tightened the ropes and made one of the bells above give a sonorous clang, which sounded like a knell to the groaning clerk.

"How are you going to do it?" he cried at last.

"Going to do what?" said the spirit.

"Going to—to—to—make an end of me?" said Asher.

"Oh!" said the spirit, "I shan't have anything to do with it. Some of those to come will do that; I shall be gone. I suppose they'll only put your head under the big hammer which strikes the hour, and it will do all that, so that people will say it was an accident. Only twenty-five minutes now."

Asher turned as white as the parson's surplice, and his teeth chattered as he groaned out:—

"Oh! what for? what for?"

"Why, you see, you are no good," said the spirit, "and only in the way, so some one else may just as well be in your place. What do you know of love, or friendship, or affection, or anything genial? Why you're cold enough to chill the whole parish. Only a quarter of an hour now."

Ten minutes after the little spirit told the trembling man that he had but five minutes more, and four of these were wasted in unavailing struggles and prayers for release, when all at once Asher felt himself seized by hundreds of tiny hands. The cords were tightened till their pressure was agonising; and then he seemed to be floated up into the great open floor where the bells hung in the massive oaken framework, and though he could not see it, he knew well enough where the tenor bell was, and also how the great iron clock hammer was fixed, which would crush his skull like an egg-shell.

Asher struggled and tried to scream, but he felt himself impelled towards the bell, and directly after his cheek was resting upon the cold metal on one side, while the great hammer barely touched his temple on the other, and he knew when it was raised that it would come down with a fierce crash, and he shuddered as he thought of the splashed bell, and the blood, and brains, and hair clinging to the hammer.

"And they'll say it was an accident," muttered Asher to himself, quoting the spirit's remark. "They'll never give me credit for doing it myself. I'm the wrong sort." And then the thoughts of a life seemed crowded into that last minute, and he shuddered to see what a little good he had done. Always money and self, and now what was it worth? He had pinched and punished all around him for the sake of heaping up riches, and now above all would come in those words—

"Thou fool, this night thy soul shall be required of thee."

Thoughts crowded through the wretched man's brain thick and fast. He seemed living his life through in these few remaining seconds, while above all there was the reproaching face of the poor widow whom he would have cast out that night homeless and friendless upon the bitter world. He could not explain it to himself, but it seemed that this face kept him down where he was more than anything else. There was no anger upon it, nothing but bitter sorrowful reproach, and though he would have closed his eyes he could not hide from his gaze that sad countenance. But now came the horror of death, for he seemed to see the little spirits glide down the pendulum far beneath him, rest for a moment upon the bob, and then as one was beaten off, up rose the hammer, and he felt its cold touch leave his temple. Up—up—higher—higher—and now it was about to come down and would dash out his brains. It was coming, and all was over, and for that second the agony he suffered was intense. Then down it came, after seeming to be poised in the air for an awful space of time, and at last came the fearful stroke.

"Clang," and his brain rocked and reeled as the blow fell upon the sonorous metal close by his forehead. The piercing tones rang through him, but before he could collect his thoughts—"Clang" went the hammer again again, and yet his heart did not revive, for he felt that it would be the *last* stroke which would crush him.

"Clang—clang—clang—clang" came the solemn tones of the great bell; solemn, although they seemed to split his head with the noise, and now he had counted eleven, and the last blow was about to fall. The hammer was rising—slowly rising—and in less than a moment he felt that the blow would come. He could not struggle, though he was being impelled nearer and nearer. He could not cry. He could not move; and at last, after an agonising suspense, during which the widow's imploring, reproachful face was pressing closer and closer, down came the great hammer for the twelfth stroke—

"Crash!"

"The clock stopped; and the bells won't ring," said a cheery voice; "and on a Christmas-morning, too. Let me try."

Asher Skurge heard the voice, and directly after he shrieked out with pain, for he felt something cutting into his leg, and this caused him to open his eyes, and to see that his lanthorn lay close beside him; that he was regularly wrapped, tied, and tangled with the bell-ropes, while the clock cupboard lay open before him—the clock at a standstill—probably from the cold; while, as for himself, he was quite at a lie-still, and there had been some one dragging at one of the ropes so as almost to cut his leg in two.

Directly after the head of young Harry Thornton appeared above the trap-door, and then at his call came the sexton; but more help was needed before Asher Skurge could be got down the ladders and across the churchyard to his cottage, where, what with rheumatics and lumbago, the old man is not so fond of winter night walks as of old.

But though Asher would as soon of thought of turning himself out as Widow Bond, he did not have her long for a tenant, for her husband's ship was not lost; and after three years' absence, Frank Bond came back safe and sound, but so weatherbeaten as hardly to be recognised.

But Asher Skurge was ever after an altered man, for it seemed to him that he had taken out a new lease of his life, and in spite of neighbourly sneers, he set heartily to work to repair his soul's tenement. You can see where it has been patched; and even now it is far from perfect, but there are much worse men in the world than Asher Skurge, even if he does believe in spirits, and you might have a worse man for a landlord than the obstinate old clerk, who so highly offended the new vicar because he would not go and wind up the clock after dark.

## Chapter Eighteen.
## Munday's Ghost.

"Shoot the lot, Sir, if I had the chance. I would, O by Jove; that is, if I had dust shot in the gun—a set of rogues, rascals, scamps, tramps, vagabonds, and robbers. Don't tell me about pheasants and partridges and hares being wild birds—there don't laugh; of course, I know a hare isn't a bird—why, they're nothing of the sort, and if it wasn't for preserving, there wouldn't be one left in a few years. Try a little more of that bread sauce. Fine pair of tender young cocks, ain't they? Well, sir, they cost me seven-and-sixpence a bird at the very least, and I suppose I could buy them at seven-and-sixpence a brace at the outside. Game preserving's dear work, sir; but there, don't think I want to spoil your dinner. I aint reckoning up the cost of your mouthfuls, but fighting upon principle. How should you like me to come into your yard, or field, or garden, and shoot or suffocate or wire your turkeys or peafowl?"

"But, my dear, sir," I said, "I don't keep turkeys or peafowl."

"Or cocks or hens, or pigeons, or ducks," continued my uncle, not noticing my remark.

"But we don't keep anything of the kind in London, my dear sir; the tiles and leads are the unpreserved grounds of the sparrows."

"Don't be a fool, Dick," said my uncle, pettishly. "You know well enough what I mean. And I maintain, sir," he continued, growing very red-faced and protuberant, as to his eyes, "that every poacher is a down-right robber, and if I were a magistrate I—"

"Wouldn't shoot them; would you, sir?" said Jenny, roguishly.

"Hold your tongue, you puss," said my uncle, shaking his fist playfully at the bright, saucy-eyed maiden; "you're as bad as Dick."

Oh, how ardently I wished she was in one particular point of view.

My uncle continued. "Ever since I've been in the place, the scoundrels have gone on thin—thin—thin—till it's enough to make one give up in despair. But I won't; hang me if I do! I won't be beaten by the hypocritical canting dogs. Now, look here; one hound whines out that he did it for hunger, but it won't do, that's a tale; while 'fore George, sir, if a man really was driven to that pitch, I'd give him the worth of a dozen of my birds sooner than have them stolen."

Well, really, one could not help condoling with the old gentleman, for he was generous and open-handed to an extent that made me wonder sometimes how my portion would fare, and whether the noble old fellow might not break faith through inability to perform his promises. Ever since he had settled in Hareby, and worked hard to get his estate into condition, the poaching fraternity seemed to have made a dead set at him, leading his two keepers a sad life, for one of them had passed two months in hospital through an encounter; while one fellow, who was always suspected of being at the head of the gang, generally contrived to elude capture, being "as cunning as Lucifer, sir," as my uncle said.

I was down at Hareby to spend Christmas, as had been my custom for years, and on going out the day after my arrival—

"You see, sir," said Browsem, the keeper; "there's no knowing where to take him. I've tried all I knows, and 'pon my sivvy, sir, I don't know where to hev him. It warn't him as give me that dressing down, but it were some of his set, for he keeps in the back grun', and finds the powder and shot, and gets rid o' the birds. War-hawk to him if I do get hold on him, though—"

"But do you watch well?" I said.

"Watch, sir? I've watched my hyes outer my head a'most, and then he's dodged me. Hyes aint no good to him. Why, I don't believe a chap fitted up with telescopes would get round him. The guv'nor swears and goes on at me and Bill, but what's the good o' that when

74

you're arter a fellow as would slip outer his skin, if you hed holt on him? Now, I'll jest tell you how he served me last week. I gets a simple-looking chap, a stranger to these parts, but a regular deep one, to come over and keep his hye on this here Mr Ruddle. So he hangs about the public, and drinks with first one, and then with another, so that they thinks him a chap outer work, and lars of all he gets friendly with Ruddle, and from one thing to another, gets on talking about fezzans and 'ares.

"'Ah,' says my chap, 'there's some fine spinneys down our way. Go out of a night there, and get a sackful of birds when you likes.'

"'Nothin' to what there is here,' says another.

"'Why,' says my chap, 'we've one chap as is the best hand at a bit o' night work as ever I did see. You should see him set a sneer or ingle, he'd captivate any mortial thing. Say he wants a few rabbuds, he'd a'most whistle 'em outer their holes. Fezzans 'll run their heads into his ingles like winkin'. While, as fur 'ares, he never sets wires for them.'

"'Why not,' says one on 'em.

"'Oh,' says my chap, 'he goes and picks 'em up outer the fields, just as he likes.'

"'Ha, ha, ha!' laughs lots on 'em there; all but Ruddle, and he didn't.

"'What d'yer think o' that, ole man,' says one.

"'Nothin' at all,' says Ruddle. 'Do it mysen,' for you see he was a bit on, and ready to talk, while mostlings he was as close as a hegg.

"'Bet you a gallon on it,' says my chap.

"'Done,' says Ruddle, and they settles as my chap and Buddie should have a walk nex' day, Sunday, and settle it.

"Nex' day then these two goes out together, and just ketching sight on 'em, I knowed something was up, but in course I didn't know my chap, and my chap didn't know me, and I sits at home smoking a pipe, for I says to myself, I says: Browsem, I says, there's suthin' up, an' if you can only put salt on that 'ere Ruddle's tail, you'll soon clear the village. You see, I on'y wanted to bring one home to him, and that would have done, for he'd on'y got off two or three times before by the skin of his teeth, and while three or four of his tools was kicking their heels in gaol, my gentleman was feathering his nest all right.

"So my chap and Ruddle goes along werry sociable, only every now and then my chap ketches him a cocking one of his old gimlet eyes round at him, while he looked as knowing and deep as an old dog-fox. By and by they gets to a field, and old Ruddle tells my chap to stop by the hedge, and he did, while Ruddle goes looking about a bit slowly and quietly, and last of all he mounts up on a gate and stands with his hand over his hyes. Last of all he walks quietly right out into the middle of the pasture and stoops down, picks up a hare, and holds it kicking and struggling by the ears, when he hugs it up on his arm strokin' on it like you'd see a little girl with a kitten.

"My chap feels ready to burst himself with delight to see how old Ruddle had fallen into the trap. First-rate it was, you know—taking a hare in open daylight, and in sight of a witness. So he scuffles up to him, looking as innocent all the time as a babby, and he says to him, he says—

"'My, what a fine un! I never thought as there was another one in England could ha' done that 'ere. You air a deep 'un,' he says, trying hard not to grin. 'But aintcher going to kill it?'

"A nasty foxy warming, not he though, for when my chap says, says he, 'Aintcher going to kill it?'

"'What,' he says, 'kill the pooty creetur! Oh, no; poor soft pussy, I wouldn't hurt it; let it go, poor thing.'

"When if he didn't put it down and let it dart off like a shot, while my chap stood dumbfounded, and staring with his mouth half open, till Ruddle tipped him a wink, and went off and left him. No, sir, there ain't no taking that chap nohow, and they do say it was his hand that fired the shot as killed Squire Todd's keeper in Bunkin's Spinney."

Three nights after Christmas was mild and open, and I was watching a busy little set of fingers prepare the tea, while my uncle was napping in his easy-chair, with a yellow silk handkerchief spread over his face. I had been whispering very earnestly, while all my impressive words had been treated as if airy nothings; and more than once I had been most decidedly snubbed. I was at last sitting with a very lachrymose countenance, looking appealingly at the stern little tyrant, who would keep looking so bewilderingly pretty by trying to frown with a beautiful little white brow that would not wrinkle, when the parlour-maid came up and announced Browsem.

"No, sir," muttered my uncle; "I'll put a stop—stop—" the rest was inaudible.

"The keeper waits to see you, uncle dear," whispered his late sister's child, in her soft kittenish way.

"Keeper, sir; yes, sir, I'll give him—Bless my heart, Jenny," exclaimed the old gentleman starting up, dragging off his handkerchief and bringing the hair down over his forehead; "bless my heart, Jenny, why I was almost asleep."

"Here's Browsem, uncle," I said.

"Show him up; show him up," cried my uncle, who would not have accorded more attention to an ambassador than he did to his keeper—that gentleman being prime minister to his pleasures.

Browsem was shown up—a process which did not become the keeper at all, for he came in delicately as to pace, not appearance, and held his red cotton handkerchief in his hand, as if in doubt whether to employ it in dabbing his damp brow, or to spread upon the carpet for fear that his boots might soil the brightness.

"Now Browsem," cried the old gentleman, as the keeper was pulling his forelock to Miss Jenny, thereby making the poor fellow start and stammer. "Now Browsem, whom have you caught?"

"Caught, sir? No one, sir, only the cat, sir. Ponto run her down, but she skretched one of his eyes a'most out."

"Cat; what cat?" said my uncle, leaning forward, with a hand upon each arm of the chair.

"Why, you see, sir," said Browsem, confidentially, "there's a dodge in it;" and then the man turned round and winked at me.

"Confound you; go on," cried my uncle in a most exasperated tone of voice, when Browsem backed against Jenny's little marqueterie work-table, and, oversetting it, sent bobbins, tapes, reels, wools, silks, and, crochet and tatting apparatus into irremediable chaos.

"There, never mind that trash," shouted the old man; "speak up at once."

"Well, sir," said Browsem, "they've been a-dodgin' of me."

"Well?" cried my uncle.

"Tied a lanthorn to a cat's neck, and sent her out in the open, to make belief as it were a dog driving the partridges."

"Well?"

"And we've been a-hunting it for long enew, and Ponto ketched her at last."

"Well?"

"And this was only to get us outer the way, for I heard a gun down Bunkin's Spinney."

"Well?" shouted my uncle.

"And I've come to know what's right to be done."

"Done," roared my uncle; "why run down to the Spinney, or there won't be a pheasant left. Here, my stick—my pistols—Here, Dick—Confound—Scoundrels. Look sharp." And then he hobbled out of the room after the keeper, when warm with the excitement of perhaps having a brush with the poachers, I was following, but a voice detained me on the threshold.

"Richard," whispered Jenny; and there was something in the earnest eyes and frightened look that drew me back in an instant. "Richard, you won't go—those men—danger—Oh! Richard, pray! There, don't. What would your uncle say?"

I didn't know, neither did I pause to think, for that newly-awakened earnestness whispered such sweet hopes that, darting back, I was for the instant forgetful of all propriety, till some one stood blushing before me, arranging those bright little curls so lately resting upon my arm.

"But you won't go?" pleaded Jenny. "For *my* sake Richard?"

"Di-i-i-i-i-ck," roared my uncle, and, wresting myself from the silken chains, I darted down into the hall.

"Here lay hold of that stick, my lad," cried my uncle, flourishing a large bludgeon, while Browsem grinning and showing his teeth, was quietly twisting the leathern thong of a short stout staff round his wrist.

"All right my darling," said the old man, turning to the pale-faced Jenny, who had come quietly downstairs to where we stood. "Don't be alarmed, we shall take care of one another, and march half a dozen poaching—here, come along, or me shall miss the scoundrels."

Browsem led the way at a half-trot, and grasping my arm, the old gentleman followed as fast as his sometimes gouty leg would allow him. We were soon out of the grounds, and, clambering a gate, made our way towards the wood, where the keeper had heard the gun.

"Confound them," growled my uncle, "that's where that poor fellow was shot ten years ago."

"Bang—bang."

"There they are, sir," growled the keeper, halting to let us get up alongside; and now I started, for in the dusk behind me, and apparently dodging my heels, was a tall figure.

"It's only Todds, sir," growled the keeper, and Todds his helper growled in response.

"That is right."

"Amost wonder as they came here, sir," whispered Browsem. "Never knowed 'em do it afore, 'cause they're feared o' Munday's Ghost."

"Munday's Ghost?" I said.

"Yes, sir; pore chap as were shot. They do say as he walks still, but there's a sight o' pheasants here."

It was one of those dark heavy nights late in winter, when the last oak-leaves have fallen, and every step you take through the thickly strewn glades rustles loudly. The wind just sighed by us as we pressed on along a path through a plantation, and then once or twice I fancied I heard guns to the right, far off behind the house. But I forgot them the next moment, for my heart beat, and the excitement increased, for just on in front came two loud and distinct reports.

"They're at it," growled my uncle, forgetting his gout, and loosing my arm. "Now Browsem, you and Todds go round, and we'll come forward, only mind when I whistle, it's for help."

The next moment I was going to speak to the keeper, but I started, for he was gone, and on looking behind I found Todds had also vanished, quiet as a snake, for my uncle and I stood alone.

"You'll stick to me, Dick?" whispered the old gentleman.

"Conditions," I said in the same voice.

"What? the white feather," growled the old gentleman.

"No, no," I said, "but if I enlist now on your side, will you join me in a siege afterwards?"

"Siege? what the deuce? Why don't you speak plain, sir?"

"Well," I said, "I mean about—about—a certain young lady at the Priory, you know."

"Confound your thick head, sir. Why, if you had had an ounce of brains, you could have seen what I meant, and—"

"Bang, bang!" from the wood.

"Forward," shouted my uncle, and crossing a small open field, we entered the Spinney.

Now, if I were to say that I was brave, the assertion would be a fib, for I possess but few of the qualifications for making a good soldier; but all the same, as we pushed our way in that night amongst the thick hazel stubs, I felt a sort of tingly sensation in my arm, which made me grasp my weapon more tightly, and feel as if I wished there was something to hit.

"Keep your eyes well open, Dick," whispered my uncle, "and if you come across a tall thin squinting rascal with his nose on one side, mind, that's Ruddle's. Fell him to the ground in an instant, sir. No mercy: capture him as you love me, and if you do take the scoundrel, you shall have another cool thousand down on your wedding morning."

"And if I don't?" I whispered.

"Hold your tongue, you dog, and don't talk nonsense."

On we went in silence as to our tongues, but with the leaves rustling and sticks cracking as we pushed on. Now I could hear my uncle ejaculating; then he'd stumble and mutter, while once I had to haul him out of a small hole half full of water.

"Confound it!" growled the old gentleman; "but I'll pay some one for all this. Open out a bit to the right, Dick."

I separated from the main body, and on we still pressed, rustling and crackling along, while now and again I could make out the well-defined forms of pheasants roosting amidst the low branches of the trees. All at once I heard my uncle stop short, for about a hundred yards to my right there came again a sharp "bang, bang" of two guns.

"Push on, my boy," whispered the old gentleman, closing up; and then, as fast as we could for the dense undergrowth, we made our way in the direction of the sounds. "They're out strong, my boy, but we're four determined men with right on our side, and a prize to win; eh, you dog?"

"Oof!" I involuntarily exclaimed, for just then my uncle gave me a poke in the ribs with his stick—very facetiously, no doubt; but it hurt.

We were now in the thickest part of the wood; and, after going a little farther, I felt my shoulder clutched, and "Here they come," was whispered in my ear. "Seize one man, Dick, and hold on to him like a bull-dog."

Just then I could hear in front the sharp crackling and rustling made by bodies being forced through the underwood; and, grasping my staff and pressing eagerly forward, I waited with beating heart for the coming of the enemy.

I did not have to wait long, for the next moment I was face to face with Browsem.

"Lord, sir! I thought it had been one on 'em," he exclaimed, and then a whispered consultation having been held, we opened out about twenty yards apart, and went straight away in the direction we supposed the poachers to have taken.

On, slowly and painfully, with the twigs flying back and lashing our faces, roots trying to trip us up, and the night growing darker and darker. Right and left I could hear my uncle and Browsem, while right off beyond the old gentleman, Mr Todds, the reticent, was making his way. Every eye was strained and every ear attent to catch the slightest sound; but for quite ten minutes we crept on until right in our rear came the sharp, loud report of a gun; and then, after the interval of a few moments, another louder and apparently nearer.

"Back again!" cried my uncle; and then, casting off all caution, we all pushed forward eagerly, closing in as we went, till we were only separated by a few bushes, so that I could hear the hard breathing on either side. Hard work blundering and stumbling along; but the will was good, and at last we all drew up again in a small opening, panting, hot, and regularly breathed.

"Hist!" whispered my uncle, and we all listened eagerly; but, with the exception of a wild, strange cry some distance off, all was silent.

"What's that?" I whispered to Browsem.

"Only a howl, sir," he whispered again. "Blessed rum start this, ain't it?"

"Bang, bang!" again a hundred yards off.

"Come on!" roared my uncle furiously, "there won't be a bird left in the place;" and away we dashed again, but only to pull up once more, regularly puzzled.

"'Tain't no good, sir," whispered Browsem. "We might go on like this all night, and ketch no one."

"Why?" I said, mopping my brow.

"That 'ere, sir, as I said was a howl, must ha' been Munday's Ghost, and them 'ere shots as we keeps hearing's the ones as killed the poor fellow, and that's why the poachers never comes to this bit."

"Browsem," puffed my uncle.

"Yes, sir," said Browsem.

"You're a fool, Browsem," puffed my uncle.

"Thanky, sir," said Browsem.

"What do you mean by that, sir?" cried my uncle, fiercely.

"Nothing, sir," said the keeper, mildly.

"For two pins, sir," cried my uncle, fiercely, "I'd discharge you, sir. D'yer hear? discharge you, sir, for talking such foolery. Ghosts—posts! pooh! bah! puff! stuff! yah! Forward."

Mr Todds, who was at my elbow, murmured his approval of his superior's language, but gave a superstitious shiver at the same moment. And then once more we opened out, and tramped through the wood, till regularly beaten out; and, without having heard another shot or seen a single enemy, we reluctantly retraced our steps to the Priory.

The next morning, at breakfast, the parlour-maid again announced Browsem—for my uncle abjures men-servants in the house—and the keeper, looking puzzled and long-faced, appeared at the door.

"Now, then," sputtered my uncle, "have you caught them?"

"They cleared Sandy Plants last night, sir," growled the man.

"Who? what?" cried my uncle, upsetting his coffee.

"Some on 'em—Ruddles's, I s'pose," said Browsem. "Don't b'leeve there's a tail left out'er scores," said the man.

"There, go down and wait, and I'll come directly after breakfast."

But to all intents and purposes my uncle had finished his breakfast, for nothing more would he touch, while his face grew purple with rage. Gout—everything—was forgotten for the time; and half an hour after, Browsem was pointing out the signs of the havoc made on the preceding night in the fir-plantation. Here and there lay feathers, spots of blood, gun-wads; and many a trunk was scarred and flayed with shot. In one place, where the trees were largest, the poachers seemed to have been burning sulphur beneath the boughs, while twice over we came upon wounded pheasants, and one dead—hung high up in the stubbly branches, where it had caught.

My uncle looked furious, and then turning in the direction of the scene of the last night's adventures, he strode off, and we followed in silence.

On reaching the wood, we very soon found, from the trampled underwood and broken twigs, traces of our chase; but the birds seemed plentiful, and no feathers or blood-stains were to be found.

"They didn't get many here, at all events," muttered my uncle.

Both Browsem and Todds shook their heads at me, and looked ghosts.

"Strange thing, though," muttered my uncle. "What do you think of it, Browsem?"

The keeper screwed up his face, and said nothing.

"Confound you for a donkey!" ejaculated the irascible old gentleman. "What Tom-fool rubbish you men do believe. Hullo! though, here's a wad;" and he stooped and picked up a wadding evidently cut out of an old beaver hat. "That don't look ghostly, at all events; does it, booby?"

Browsem only screwed up his phiz a little tighter.

"Why, tut, tut, tut! Come here, Dick!" shouted the old gentleman, excitedly. "We've been done, my lad; and they've cleared out the plantation while we were racing up and down here."

I followed the old gentleman to one of the openings where we had stopped together the night before, when Todds, who was close behind, suddenly gave a grunt, and stooping down, picked up a half-empty horn powder-flask.

"That's Ruddles's, I'd swear," growled Browsem.

"Of course," said my uncle. "And now, look here, Dick," he cried, pointing to the half-burnt gun-wads lying about near a large pollard oak. "There, shin up, and look down inside this tree."

With very little difficulty, I wonderingly climbed up some fifteen feet, by means of the low branches, which came off clayey on my hands, as though some one had mounted by that same means lately, and then I found that I could look down right through the hollow trunk, which was lighted by a hole here and there.

"That'll do; come down," cried my uncle. "If I'd only thought of it last night, we could have boxed the rascal up—a vagabond! keeping us racing up and down the wood, while he sat snugly in his hole, blazing away directly we were a few yards off."

I was certainly very close to Jenny that afternoon when my uncle, whom we thought to be napping in his study, rushed into the room.

"Hurrah, Dick! Tompkins has peached, and they sent fifty pheasants up in Ruddles's cart this morning; but the old rascal's locked up, and—hum! That sort of thing looks pretty," he continued, for we were certainly taken somewhat by surprise. "But, you dog," he roared, as Jenny darted from the room, "you did not catch the scoundrel."

However, after that morning's take, even if a hundred pheasants had been sent in the cart, my uncle would have been plastic as clay, while, an hour afterwards, he exclaimed:

"Why, Dick, I'd almost forgotten my gout."

## Chapter Nineteen.
## The Spirits of the Bells.

  Heart-sore and spirit-weary,
   Life blank, and future dreary,
Mournfully I gazed upon my fire's golden glow,
   Pondering on idle errors,
   Writhing under conscience terrors,
Gloomily I murmured, with my spirits faint and low.

  I had drained the golden measure,
   Sipped the sweets of so-called pleasure,
Seeing in the future but a time for newer joy;
   Now I found their luscious cloying,
   Ev'ry hope and peace destroying,
Golden visions, brightest fancies - bitter, base alloy.

  Riches, comfort spoke then vainly,
   To a brain thus tinged insanely,
   Wildly throbbing, aching, teeming,
   Fancy-filled with hideous dreaming,
Speaking of an aimless life, a life without a goal:
   While as if to chide my murmur,
   Came a voice which cried, "Be firmer,
Would'st be like the beasts that perish? Think thou of thy soul."

  Starting from my chair and trembling,
   Vainly to my heart dissembling,
'Twas an idle fancy that had seemed to strike my ear;
   Still the words came stealing round me,
   Horror in its chains had bound me;
Dripping from my aching brow, were beads of deepest fear.

  Hurrying to my moonlit casement,
   Throwing up the sash,
  Highest roof to lowest basement
   Seemed to brightly flash,
  Glitt'ring white, with Winter's dressing;
  While each crystal was caressing
Purest rays that glanced around it from the moon's pale light.
   Nature slept in sweetest beauty,
   Gleaming stars spoke hope and duty:
Calmer grew my aching brow, beneath the heavenly sight.

  Christmas-Eve! the Christian's morrow
  Soon would dawn on joy and sorrow,

Spreading cheer and holy pleasure brightly through the land;
    Whilst I, lonely, stricken-hearted,
    Under bitter mem'ries smarted,
Standing like an outcast, or as one the world had banned.

    Sadly to my chair returning,
    By my fire still brightly burning,
Battling with the purer rays that through the window gleamed;
    Like two spirits floating o'er me,
    Vividly rays played before me,
Each to wrap me in its light that on my forehead streamed.


    The glowing fire with warm embracing
    Told of earthly, sinful racing:
Warmth and pleasure in its looks, but in its touch sharp pain;
    While the moonbeams, paler, purer,
    Spoke of pleasures, sweeter, surer,
Oft rejected by Earth's sons for joys that bear a stain.

    Suddenly with dread I shivered,
    As the air around me quivered,
Laden with the burden of a mighty spirit-tone,
    Rolling through the midnight stilly,
    Borne upon the night-wind chilly,
Rushing through my chamber, where I sat in dread alone.

    "Soul!" it cried, in power pealing,
    "Soul!" the cry was through me stealing,
Vibrating through each fibre with a wonder-breeding might.
    "Soul!" the voice was deeply roaring;
    "Soul!" rang back from roof and flooring,
Booming thro' the silence of the piercing winter night.

    Now came crashing, wildly dashing,
    Waves of sound in power splashing,
    Ringing, swinging, tearing, scaring,
    Shrieking out in words unsparing,
    "Soul of sorrow! murm'ring mortal!"
    Roaring through my chamber portal,
    Borne thro' window, borne thro' ceiling
    Ever to my sense revealing,
    Still the bells these words were pealing,
    "Soul of sorrow! murm'ring mortal!"
    "Soul of sorrow! murm'ring mortal!"
Till my room seemed filled with bells that rang the self-same strain;
    While, above the brazen roaring,
    Mightily the first tone pouring,
Boomed out "Soul!" in mighty pow'r, and linked in with the chain.


    Then an unseen presence o'er me
    Leant, and from my chamber tore me:
Out upon the night-wind I was swept among the sounds,
    Whirling on amid the pealing,
    Warning to the city dealing

Of the coming morrow, in reverberating rounds.

    Still they cried, as from doom's portal,
    "Soul of sorrow! murm'ring mortal!"
Shrieking all around me as I floated with the wind,
    Ever borne away and crying,
    Every bell-tone swiftly flying
O'er the silent city, to its slumber now consigned.

    Hurried round each airy tower,
    Writhing with the unseen power
Vainly, for a spirit-chain each struggling limb would bind;
    Doomed to hear those words repelling,
    Ever on my senses knelling,
Still - a booming hurricane - we wrestled with the wind.

    Sweeping o'er the sluggish river,
    Where dark piles the waves dissever,
    'Neath the bridges, by the shipping,
    Sluice-gates, with the waters dripping,
    By the rustling, moaning rushes,
    Where the tribute-water gushes;
    Forced to gaze on ghastly faces,
    Where the dread one left his traces,
Faces of the suicide, the murdered floated on,
    Whose blue, leaden lips, unclosing,
    Shrieked out words, my brain that froze in,
Crying I had stayed my help in hours long passed and gone.


    "Hopeless, hopeless!" ever crying,
    "Hopeless we are round you dying,
Asking vainly for the aid withheld in selfish grasp;
    Hopeless, from the crime that's breeding,
    Ever to new horrors leading,
    Horrors, growing, flow'ring, seeding,
Soon to spread a poison round more deadly than the asp."

    Still an unseen presence bound me;
    Still the bells were shrieking round me,
    "Soul of sorrow! murm'ring mortal!"
    "Soul of sorrow! murm'ring mortal!"
    Rising, falling, ever calling,
    Thought and mem'ry, soul appalling,
    Borne away and louder crying,
    In the distance softly dying;
    Here in gentle murmurs sighing,
    Then again far higher flying,
    Swiftly o'er the houses hieing;
    While around these fear-begetters
    Bound me in their brazen fetters.
    On I sped with brain on fire,
    'Mid the bell-tones, higher, higher,
    List'ning to their words upbraiding,
    Each with dread my soul new lading.
    Now away, the mighty chorus

Swept around a church before us,
In whose yard were paupers lying.
From their graves I heard them crying,
Joining in the words upbraiding,
Loudly piercing, softly fading:
"Soul of sorrow! murm'ring mortal!"
"Soul of sorrow! murm'ring mortal!"
"Cease your murmurs, cease your sorrow,
From our fate a lesson borrow:
Never heeded, lost to pity,
Dying round you through the city.
Leave us to our peaceful sleeping,
Freed from hunger, care, and weeping."


O'er and o'er the hillocks grassy,
Now away o'er buildings massy:
Ever cries, as from doom's portal,
"Soul of sorrow! murm'ring mortal!"
Thro' the wards where pain was shrieking,
Where disease was vengeance wreaking,
Still the sounds were hurrying, crying,
As in emulation trying;
Many a fev'rish slumber breaking;
O'er the lips that knew no slaking.
All were crying, help imploring;
While the bells from roof to flooring,
Still, as from the first beginning,
Still the self-same burden dinning,
Spite of all my writhing, tearing,
Onward still my spirit bearing
Far away in booming sallies,
Rushing thro' the crowded alleys,
Where grim Want his wings was quiv'ring
O'er the pinched forms, half clad, shiv'ring;
Where disease and death were hov'ring;
Where deep sorrow earth was cov'ring.

Away, again, where life was failing;
Away, again, by orphans wailing;
Thro' the prison bars now darting,
Where the fettered wretch lay smarting,
Wakened from his sleep, and starting,
He too shrieked in bitter parting
Curses on my aid withholden,
In the glorious hours golden,
Wasted, thrown away in madness—
Hours that might deep sorrow, sadness.
Misery, have chased from numbers,—
Chased the want the earth that cumbers.


Away, away, and faster speeding,
Away, the tones seemed round me pleading
Lessons to my madness reading,
From the scenes I'd lived unheeding.

Still the unseen fetters bound me;
Still the burden floated round me:
"Soul of sorrow! murm'ring mortal!"
"Soul of sorrow! murm'ring mortal!"

But the words came softer, lower,
  Calmer still, and sweeter, slower,
Till they murmured off in silence on the wintry air;
  Save returning, booming, rolling,
  Came that one vast warning, tolling
"Soul!" as when at first it called me, sitting in my chair.

Now again from earth rebounding,
  Quick and fast, the bells were sounding,
And I sprang from out my seat, with wild and startled look.
  'Twas the blest Redeemer's morning!—
  Sunshine brightly Earth adorning,—
And the Christmas jocund peal my brightened casement shook.

Hope has risen clearer, purer,
  O'er my life-course firmer, surer,
Since that eve, when gloomily I pondered on my life;
  When I heard, as from doom's portal,
  "Soul of sorrow! murm'ring mortal!"
Booming on my aching brain, with murmurs thickly rife.

## Chapter Twenty.
## A Rogue and a Vagabond.

"You must fetch the doctor," says Dick, as I stood over him looking at his poor worn face, all drawed with pain and hollow-looking, although he'd got his paint on and the band and spangles were round his head, though his black hair was all rough with him a-tossing about.

There was the bit of candle flaring away and guttering down, the wind flapping the canvas backwards and forwards and coming in fierce through the holes, while the rain was dripping from the top because the canvas hadn't got well soaked and tight, and I couldn't help thinking about what a miserable place it was for a sick man. There was the drum a-going and the clarinet squeaking, while another of the company was rattling away at a pair o' pot-lid cymbals; the grease-pots were flaring in front of the stage, and them all a dancing and one thing and another over and over again, while Balchin's voice, husky and bad with his cold, could be heard telling people to walk up for the last time that night; but they wouldn't, for it was wet and miserable and spiritless as could be.

Poor Dick had been out ever so long in his tights and fleshings doing his summersets and bits o' posturing, till his thin things were wet through, when he comes in at last to me, where I was nursing little Totty, hard at work to keep her quiet, and he says with a bit of a groan—

"I'm knocked over, lass. It's like a knife in my chest," and I could hear his breath rattling hard, as he looked that ill I couldn't keep the tears back. You see he'd been bad for days and taking medicine for his cough; but then what good was that with us, going from place to place in wet weather and him obliged to take his turn with the rest, and we always sleeping under the canvas. Why, he ought to have been in a house and with a doctor to him, though he wouldn't hear of it when I talked about it.

"Can't afford it, Sally," he'd say, and then, poor fellow, he'd sit up in bed and cough till he'd fall back worn out, when as soon as he was laid down, back came the cough again worse than ever, and I've lain quiet and still, crying because I couldn't help him. Don't know anything more sad and wearying than to hear some one cough—cough—cough the whole long night through, with it resting a little when sitting up, and then coming on again worse and worse as soon as you lie down.

And that's how it was with poor Dick, but he had a heart like a lion and would never give up. All the others used to lodge about at the public-houses, 'cept Balchin, who lived in the van, but Dick said he liked being under the canvas best, for you were like in your own place, and there was no noise and bother with the landlords, besides sleeping in all sorts of dirty places after other people, so we always kept to the corner of the tent and under the stage, making use of a bit of charcoal fire in a stand.

And Dick wouldn't have the doctor till that night, when he says at last, "you must fetch him." I'd been watching him lying there hardly able to breathe, and sometimes, when his eyes were nearly shut, you could only see the whites, while his hands tore like at the covering, he seemed in such pain.

Just then in came Balchin, looking very cross and out of humour, for there was the ground to pay for, and he'd taken next to nothing that night.

"What did you sneak off like that for, Dick Parker?" he says, and then Dick started up, but he fell back with a bit of a groan, when Balchin grumbled out something, and turned round and went off.

"Could you mind little Totty?" I says to Dick, for I didn't like to take the child out in the wet.

He didn't speak, but made a place aside him for the little thing, and the next minute the poor little mite had nestled up close to him, and I turned to put on my shawl, when who should lift up the canvas and come in but Balchin, with a steaming hot glass of whisky and water in his hand?

"Here we are, my boy," he says, in his rough cheery way, that he could put on when he liked. "Now is the sun of summer turned to glorious winter, so away with discontent and a merry Christmas and a happy noo year to you, my boy. You're a bit outer sorts you are, and so was I just now, but I'm what you're going to be directly, so tip some of this up."

But Dick only shook his head and smiled, and then whispering him to please stop till I got back, I slipped out to fetch the doctor.

It isn't hard to find the doctor's place in a town, and I was soon there standing, ring, ring, ring, while the rain, now half sleet and snow, began to come down so, that I shivered again. But I hardly thought about it, for my mind was all upon poor Dick, for a terrible thought had come into my head, and that was, that my poor boy was going to leave me. Everything now seemed to tell me of it: the cold howling wind seemed to shriek as it tore away through the long street, the clock at the big church seemed to be tolling instead of striking twelve, while the very air seemed alive with terrible whispers of something dreadful going to happen.

At last a window upstairs was opened, and I asked if the doctor was at home.

"Who wants him?" said a voice.

"I want him to come to my poor husband, for he's—" I couldn't finish the word for a sob that seemed to choke me.

"Where do you live?" said the same voice.

"At the show in the market-place," I said, feeling all the while half ashamed.

"You'd better go to Mr Smith, he's the parish doctor," said the voice, and then the window was shut. And I stood half blind with the tears that would come, as I dragged my shawl closer round me, and stood shivering and wondering which way to turn so as to find the parish doctor. The wind was sweeping and howling along; the snow came in heavy squalls which whitened me in a few moments, while the cold seemed to chill one's very marrow; but I hardly thought of it, for I was all the time seeing poor Dick lying in our miserable bit of a bed by the light of the flaring candle, while above the howling of the wind I seemed to be hearing his low hacking cough.

Oh! it was pitiful, pitiful, standing out there on that bitter night, close to Christmas-time, when people's hearts are said to be more charitably disposed; but now, though bright lights shone in windows here and there, I was alone, alone, in the bitter storm, without a soul to direct me or teach me where to go for a doctor. I hurried to the end of the street—then back along the other side, up one street and down another, eagerly looking for a lighted lamp over a door, or for some one to tell me; but not a soul was to be seen, and every public-house was shut.

On I went again, growing almost frantic, for the howling wind seemed to form itself into cries—wild, appealing cries to me for help for my boy, who lay suffering in our wretched wandering home; and at last I ran up to a door and rang the bell, but no one answered. Then I heard the muffled sound of wheels, and stood listening. Yes, they were coming nearer and nearer—they were in the street, and I ran into the road to try and stay the driver, as I shrieked for help, for I was most mad with anxiety; but there was the sharp stinging cut of a whip across my cheek, and half-blinded and smarting, I started back, and the next minute the round of the wheels had died away.

"Oh, oh, oh!" I moaned piteously, wringing my hands; what shall I do, what shall I do? But the next moment my heart leaped, for by the light of one of the street lamps I saw a man approaching and hurried up to him.

"Sir, sir," I cried; "the doctor—the—" But an oath and a rude push, which sent me staggering off the pavement to fall in the mud and snow of the road, was my answer, and then, as half bewildered I slowly got up, I heard a harsh laugh and the man began whistling.

I could not sob now, but felt as if something was clutching at my heart and tearing it, but again I hurried along half blind with the heavy snow, and now once more I saw a man in front, but dimly seen through the heavy fall.

"Help, help," I cried hoarsely, with my hands clasped together.

"Eh! what?" he said.

"Oh, sir, a doctor, for God's sake—for pity's sake—my poor boy!"

"Who, who?" he said, taking hold of my arm.

"My poor husband," I said, "he's dying."

The next moment he was walking beside me, as I thought to show me where the doctor lived, and it was nearer the market-place where the show stood.

"Come in here," he said, opening a door with a key, when feeling trembling and suspicious, I hung back, but the light falling upon my new companion, showed me a pleasant faced old man, and I followed him into a surgery, where he put something into a bottle, and five minutes after we were standing in the booth where Balchin and his wife and a couple more of the company were standing about the bed where poor Dick lay, breathing so heavily that it was pitiful to hear him, and me not daring to wake him for fear of his cough.

"God bless my soul," muttered the doctor I had so fortunately met; "what a place and what a night! Can't you move him to a house?"

"No," said Dick, suddenly sitting up. "I'll die here. This is good enough for a rogue and a vagabond of a strolling player. But doctor," he said, with his eyes almost blazing, "can you cure my complaint?"

"Well, well! we'll see," said the doctor, laying his hand upon poor Dick's chest.

"No, no; not there, sir," said Dick. "It's here—here—in my heart, and it's sore about that poor girl and this little one: that's my complaint, not this cough. What are they to do? Where are they to go? Who's to keep them when I'm gone? Not that I've done much for them, poor things."

"Dick, Dick," I said, reproachfully.

"My girl!" he says, so softly and tenderly and with such a look, that I was down next moment upon my knees beside him, when he threw one arm round my neck and rested his head again my cheek so loving, so tender, while his other arm was round the little one now fast asleep.

And there we all stayed for a bit; no one speaking, for the doctor stood with his head bent down and his hat off, while the light of the candle shone amongst his silver-looking hair. Two or three times over I saw Balchin and his wife and the others look hard at him, and once Balchin touched him on the sleeve, but he stood still looking on, while poor Dick lay there with his head upon my shoulder, and me, not crying but confused and struck down, and dazed like with sorrow.

At last every one seemed so still and quiet, that I looked up wondering to see the doctor hold up his hand to the others to be silent, when, whispering to me that he would be back in a few minutes, he hurried away. And still no one moved for perhaps a quarter of an hour, when through being half blind now with the tears that began to come, I could not see the doctor come back; and this time he had something in his hand which he made as though he would give to Dick, but he shrunk back next moment shaking his head, gave the glass to Balchin to hold, and then as Mrs Balchin began sobbing loudly, the doctor knelt down beside the bed and said some words in a low tone at first, but getting more earnest and loud as he went on and then he was silent, and Dick seemed to give a deep drawn sigh.

Then I waited to hear the next sigh, for all was still and quiet; Balchin and his wife stood with their heads bent down, and Mrs Balchin had left off sobbing; the others stood about, one here and one there, and the good doctor was still upon his knees, and I couldn't help thinking how calm and easy poor Dick's laboured breathing had become, when all at once little Totty began to say some prattling words in her sleep, and then as if some bright little dream was hers she began to laugh out loud in her little merry way, and nestled closer to her father.

All at once I started, for a horrible thought came into my mind, and turning my face I looked as well as I could at poor Dick's eyes. The light was very dim and I could only see that they were half open, while there was a quiet happy smile upon his lip. Then I eagerly held the back of my hand to his mouth to feel his breath, but there was nothing. I felt his heart—it was still. I whispered to him—

"Dick! Dick! speak to me," and I fancied there was just another faint sigh, but no answer—no reply—for with his arms round all he loved and who loved him on this earth, he had gone from us—gone without me fancying for a moment it was so near. And then again for a moment I could not believe it, but looked first at the doctor, and then at first one and then another, till they all turned their heads away, when with a bitter cry I clasped him to me, for I knew poor Dick was dead.

### Chapter Twenty One.
### A Spirit of the Past.

Of course they were—the good old times, or, as Macaulay has it, "the brave days of old." Things are not now as they used to be; and mind, O reader, these are not my words, but those of a patriarch. Things are not as they used to be; the theatres even have not the casts now that they had fifty years since; those were the fine old coaching times, when team after team started from the old Post-office in style. There were beaux and bucks, and men of spirit then—men who could dress, and spent their money as it should be spent. Gambling, duelling, and such spirited affairs were common, and really, there can be no doubt of it, times are altered.

I am foolish enough to think for the better—but then I am only a unit,—and I think so in spite of the incessant mess the railway, gas, water, telegraph, pneumatic, and all the other companies are making of our streets. One cannot help admiring our monster hotels, gigantic railway schemes, palatial warehouses, etcetera, etcetera, but then we miss many of our delightful old institutions. Where are the dustmen's bells of our childhood? Surely those polished articles in our railway stations, always reposing upon a wooden block when one is at a distance, but which our approach seems to be the signal for the "stout porters" to seize and jangle harshly in our ears—surely those are not the "bells, bells, bells" so familiar of old. Where are the organs with the waltzing figures turning round and round to the ground-up music of Strauss or Weber, then in their popularity? Where the people who so horrified our diaper pinafore-encased bosom by walking upon stilts to the accompaniment of drum and Pan pipes? Where the ancient glories of Jack in the Green and Guido Fawkes? Where are numbers of our old street friends who seem gone, while Punch alone seems immortal, and comes out yearly with fresh paint covering his battered old phiz? Certainly we had in the street "twopence more and up goes the donkey," though no man had the good fortune to be present when the twopence more was arrived at, and the miserable asinine quadruped was elevated upon the ladder and balanced upon its owner's chin—certainly we had that; but after all said and done, how our acrobats have improved, how much brighter are the spangles, how much better greased the hair and developed the muscles. Look at that tub feat, or the man balanced upon the pole, of course an improved donkey trick. Look at—look at the length of thy article, oh! writer.

It seems only yesterday, but some years have passed now since we used to lie in bed of a cold, dark winter's morning, and listen to the prolonged rattle of the sweep's brush upon some chimney-pot far on high, and then hear the miserable little fellow's doleful "halloo, halloo, halloo," by way of announcement that he had achieved his task, and had head and shoulders right out of the pot. And it seems only yesterday, too, that, by special favour, our household Betty allowed me to descend and see the sweeps do the kitchen chimney, when I stood trembling in presence of our blackened visitors and the smoke-jack, and then saw the great black pall fastened before the fireplace with three forks, when the sooty boy covered his head and face with a cap, grinning diabolically at me before he eclipsed his features, and then by the light of the blackened tallow candle I saw him disappear behind the cloth.

That was quite enough, and I could stand no more, but turned and fled upstairs, feeling convinced that he would never come down again.

And it really was but yesterday, comparatively speaking, when, in the depth of winter, a few days before Christmas, Mrs Scribe and self were staying at a friend's house in Lower Bleak Street, Grimgreen Square, close by Glower Street, North. I had a cold whose effect was to make me insufferably hot and feverish, and as I lay in bed, somewhere about what seemed the middle of the night, by which I mean the middle of one's sleeping night, not twelve o'clock, when one has just plunged into bed—about the middle of the night, while I was dreaming of being where there were rows upon rows of lights, through which I was being somehow propelled at the risk of being dashed against an indescribable object, while my hands were apparently swelling out to a large size, and I was in a wild, semi-delirious dream, from which it was a charity to wake me, I felt my arm roughly grasped, and a well-known voice whispered in my ear—

"Are you awake?"

As soon as I could collect myself and make sure that I really was in the required state, I said, "Yes." But that was not until some few seconds had passed.

"Only listen, dear," there's some one in the room, the voice whispered again in an agitated manner.

"Pooh, nonsense," I said perversely, "I know that. There's been some one all night." And then I stopped short, for though I knew that I had fastened the door when we came to bed, I could hear a gentle rustling noise, as of some one in a silk dress slowly gliding about the room very slowly, and then coming to a stop, and apparently agitating the robe, when again the rustling began, and it appeared just opposite the foot of our bed.

"What shall we do?" gasped Mrs Scribe in a smothered voice, from beneath the clothes.

I didn't know, so of course I could not tell her. I knew what I ought to do, which was to have leaped boldly out of bed, and grappled the intruder, but then the rustling was like that of a silk dress, and if a ghost, of course it was of the feminine gender, and one could not help studying decorum.

"Hadn't you better get up and see what it is?" said Mrs S, accompanying the remark with a touch from her elbow.

"I'm in such a perspiration, I daren't stir," I whispered. "Remember what a cold I have." And how I blessed that cold just then, for to a man not too brave in his constitution, it did seem such a neat creephole, for if one is no hero to his valet, one likes to be somebody in the eyes of a wife. But still I must confess to a horrible dread of ghosts, owing no doubt to the fact, that in our old house in Pimlico, where I dwelt till the age of five, there was a huge black bogie who had his habitat in the cellar, and though I never saw him, I was assured of his existence upon the competent authority of both maids, and consequently always had a wholesome dread of the coal-scuttle and the coals, over which he must have walked.

"But what shall we do?" whispered Mrs Scribe again. "You really must get out, dear."

Which was likely, wasn't it, to jump out of bed in the dark on purpose to attack an unseen form in a rustling silk dress, creeping and gliding about apparently by the wall? Why, to have attacked a ghost one could have seen would have been bad enough, but in the dark when it could take one at such disadvantage, it was not to be thought of, so I said by way of compromise—

"Stop a minute," and there I lay listening to the horrible, creeping, gliding, rustling noise. Ah! I could see it all plainly enough in my imagination. We were in one of the old houses of the past century, and here no doubt there had been a lady murdered after betrayal, and concealed behind the wainscot. And now I remembered a peculiar smell there was in the place when we entered it, a smell that I could not name then, but which I know now, from having experienced it in the British Museum—it was a mummy. There it was, all as plain as could be, a tall slight figure in a brocaded silk dress extended with hoops, short sleeves, and long lace trimmings hanging over the soft well rounded arms; and there she was with her hair built right up, and secured by a great comb, slowly gliding along by the wall, not on the floor, but some feet up, and slowly rising higher and higher towards the ceiling.

All at once I fancied she turned her face to me, and, horror of horrors, it was fleshless—nothing but the gaping sockets of the eyeballs, and the grinning white teeth of a skull, and then I could bear no more, but tried to cover my eyes with my hands, but found they did not need the cover as the clothes were already to a certain extent over them. I solemnly protest, however, that this must have been the act of Mrs Scribe, for I could not have done such a thing.

This convinced me that I could not have seen the figure, so I raised myself upon my elbow, urged thereto by the words of Mrs S, who exclaimed—

"Do pray get up, dear, or I shall faint."

"I wish you would," I muttered to myself, but then, thinking of the cruelty of the remark, I added, "or go to sleep," and then I tried to pierce the thick darkness, but found that I was unable even to distinguish the parts of the bedstead, and there, all the while, was the noise, "rustle, rustle, rustle"—then a stoppage, and a sound as if a hand beat against the wall, and at last the rustling quite ceased, and was succeeded by a peculiar scraping sound, at times quite loud, and then dying away, or stopping, and seeming as if it was not in the room at all.

"Is it gone?" whispered Mrs S, and then, as I did not answer, and she could not hear any noise, sitting up in bed by my side, "Oh! how dreadful it is—isn't it, dear?" she whispered. "Pray do get up and see what it can be."

The catarrh had made me so weak, and preyed so upon my nerves, that I was obliged to take refuge again under my cold, and plead perspiration and sudden check, and then, with the exception of the grating noise, all seemed quiet; and I was about thinking of lying down again, when "rustle, rustle," came the sound again, and Mrs S collapsed, that is to say, sank beneath the clothes, while I—well I *didn't* leap out of bed, and try to grapple with our nocturnal visitant. I knew there were matches upon the table, and I remembered exactly where the candle stood, but I put it to the reader, who could get out of bed and try to light a candle when there was a ghost in the room in a brocaded silk dress, rustling about from place to place, and seeming as if the floor was no necessity at all, for sometimes the noise came from far up, and sometimes from low down; and at last, as I sat there in a regular Turkish Bath, minus the shampooing, it seemed that the tall figure I imagined to be there gliding about by the wall grew shorter and shorter until but a foot high, then a few inches, and at last it was upon a level with the floor, and then the noise grew fainter and fainter, and at last was gone entirely, leaving a deep silence as intense as the darkness which closed us in upon all sides.

With what a sigh of relief I fell back in the bed, and exclaimed—

"She's gone?"

"Then get up and light the candle, dear," exclaimed Mrs S; but suffering as I was from catarrh, I might have made myself worse—at all events, such a proceeding would have been imprudent—so I lay quite still, thinking that, perhaps, after all, it was but a delusion and a snare, and that I might be attacked as soon as I got out of bed; or even if the ghost were gone, might she not come back again?

It was of no use though. I fought hard, but some women are so powerful in their arguments; and before ten minutes had passed, I was standing shivering by the dressing-table, fumbling about after the matches, which I could not find until I had knocked over the candlestick and a scent-bottle, and then put my foot upon one of the broken pieces. Then, when I opened the box and took hold of a match, it would come off all diabolical and phosphorescent upon my fingers, but no light could I get. Sometimes it was the wrong end I was rubbing upon the sand-paper; sometimes the head came off, and I could see it shining like a tiny star upon the carpet. The beastly things would not light upon the looking-glass, nor yet upon the table; but after I can't say how many tries, I managed to get a light, though it went out again in an instant, and there I stood trembling and expecting to be clutched by a cold hand or to be dragged back.

Light at last though, for, drying my damp hands as well as I could, I tried again by rubbing the match upon the paper of the wall, and then, though the candle would not ignite with the extinguisher upon it, yet I managed to get it well alight at last, and then tremblingly began to search the room.

The door was fast, and at the first glance there was nothing to be seen anywhere; but I examined behind the curtains, beneath the bed, in the cupboard, and, as a last resource, up the chimney, and found—nothing.

"Why, it was fancy," I said, quite boldly, putting down the candle upon the dressing-table, and looking at my watch, which, for the moment, I made sure was wrong, for it pointed to seven.

"Don't put out the candle," said Mrs S, and I left it burning; but I had hard work to make her believe it was so late.

"But not another night will I stop," she exclaimed. "I could not bear it, for my nerves would be completely shattered if I had to put up with this long. The place must be haunted."

Hot water and daylight put a stop to the dissertation which we had upon the subject, and soon after—that is to say, about nine o'clock—we made our way to the breakfast-parlour, where our host and hostess did not appear for another quarter of an hour, and then it was nearly half an hour more before we began breakfast, on account of delays in the kitchen relating to toast, eggs, bacon, hot water, and other necessaries for the matutinal repast.

"You see, it happened so unfortunately," said our hostess; "but I'm sure you will look over it, as we wanted to be all clear for Christmas-day."

"Oh, don't name it," said Mrs S; "we are often later than this, for Mr S will keep such late hours, especially if he is interested in anything he is reading or writing."

"I'm sure I need not ask if you both slept comfortably," said our hostess, "for you both look so well."

"Hem!" said Mrs Scribe; and I supplemented her cough with another much louder.

"Surely the bed was not damp," exclaimed our hostess.

"Oh, no," said Mrs S; "but—but—er—did you ever hear any particular noise about the house of a night?"

Our hostess shook her head, and then looked at me, but my face appeared so placid and happy, that she looked back at Mrs S, who was telegraphing for me to speak.

"No," said our host, putting down his letters, "no, I don't think we are much troubled with noises here of a night. I often thought I should like a good haunted house. But surely you heard nothing?"

"Oh, yes," said my wife, excitedly; "but pray ask Mr S—he will explain;" and she again telegraphed for me to act as chief speaker.

"Well, what was it, Scribe?" exclaimed our host. "What did you hear?"

"What did I hear?" I said, for I had smelt out the rat—or the soot. "Oh, I heard nothing but the sweeps."

Mrs S looked daggers.

## Chapter Twenty Two.
## A Goblin Ditty.

"You don't believe in ghostsh?"

"No, I don't believe in ghostsh."

"Nor yet in goblinsh?"

"No, nor yet in goblinsh, nor witches, nor nothing of the kind, I don't," cried Sandy Brown, talking all the while to himself as he was making his way home from the village alehouse on Christmas-eve. "I'm the right short I am, and I ain't 'fraid o' nothin', nor I don't care for nothin', an' I'm aw' right, and rule Britannia never shall be slaves. I'm a Hinglishman, I am, an' I'm a goin' crosh the churchyard home, and I'll knock the wind outer any ghosht—azh—azh—azh—you know—ghosht, and who shaysh it ain't all right? I never shee a ghosht yet azh could get the better o' me, for I'm a man, I am, a true born Briton if I am a tailor. And when I getsh to the head of affairsh I'll do it p'litically, and put a shtop to ghoshts, and all the whole lot of 'em, and my namesh Brown, and I'm a-going home through churchyard I am."

And a very nice man was Sandy Brown, the true born Briton, as he went rolling along the path that gloriously bright Christmas-eve, when there were myriads of stars in the East, and the whole heavens above seemed singing their wondrous eternal chorus—

"The hand that made us is Divine."

The moon shone; the sky was of a deep blue; the stars gemmed the vast arch like diamonds; ay, and, like the most lustrous of jewels, shone again the snow and frost from the pure white earth, while from far away came the northern breeze humming over woodland, down, and lea, turning everything to ice with its freezing breath, so that river and brook forgot to flow, and every chimney sent up its incense-like smoke, rising higher and higher in the frosty air.

The bells had been ringing, and the ringers had shut up the belfry-door. The curate's and rector's daughters had finished their task, so that the inside of the church was one great wreath of bright evergreens; while many a busy housewife was hard at work yet, even though past twelve, to finish dressing the goose or stoning the plums.

And what a breeze that was that came singing over the hills, sharp, keen, and blood dancing. Why, it was no use to try and resist it, for it seemed to make your very heart glow, so that you wanted to hug everybody and wish them a merry Christmas. Late, yes, it was late, but there were glaring lights in many a window, and even bright sparks dancing out of the tops of chimneys, for wasn't it Christmas-eve, and was not the elder wine simmering in the little warmer, while many a rosy face grew rosier through making the toast? And there, too, when you stood by Rudby churchyard and looked at the venerable pile, glittering with snow and ice in the moonlight, while the smooth, round hillocks lay covered as it were with white fur for warmth, the scene brought then no saddening thoughts, for you seemed only gazing upon the happy, peaceful resting-place of those who enjoyed Christmas in the days of the past.

For it's of no use, you can't help it, it's in the bells, or the wind, or the time, or something, you must feel jolly at Christmas, whether you will or no, and though you may set up your back and resist, and all that sort of thing, it's of no avail, so you may just as well yield with a good grace, and in making others enjoy themselves, enjoy yourself too. Selfishness! Bah, it's madness, folly: why, the real—the true enjoyment of life is making other people happy, but Sandy Brown thought that making himself the receptacle for more beer than was good for him was being happy; and Sandy Brown was wrong.

And perhaps you'll say, too, that you don't believe in ghosts, goblins, and spirits? Hold your tongue, for they're out by the thousand this Christmas-time, putting noble and bright inspirations into people's hearts, showing us the sufferings of the poor, and teaching us of the good that there is room to do in this wicked world of ours. But there, fie! fie! fie! to call it this wicked world—this great, wondrous, glorious, beautiful world, if we did not mar its beauty. But there, it's Christmas-time, when we all think of the coming year, and hopefully gird up our loins for the new struggle.

Sandy Brown had left his wife and child at home, while he went out to enjoy himself after his fashion, which was to drink till he grew so quarrelsome that the landlord turned him out, when he would go home, beat his wife, and then lay upon the bed and swear.

Ah, he was a nice man, was Sandy, just the fellow to have had in a glass case to show as a specimen of a free-born Briton—of the man who never would be a slave—to anything but his own vile passions.

It was very bleak at Sandy's cottage that night, for the coals were done, and there was no wood. Little Polly could not sleep for the cold, and her mother eat shivering over the fire trying to warm the little thing, who cried piteously, as did its mother. There were no preparations for spending a happy Christmas there, but poor Mrs Brown, pale, young, and of the trusting heart, sat watching and waiting till her lord and master should choose to return.

"There," said Sandy, blundering through the swing-gate and standing in the churchyard. "Who'sh afraid? Where'sh yer ghosh—eh?"

"Hallo!" said a voice at his elbow, while it seemed that a cold, icy, chilling breath swept over his cheek.

"Where'sh yer ghosh?" cried Sandy, startled and half sober already.

"Don't make such a noise, man, we're all here," said the voice, "come along."

"Eh?" cried Sandy, now quite sober and all of a shiver, for a cold breath seemed to have gone right through him, and he looked behind him on each side and then in front, but there was nothing visible but the glittering snow—covered graves and tombstones sparkling in the brilliant moonlight.

"Bah!" cried Sandy, "I don't believe—"

"Yes, you do," said the same voice, and again the cold breath seemed to go through Sandy and amongst his hair, so that it lifted his hat, already half off, and it fell to the ground.

"N-n-no, I don't," cried Sandy, trying to start off in a run, but he stopped short, for just in front of him stood a bright, glittering, white figure, apparently made of snow, only that it had jolly rosy cheeks, and a pair of the keenest eyes ever seen.

"Yes, you do, Sandy Brown," said the same voice, "and so don't contradict. Bring him along."

In a moment, before he could turn himself, there came a rushing sound like when the wintry breeze plunges into a heap of leaves, and whirls and rustles them away, when Sandy felt himself turned in a moment as it were to ice, and then rising higher and higher as he was borne round and round for some distance; when in the midst of myriads of tiny, glittering, snow-like figures, he was carried all at once right over the church; while like a beam of light the figures swept on after him as now rising, now falling, then circling, he was at last wafted round and round the old church, till he was placed upon the tower top, and like a swarm of bees in summer, the tiny figures came clustering and humming round him till they were all settled.

"Let me go home, please," cried Sandy, as soon as he could speak, but before the last word was well said, the first figure he had seen clapped its hand upon his mouth, when the tailor's jaw seemed to freeze stiff, so that he could not move his jaw.

"How dare you?" cried the spirit angrily.

"Dare I what?" Sandy said with his eyes.

"Profane good words," cried the spirit, in answer. "How dare you talk about home, when you have murdered it, and cast the guardian spirit out? Freeze him. But there, stop a bit."

Hundreds of the little fellows round had been about to make a dash at Sandy, but they fell back once more, and the tailor sat immoveable.

"There, look there," said the cold voice; "that's what you have spoilt." And Sandy began to weep bitterly, so that his tears froze and fell in little hard pellets of ice on to the snow before him, for he was looking upon the happy little home he had once had before he took to drinking, and watching in the humble but comfortable spot the busy wife preparing for the next day's Christmas feast, while he, busy and active, was finishing some work to take back.

"Now, look," cried the cold voice, and in an instant the scene had changed from light to darkness, for he could see his own dissipated, ragged self standing in the open door of his cottage, with the moonlight casting his shadow across the figure of his wife, lying cold and pale, with her child clasped to her breast. The black shadow—his shadow—the gloomy shade of her life cast upon her; and in speechless agony Sandy tried to shriek, for it seemed that she was dead—that they were dead, frozen in the bitter night while waiting for him.

The poor wretch looked imploringly at the figure before him, but there was only a grim smile upon its countenance as it nodded its head; and then, as if in the midst of a storm of snow flakes, Sandy was borne away and away, freezing as he went, now higher, now lower; now close up to some bright window, where he could see merry faces clustering round the fire; now by the humblest cottage, now by the lordly mansion; but see what he would, there was still the black shadow of himself cast upon those two cold figures, and he turned his eyes imploringly from tiny face to tiny face, till all at once he found that they were sailing once more round and round, now higher, now lower, till from sailing round the church the tiny spirits began to settle slowly down more and more in the churchyard, till they left Sandy, stiff and cold, lying between two graves, with the one tall ghostly figure glittering above him.

And now began something more wondrous than ever, for the bright figure glittering in the moonlight began to hover and quiver its long arms and legs above the tailor, and as it shook itself it seemed to fall all away in innumerable other figures, each one its own counterpart, till there was nothing left but the face, which stayed staring right in front.

The old clock struck four, when, groaning with pain and trembling with fear and cold, Sandy Brown slowly raised himself, keeping his eyes fixed upon a stony-faced cherub powdered with snow, which sat upon a tombstone in front, and returned the stare with its stony eyes till Sandy slowly and painfully made his way across the churchyard, leaving his track in the newly fallen snow; while, after an hour or two's overclouding, the heavens were once more bright and clear, so that when Sandy stood shuddering at his own door he feared to raise the latch, for the moon shone brightly behind him, and he trembled and paused in dread, for he knew where his black shadow would fall.

But in an agony of fear he at length slowly and carefully raised the latch, gazed upon his shadow falling across his wife and child, and then, in the revulsion of feeling to find that they only slept, he staggered for a moment, and as his frightened wife shrieked, he fell to the ground, as if stricken by some mighty blow.

But joy don't kill, especially at Christmas-time, and when Mrs Brown rose rather late that morning, she could not make out why Sandy was gone out so soon, for his usual custom was to lie half the day in bed after a drinking bout. But Sandy had gone to see about the day's dinner, and—

But there, Sandy's home a year after showed the effect of his meeting with the Christmas spirits, for it was well-furnished, and his wife looked happy, plump, and rosy— another woman, in fact; while as to people saying that Sandy fell down drunk in the churchyard, and that it was the little snow storm that he saw, why that's all nonsense; the story must be true, for a man picked up Sandy's old hat just by the swing-gate, where it fell off when he felt the spirit's breath. And as to there being no spirits out at Christmas-time, why I could name no end of them, such as love, gratitude, kindness, gentleness, good humour, and scores more with names, besides all those nameless spirits that cluster round every good, true, and loving heart at Christmas; ay, and at all times. While among those who have listened to this story and thought of its moral, surely there is at this moment that most gracious of spirits—Forbearance.

## Chapter Twenty Three.
### King Boreas.

Away with a shout and a shriek from the North,
The host of the Storm King in rage hurries forth;
With the monarch to lead them away o'er the main,
Sweep with whistle and wild shriek the winterly train.

O'er the sea, o'er the waves that spring tossing in wrath,
To fly after the host in a storm of white froth,
Till they dash in their anger on sand-hill and rock,
Or make some ship shiver, and groan with their shock.

Away rush the train with a howl 'mid each cloud,
That no longer moon-silvered floats massive and proud;
But torn by the Storm King, and rent by his crew,

Wild and ragged scuds onward in murkiest hue.

'Mid the rocks, through the caves that o'er ocean's waves scowl,
Away speeds the King, and his followers howl
As they toss the dark sea-weed, and tear up the sand,
Which flies frightened in drifts at the touch of their hand.

And away, and away, where the forest trees wave,
Where the willow and silver birch drooping boughs lave
In the silver-like stream, in the mossy green vale,
That ere yet the storm cometh breaks forth in a wail.

Now crashing 'mid beech-tops, now rending the oak,
Then laying the larch low with mightiest stroke;
While through the frail willow the storm spirits tear,
And the boughs stream aloft like a maniac's hair.

Rejoicing and shrieking anew at each feat,
Away o'er the moorlands, away sharp and fleet;
By the cotter's low hovel, the steep-cresting mill,
To the town by the hill-slope, as yet calm and still.

Bursting now o'er the roofs with a brain-piercing yell,
Round the old abbey towers they mock at each bell
As the past hour's chimed, when they sweep off the tone,
And away o'er the woodlands the summons has flown.

Again with a shriek, and again with a cry,
The King and his crew keep their revel on high;
They bear the cold snow-drift aloft in their train,
The sleet-darting arrow, and icy North chain.

They bind up the streamlet, they fetter the lake,
The huge rocky mountain they shivering break;
They rage through the forest, they strew the sea-shore,
While the echoing hill-sides resound with their roar.

King Boreas passes, his revel is o'er,
But the waves still in anger toss down by the shore;
The trees lie half broken and torn by the gale,
While the streamlets are fettered and bound in the vale.

## Chapter Twenty Four.
### A Lady in the Case.

Well, no, sir, I can't complain, I've risen well in the force, and I'm very well satisfied with my position, but then there's a great deal of responsibility attached to one's office, and, I can assure you, police inspectors have something else to do besides sitting still and growing fat. Many a smart young fellow would rise and get to be sergeant, inspector, or super in his turn, but for some little failings that creep out—I have my failings, too, of course, but still somehow I've crept up till here I am on the shady side of fifty and busy as ever.

Now you want me to give you an anecdote to put into print, that's what you want, eh? Well, of course it was easy enough to tell that, and I don't mind obliging you, for, as you very reasonably say, truth is stranger than fiction. But that disposition to tattle or talk about their business has been the ruin of more than one promising young officer. Now just think for a moment and suppose us to be always ready to talk of the cases we had in hand, where should we be? Marked men would slip us, planned jobs would be stopped, and many a gaol bird, whose tail we want to salt, would be off and escape. Ah, thirty years in the force have shown me some strange sights, and laid bare some curious tricks, all planned for the purpose of getting hold of somebody's money. I've seen and had to do with robbery, and murder, and garrotting, and burking, and suicide, and swindling, and embezzlement, and every kind of felony or larceny you can find a name for.

You know, our part is decidedly, I think, more lively than the city, for with the exception of a good bold robbery now and then at a bank or big gentleman's, there's seldom anything much there, while in our part we're always busy. For somehow or another there's always so many really clever rascals laying their heads together and making schemes, and then you have something new coming out all at once, like a clap of thunder over the town, and people are very much disgusted because the police have not bad more foresight, when all the while it's like a game of chess, and though we who play with the white pieces can to a certain extent see through the manoeuvres of black, yet we cannot see through everything as a matter of course.

Now I'm going to tell you of a little affair that happened one Christmas-night about twenty years ago, when I was only number so and so. It was a bright, clear, frosty night; no moon, but plenty of snow had fallen, quite late in the evening, so that the streets were regularly muffled; and in spite of feeling a bit ill-tempered at having to be on duty while other people were enjoying themselves, I could not help thinking of what a seasonable night it was, and how jovial and pleasant every place seemed to look. There were the bright lights and glowing fires, shining ruddy and warm through the drawn curtains; music and laughing might be heard every here and there, and more than once I stopped to hear a sweet voice singing, and felt envious like of the comforts other people enjoyed. Everywhere there seemed jollity and festivity, but in the midst of my growling I could not help recollecting that my beat that night was all in the better part, while down in the slums there was plenty of misery, enough to make even a policeman's heart sore.

Well, I felt better then, and I went on quietly through the deep snow, now making a little noise where it was a bit trampled, and now stealing along as quietly as could be. Once I caught myself humming a bit of a song I had just heard some one singing, then I whistled a bit, and still I kept on, buttoned up and gloved, thinking how pleasant it would have been spending Christmas at some jolly farm-house in the country, far away from the noise and worry of London.

All at once I came upon a merry party of some half-dozen ladies and gentlemen, just going in at a large house, when one of the gentlemen stopped and gave me quite a cheerer.

"How long are you on for, my man?" he says.

"Six o'clock to-morrow morning, sir."

"Hum; long hours on a bitter night like this. Bring a glass, John."

And then I heard him rattle his keys as he says, "stop a minute," and directly after he came back into the large, handsome hall with a decanter in his hand, while just about the same time the servant brought a wine glass on a little silver tray.

"There, my man," says the jolly-looking old gentleman, filling me up a glass of wine. "You take care of us, so it's only fair that we should take care of you. Thank you, my man, I hope I may have good health. There tip it down and have another glass. That's twenty port, that is, and a couple of glasses of that won't hurt you. Here, take hold of this lump of cake."

I didn't know anything then about twenty port, but I thought I should like twenty glasses of the rich red wine, which trickled down your throat like molten sunshine, and made you feel as if it was a jolly thing to be out on a cold Christmas-night; so I drank my second glass, wishing the pleasant, smiling old chap a merry Christmas, and then next minute, feeling like a new man, I was slowly tramping down the long street.

As I told you, in places I went along as quiet as a mouse, when I suppose it was about one o'clock that, in the middle of one street, I came all at once upon a tall, well-dressed young fellow inside some area railings, same as you may have seen, sometimes, where, beside the rails, the top of the area is all covered with iron bars, which make it like the top of a cage; while, as a matter of course, you can walk up to the dining-room windows.

Well, that's what this young fellow had done; and, as I went quietly up, there he was, close up, resting one foot on a ledge of the stucco, while one hand was on the sill of the open parlour window.

"Hallo!" I said quietly, for I had taken my gentleman quite by surprise; and I felt very good-tempered and comfortable from the effects of those two glasses of sunshine; so "Hallo!" I said, "what is it?" knowing all the while that I must have my gentleman, for he was regularly caged, and looking at me through the bars.

"Hush!" he said, not in the least taken aback; "Hush! hold your tongue: there's a lady in the case. Here, catch hold, and be off, there's a good fellow;" and then he gave me half-a-crown.

Now, seeing that it was light enough for me to make out that he was a well-dressed, smart-looking young chap, I took the half-crown, and as it didn't seem to be part of my work to interfere with a bit of billing and cooing, I went on, leaving my friend whispering to some one inside.

"All right, my fine fellow," I said to myself, turning it over in my mind; "All right, but I don't mean to be done if there's anything else on the way." So I went slowly on, and turned the corner; and then, knowing that my steps couldn't be heard, I slipped into a doorway, and made myself as small as I could.

Well, I hadn't been there a minute before I fancied I heard a sound like somebody sneezing, and trying to smother it down; and then my heart beat a little heavier, for I knew there was something more than a lady in the case; while, as I stood squeezed up there, I could make out my friend coming along by the shadow sent forward by the gas-lamp just round the corner. At last, very slowly he peeped round to look along the street where I was, but he could make nothing out, for I kept very snug in my doorway; though, if he had only come down half-a-dozen yards, he must have seen me, for there was a light burning over the door.

But the very openness of the place concealed me, and I breathed easier again as I made out by the shadow that he was going back.

"My turn now," I said; and then, going down on hands and knees, I crawled quietly and quickly over the snow, and had my peep round the corner after him, when there he was, slipping along as fast as he could go. "Stop a minute, my boy," I said, and then I runs as hard as I could down two streets to where I knew I must meet our sergeant and another man; for, you see, we all have our points to cross one another at certain times of the night, so that one man acts as a check on another; and the sergeant soon knows that, if a man's not at his place, there's either something wrong or the constable's neglecting his duty.

Just as I thought, there were the sergeant and the man, and the next minute we were going over my ground again, so as to pass along the street and come up to the open window, as I did at first. They were close behind me when I reached the street, and down on my knees I went again, held my hat behind me, crept to the end of the railings, and peeped like a boy playing "whoop."

"All right," I whispered back to the sergeant, for there was my friend at the other corner down on his hands and knees peeping round too, and watching for me to come back again.

Well, we sent our man back through the mews behind the houses to try and catch the watcher, while the sergeant and I crawled very quietly along close to the railings towards the open-windowed house, and next moment we were safe in the doorway, when I saw a head pop back from the open window as we came up; and so did the sergeant—by the way he nipped my arm. But there, we waited quiet and still for our other man to do his work and take number one, as I'll call the generous half-crown gentleman, when we meant to take proceedings against the one or two inside.

About five minutes slipped away very slowly when the sergeant whispered, "He's a very long time!" But the words were hardly out of his mouth before we heard some one coming down the street as hard as he could run, with another in full chase. So we let the first come on without our showing ourselves, when, as he came near the open window, he gave a low, peculiar whistle—one which was replied to from inside by a sort of warning chirrup. But, if meant for a warning, it was of no use, for, stooping in the shadow of the railings, we darted out just at the right moment, tripped my amorous friend up; and, though he tried to jump clear, it was of no use, for down he went, over and over in the snow, our other man atop of him, and then we had the "darbies" on him in a moment.

"I hope we shan't alarm that lady that's in the case," I said to my friend, as we hauled him up into the doorway; and then with another pair of bracelets we fastened him tight to the scraper, where he was quite safe till we liked to take him off.

"Hum," said the sergeant; then, looking at me and chuckling, as he stood brushing the snow off the knees of his trousers; "Hum, that's the cock bird, Jones, but I'm afraid the hen will prove rather tough."

"Yes," I says, "and I'm afraid there'll be one or two awkward chicks as well."

The next thing the sergeant did was to ring well at the door after sending another man, who now came up, round to the mews at the back to be on the look-out for escaping in that direction; and then, as he climbed over the railings to get at the parlour window, we heard a most tremendous screaming.

"Come now, there is a lady in the case after all," said the sergeant; and then, telling our other man to mind the prisoner, he made ready to get in at the window, where all looked very uncomfortably dark and treacherous.

"Shall I go first?" I said, all in a fidget at the same time lest he should say "Yes," for I don't mind owning that it looked uncommonly like putting one's head in a trap to go in at that window; and I felt a bit nervous, if not frightened.

The next moment I was over the railings too; and, holding my bull's-eye so as to throw all the light into the room I could, when in went the sergeant, and directly after, almost before you could say "Jack Robinson," there was a bit of a scuffle and the sound of a heavy blow, and some one went down with a crash; while, as I leaned forward and held in my light, I just caught a glimpse of some one, and at the same moment a heavy, numbing blow came down on my hand, and the lanthorn was knocked out, and fell with a clang under my feet in the area, while the silence which followed showed me plainly enough that it was not the lady in the case who had been knocked down, but the sergeant.

"Now, my lad," I said to the other policeman, as I stood rubbing and shaking my hand, "one of us must go in; sergeant's down, safe."

"Well," he said, "you've been longest in the force, you'd best go."

"Wrong," I said; "you were in before me."

"Well, but," he said, "I'm a married man, and you ain't."

"Wrong again," I said; "I'm married, and have two little ones."

Well, perhaps, you'll say it was cowardly not to have dashed in at once to help the sergeant. Perhaps it was; but, mind you, all this didn't take many seconds, as we whispered together; and, besides, I knew well enough that I should be taken at a disadvantage; for, though I couldn't see him, I was sure enough that there was a fellow armed with a life-preserver or a poker just behind the large window-curtain, so I wanted to plan a bit. And, mind you, I didn't want to go; but, as my fellow-constable did not seem disposed, and I stood close to the window, there was nothing for it, but to take off my great coat and jump in. So I drew out my staff, when my fingers were so numbed that I could hardly hold it; and then I said to myself, "Now for it, my boy;" when, making plenty of noise, I tried a very stale old trick—one that I didn't for a moment expect would take; and I tell you what I did. I got my fellow-constable's bull's-eye, opened it, and set it on the window-sill, so that the light was shining into the room, and then in went one leg, and I made believe to be jumping in with a rush; but, instead of doing so, I pushed in my hat as far as I could reach on the end of my staff, when "bang, crash," down came something right on the hat, beating my staff out of my hand, and making my fingers tingle again, it came so hard.

That was my time, though, and I leaped in so quickly that, before there was time for another cut, I had tight hold of somebody, and there I was engaged in the fiercest struggle I ever had. There were the chairs knocking here, there, and everywhere, while I could feel somebody's hot breath against my neck as, locked together, we swayed backwards and forwards. Once I was forced right back upon the dining-room table, but I sprang up again, and the next moment, whoever it was I struggled with had his head through the glass; while, as to the darkness, it was something fearful, for the lanthorn was knocked over, and only shone just in one corner by the floor. Jangle went a piano once as I was forced back on to it, and then the noise grew louder, for I could hear above the wild beast, worrying noise we made, the people upstairs screaming worse than ever.

"Well, there must be help come soon," I thought, as now down, now up, we struggled on. I wanted to shout to my fellow-constable to come in, as he was not wanted outside, but I suppose he did not like the job of getting in, for he did not attempt to come, while as to calling him, I could just as soon have flown, for my adversary seemed quite satisfied with my company, and held on by my throat so tightly, that I was almost choked.

All at once, for about the sixth time, I tumbled over the sergeant, and this time down I went undermost, while my head came against one of those tin-plate warmers, and made the most outrageous noise you ever heard in your life. Well, this rather shook the sense out of me, tin being rather a hard metal to catch your head against—so hard, that it seemed to me to quite strike fire, and then taking advantage of my being a little beaten down, this fellow got his hand inside my stock, when what with the blow and the pressure of his knuckles in my throat, lights began to dance before my eyes, and I felt about done. However, it seemed to me to be now not a struggle for capture or escape, but for life and death, and in the last despair of the moment, I got hold of the fellow's hand between my teeth, and hung on like a bull terrier.

How long this lasted I can't say; but I remember hearing a crash, and seeing the flashed light of a bull's-eye, when my lord rolled off me, and then through a sort of mist I could just see the sergeant's face looking all bloody, while directly after the light of the lanthorn was thrown two or three times upon my face.

"How are you, my lad?" said the sergeant.

But I didn't tell him, for the simple reason that I could not just then, but lay as still as could be, feeling afraid of tumbling, for the room appeared to be spinning round as fast as possible.

"How are you, my lad?" said the sergeant again directly after, but this time a little way off, and then I heard the "click, click" of the handcuffs, as he made them fast round my dear friend's wrists.

But I did not answer then; for though the room had left off spinning so hard, my tongue seemed to have turned sulky, and would not speak, though it was not my fault a bit. One feeling, however, did seem to come upon me now strong, and that was that I should like to have a look at the man on the floor, though not an inch could I move right or left.

Well, seeing that I could not answer, the sergeant called in the outside man, and then after a look round the room, he went and opened the dining-room door, and called out:—

"Come down, and bring a light. We are the police."

But before he had well said the words, there came a bang like thunder, and I could hear shot go rattling down the passage.

"Here, I say! confound you; what are you doing?" shouted the sergeant. "Don't you hear? We're the police." When, bad as I was, I could not help laughing to see the way our poor sergeant jumped. Though certainly it was enough to make him, you'll say.

After a few minutes a miserable looking old gentleman, in a dressing gown, came shivering down with one of those great brass blunderbusses in one hand, and a candlestick in the other.

"Keep back," the old gentleman cried; "it's loaded again."

"Then the sooner you uncock it the better," said our sergeant; "or else, perhaps, you'll be making another mistake. But now, if you'll go with me, we will just let the other man in," and then he went and shut down the window, and drew the curtains across.

But the old gentleman seemed so scared, that he could hardly tell friends from enemies, and he did not appear to like the idea of the front door being opened, for nearly all the sense seemed frightened out of him. However, he followed the sergeant, and they unlocked the door, let down the chain, and slipped back the bolts, and then after unlocking the darby, they lugged in my friend who said there was a lady in the case, brought him into the dining-room, and set him in an easy-chair in the corner. The sergeant then set light to a pair of candles on the chimney-piece, when I could see all that went on, for I could neither move nor speak yet.

"Slip round to the station for more help, and the stretcher," said the sergeant; and my fellow-constable went, though the old gentleman didn't seem to like it, and asked if it was safe to be left with the two burglars.

Then the sergeant came and stooped over me again, and asked me how I was; but all I could do was to look hard in his face, and wink both my eyes.

Just then he asked the old gentleman if he had a drop of brandy in the house, when a decanter was brought out, and a glass held to my lips, and a few drops seemed to revive me so, that I was able to sit up, when the sergeant and the old gentleman between them got me upon a sofa, where I lay quite still and felt better.

"Dear me, dear me," said the old gentleman: "I don't like my house being turned into a hospital."

"P'raps not," said the sergeant; "but if it hadn't been for that poor fellow, you might have looked queer."

Hearing the old fellow grumble seemed to rouse me, and I still went on listening.

"It's been a stiff fight, sir," said the sergeant; "and that young fellow—"

"And you, sergeant," I said feebly.

"Oh, come; that's cheering," said he with a pleasant look, which went right over his shining face.

You can't tell how pleased I felt to be able to use my tongue once more, but there was no work in me, and there I lay watching the sergeant give a look at the two prisoners, and examine the handcuffs to see that all was right, when all at once the fellow I had such a struggle with, sprang up and fetched the sergeant the most savage of kicks in the knee—one which sent him staggering back—when, in spite of all that has been said about the police using their staves, I'm sure no one could have blamed that sergeant for bringing his staff down on the fellow's head, and striking him to the ground, where, as he lay, I had a good look at him.

And a nice specimen of humanity he looked—a great six-foot fellow, strong as a horse, while my impression is that, if the sergeant had not come so opportunely to my aid, you would not have heard this story. But the fellow was tolerably knocked about. Ah! and so was the sergeant, while, no doubt, I should have been stunned at first if the chap had not been taken in by my shallow trick.

A nice little affair that was, and I saw that I had only just got up in time, for there were two carpet-bags on the floor crammed full of plate—silver dishes and tea and coffee pots, while all the small parts were filled out with forks and spoons.

All at once the old gentleman, who had been shivering about as far off the burglars as he could, seemed to catch sight of my half-crown gentleman's face—a face that he had not appeared so far to be very proud of, for he had kept it hung down over his waistcoat the greater part of the time—when all at once the old gentleman stood still and exclaimed:—

"Why, you scoundrel, it's you, is it?" and the fellow only shrunk down more of a heap, while the old gentleman was so enraged, that he made believe to shoot the rascal with his blunderbuss, when the sergeant made no more ado, but went and took it away from him.

"Come, you know," said the sergeant; "I see you won't be happy till you've done some one a mischief with that pretty little plaything. Oh, he was your footman, was he, and you discharged him for drunkenness, did you, a month ago? Well, I'm not surprised a bit."

Just then three of our men came in, and they walked off our two gaol-birds at once, and then I got hold of the sergeant's arm, and found I could walk.

"Take a little more brandy," said the old gentleman, and he poured out with a shaking hand about half a wine-glassful, when after I had drunk it he said again:—

"You're a brave fellow, and there's something to drink my health with."

I thanked him, and then we two walked out together, and stood on the pavement amongst the snow, listening to the old gentleman and the servants locking and bolting the door after us.

"Well," said the sergeant; "I think, my lad, we've done our night's work, and after reporting at the station, we'll go off duty for a day or two; for my head is in a queer state," and then he lifted his hat, pressed his hand upon it, and looked at the blood-smeared palm under the lamp. "But what did the old fellow give you?"

I opened my hand and looked, for I had not cared to look before; in fact, I was so stupid then, and dizzy, that I felt no interest in the money.

"Just what I expected," exclaimed the sergeant; "Sixpence! Well, some men have consciences."

It was a week before the sergeant was pronounced fit for duty, but it took me a fortnight to get right; while our friends had fourteen years each. I've often thought of the way I spent that Christmas-night—the roughest I ever did pass; but then you see, there was a Lady in the Case.

## Chapter Twenty Five.
## The Ghosts at the Grange.

Whether I believe in ghosts, fetches, hobgoblins, table spirits, and the rest of the lights and shades of the supernatural world, is a question that we will not stop to discuss, but if these pages should meet the eye of any person who can introduce me to a haunted house, I shall be his debtor. Now, when I say a haunted house, I must place a few stipulations upon my acceptance of the said house, so I will at once state what I want.

I want one of those comfortably (old-fashioned) furnished, quaint, gabled houses, shut up and deserted on account of supernatural tenants who will not be evicted; a house sacred to dust, spiders, and silence, where the damp has crept in here, and the mildew there, where dry rot and desolation have fixed their abodes, where the owl hoots and the chimney swallow builds, undisturbed by the cheering fumes of a fire; where the once trim garden is weed-grown and wild; pedestals overturned; moss and ivy rampant; fountains choked, and nature having it all her own way as she has had it for years. That's the sort of place I want to meet with, one that nobody will take, and when I present myself, the agent will laugh in his sleeve, and gladly accept me as tenant on lease for a trivial rent. Yes, the agent will laugh in his sleeve at my folly in taking the place on lease, and eagerly getting the document prepared and signed.

But then about the murder once committed in the far chamber—the noises—the rustling of silk dresses—the groans—the spots on the floor—the steps along the passages—the opening and closing doors—and other horrors that have scared people to death? Well, by God's help, and the exercise of a little observation, and putting of that and that together, I fancy I could get over those little troubles in time, for if the released souls of Hades, that once strutted upon this world's stage, can come back to perform such pitiful duties as to get in table legs and hats, bang doors, rattle chains, and rustle about o' nights, why e'en let them; and as I before hinted, I'll try and get used to that part of the trouble. The birds would still be welcome visitants, for I must own to a weakness for the feathered tribe, while on their part I can easily conceive that they would be discriminating in their choice of chimneys; the mildew and damp must, of course, be ousted, along with the dust and dry rot, while, as to the spiders and their works, why, much as their untiring industry and patience must be admired, out they must go too. And after all said and done, I fancy that a spider deserves a little better treatment at our hands. As to his character: it is too bad to associate him with so much craft and insidiousness. Why, what does the poor thing do but toil hard for its living? and I maintain that friend Arachne is as reputable a member of insect society as the much-vaunted busy bee.

"Oh!" some one will say; "but look at the nasty murdering thing and the poor flies struggling in its net, while the dear bees live upon nectar and honey!"

Who killed and murdered most wilfully all those poor unfortunate chuckle-headed drones this summer, eh?

But to my haunted house once more. What a crusade against rats and mice—what inspecting of old furniture—and sending this to the lumber-room, and that to be polished and rubbed up—what choosing of suitable new objects, and fitting up the old-fashioned rooms again, mingling just enough of the modern to add to the comfort of the old, without destroying its delicious quaintness. For I like an old house, with its crooks and corners, and bo-peep passages, and closets, and steps, and ins and outs, wainscots, old pictures, and memories of the past. Why, no one with a thinking apparatus of his own can be dull in such a place for calling up the scenes of the past, and trying to trace the old place's history.

Then, again, the garden. How glorious to leave to nature her beauties, and only take away the foul and rank; cutting back here and rescuing there, and bringing the neglected place into a charming wilderness—a place that nature has robbed of its old formal primness, and, setting art at defiance, made it her own.

Yes, if some one will kindly put me in the way of getting such a place for a residence I shall be his or her debtor, while for recompense, as soon as ever matters have been a bit seen to, and the place is habitable, they shall have the honour of first sleeping in the most haunted room in the house.

This is, I am well aware, a very choice kind of house, but that there are such places every one is aware, and my story is to be about one of these old man-forsaken spots, that years ago existed in Hertfordshire. I say years ago existed, for though the house still stands, it is in a dreadfully modernised form. Wings were pulled down, wainscotings torn out, and the place so altered that a tenant was found, and the haunters so disgusted with their home that the noises ceased, and the old reputation was forgotten.

I write this story as it was told to me by a friend, in whose word I have faith sufficient to vouch for the truth of what he heard.

There was an old legend attached to the place, something relating to the right of possession, and some one coming home to oust the then holder of the estate; then followed midnight murder, the concealment of the deed, and, as 'tis said, the spirits of the murderer and murdered haunted the scene of the dread deed.

Be that as it may, family after family took the house and left in a very short time. Strange noises were heard, strange stories got about the village; servants at first could only be sent from one room to another in twos or threes for mutual protection. Jane fell down in a fit; Mary was found staring, with her eyes fixed on nothingness, and her mouth wide open; Betsey was lost, but afterwards found in the best bedroom, with the whole of her person buried beneath the clothes, when she struggled and screamed horribly at their being dragged off; cooks Number 1, 2, 3, 4, and 5 used to go about after dark with their aprons over their heads; Mary Hann would not sleep alone; Thomas said nothing, but took to wearing his hair standing on end like quills upon the fretful etcetera, or better still, in this case, like a hedgehog; and all ended by giving notice one after the other, so fast, that at last it came to a fresh servant reaching the village, hearing the character of the house, and then going back without even testing the place, for, like a snowball, the horrors said to abound, increased at a fearful ratio when slipping glibly off Rumour's many tongues. At last the house stood empty year after year. The agent who was empowered to let it did his best. House-hunters came, looked at it, asked questions, and then, after a few inquiries, house-hunters went, and the house stood empty, when, as season after season passed, the forlorn aspect of the place became worse; the paint peeled off the window frames; the gutters rotted; green mould settled upon the doors; grass grew up between the steps; while the large slab was raised right out of its place by a growth of fungus; idle boys threw stones at the windows, and then ran for their lives; shutters became loose and flapped about; while neglect and ruin were everywhere, and the house was said to be more haunted than ever.

Fortunately, The Grange was the property of a wealthy man, who did not feel the loss of the rent, and as time wore on the place was known as "The Harnted House," and no attempt was made to let it, so that it became at last almost untenable.

At length a new agent came to the neighbouring town, and after a few months' stay his curiosity became aroused, and being a quiet sensible fellow, he talked to first one acquaintance and then another, heard the story of the haunted house from different sources, and the upstart was, that a party of half a dozen, of whom my friend was one, agreed to sit up with the agent in the ghostly place, and try and investigate the matter, so as to place the strange rumours in a better light if possible.

The night fixed upon came, and well provided with creature comforts, the party adjourned to the Grange; Mr Hemson, the agent, having been in the afternoon, and seen that a supply of fuel was placed ready, and at the same time had all he could done towards making what had evidently been a little breakfast-room comfortable.

On reaching the hall door the snow was falling heavily, while a sad moaning wind swept round the house, and blew the large flakes in the unwonted visitors' faces. Dreary and dismal looked the old Elizabethan Grange, and more than one of the venturesome party felt a shiver—perhaps of cold—pass through him as a large key was thrust into the lock, and with a groan the door turned upon its hinges.

Mr Hemson had brought with him a bull's-eye dark lanthorn, and now turning it on, the party found themselves in a small square hall with a wide staircase in front, and about three doors on either side. All looked gloomy and weird, while a sensation of chill fell upon one and all as they passed across the earthy-smelling place, followed Mr Hemson down a few stairs to the right, and then stood in the little breakfast-room, where a few sparks yet remained of the large fire that had been lit.

Every man had come loaded and ready for passing a cold winter's night in the forsaken house; and soon candles were lit, a large fire was roaring up the chimney, and a cloth having been spread over an old table, spirit bottles, glasses, lemons, and sugar, all tended towards making the room a little more cheering, while, in spite of dust and cobwebs, there was some very good furniture about the place.

"Choose wood-seat chairs, gentlemen," said Mr Hemson, "for everything is terribly damp."

The advice was followed, after closing the shutters, and bringing down a cloud of dust in the performance.

Glasses round became the order of the night, and whether for the sake of getting Dutch courage or not, I cannot say, but Hollands gin was a favoured spirit. After this refresher, candles were trimmed, the lanthorn turned on, and beginning with the cellars, a careful investigation of the place was made, walls were tapped, fastenings tried, shutters shaken, and all perfectly satisfied that no one but themselves was in or could gain entrance to the place. Go where they would, there was the same dull, damp, mephitic odour; dust and cobwebs, and mildew everywhere.

But for these traces of the lapse of time, the place might have been left but a few weeks or months. The rooms were well-furnished, good carpets were down, the library shelves were full of books, and ornaments upon the chimney-pieces. In the drawing-room was an old square pianoforte, while from every wall gloomy and dark faces looked down upon the intruders. And thus the tour of the house was completed, not a closet even being left unscanned, while as they left each room the keys were turned, and at length, joking and laughing, they returned to the comparatively snug room, and assembled round the fire.

"Now," said my friend, "presuming that we have come here to listen for the strange sounds that are heard, what course are we to adopt in the event of anything taking our attention?"

"Not much fear," laughed one.

"Then let's have a little smoke and a song," said another.

"But really," said Mr Hemson, "I think we ought to do something, gentlemen; for mind you, I for one fully expect that we shall hear some strange noise, and what I want is for us to find out what it is, and see if we can't stop it for the future."

"Did you bring any holy water, Hemson?" said one of the party.

"Come, come, gentlemen," said my friend, "business, business. Now, I tell you what: we will all sit here and of course the first man who thinks he hears a sound will advise the others, when we will all go together and try and find out what it was, but in silence, mind. No man is to speak till we get back to this room, when here is paper and you have, most of you, pencils; let each man write down what impression that which he has seen and heard made upon him, writing it down in as few words as possible, and so we can compare impressions, and there will not be, as is often the case, one person modelling his ideas upon those of another."

"Very good; I second that," said Mr Hemson, while, after a few remarks, first one and then another agreed that the plan would be excellent.

Ten—eleven struck by the old church-clock, and the wind roared round the old place, rumbling in the chimney and sending the snow with soft pats up against the window-panes, so that more than once a member of the party started and looked round, but the warm glow of the fire, the social cheer, and perhaps, more than all, the spirits, tended to drive away any dread that might otherwise have taken possession of those present, and the night wore on.

Twelve struck by the old church-clock, and the wind lulled.

"Now is the witching—what's the rest of it?" said one of the party.

"Ah," said another, "now's the ghostly time."

"Don't you wish you were at home, Hemson?" said another.

"Not I," said the agent. "I'm perfectly cool, so far."

"Well, I'm not," said the first speaker, "for my shins are scorching."

"Pass the kettle this way," said my friend, "and——"

"Hush!" exclaimed Mr Hemson, and a dead silence fell upon the group.

"Well, what is it?" said my friend, holding his glass to the kettle-spout.

"I fancied I heard a noise," said Mr Hemson, while all listened attentively.

"Pooh," said my friend; "the wind," and he then filled up his glass and placed it upon the table, but the next moment he started up.

"Well, what now?" said Mr Hemson.

"Didn't you hear that?" exclaimed my friend.

"No, what?" said Mr Hemson.

"Why that noise—there!" he exclaimed, and now every man started to his feet, having distinctly heard some sounds proceeding from the direction of the hall.

"Hush, be quiet," whispered Mr Hemson, hastily examining his lanthorn. "Now then, follow me," and all hastily passed up the few steps and stood in the hall listening to the sound as of some one talking in the room right in front—the dining-room.

The hall was quite dark save where the light from the breakfast-parlour shone out and cast a long streak upon the dining-room door, while there, each man holding his breath, and armed as they were with stout walking-sticks, pokers, or whatever came to their reach, the party stood listening as the loud utterance of some voice reached their ears, succeeded by various noises, as if there were some occupant of the room.

"Now then," whispered Mr Hemson, "are you all ready?"

"Yes," was the whispered response.

Mr Hemson turned on his dark lanthorn, almost with one movement turned key and handle, threw open the door, and as every man rushed in, the light was flashed all over the room, but no one was visible. There stood the old-fashioned dining-room chairs formally against the walls, the pictures looked down grimly, the wine cooler beneath the sideboard yawned gloomily and black, but nothing more could be seen; not even a chair was out of place, though every eye was now directed to a large closet in one corner.

"Come along, gentlemen," said Mr Hemson, and he swung the door of the empty closet open.

"But the table cover," whispered my friend, pointing to the large dust-covered cloth, whose corners touched the floor.

To whisk off the great pall-like cloth from the long dining-table was but the work of an instant, and then the light was flashed beneath the table; but nothing save a cloud of penetrating dust rewarded the searchers, who then stood, pale and puzzled, looking at one another, till Mr Hemson proposed an adjournment to the little room, where, after carefully locking the dining-room door, they retook their places, every man feeling uncomfortable and put out.

But attention was soon drawn by my friend to the arrangement agreed upon, when pencils were eagerly seized, and for a quarter of an hour not a word was spoken, when the last man laid down his pencil.

"Has every man signed his name?" asked my friend.

This caused another trifling delay, for no man had placed his name at the bottom of his manuscript; but this being done, the first man's paper was read over. It was, of course, very brief, but to the effect that, while standing in the hall, he had heard the sound as of a man talking to himself in a wild, agitated manner; that it seemed that a book was thrown hastily down upon the table by some one, who then hurriedly pushed his chair back, so that it scraped along the floor, while at the same time the table gave way and cracked audibly. Then followed the hurried pacing of some one up and down the room, till the door was thrown open and all became silent.

"Precisely what I have stated," exclaimed Mr Hemson.

"Mine is almost word for word the same," cried my friend; while, with trifling exceptions, the narratives of the other watchers tallied.

Rather pale and uncomfortable, the party now eat talking in whispers, starting at every loud gust of wind or loud pat of snow upon the window, while the rattling of casement or door was enough to send a shiver through the stoutest man present. But as the night wore on and nothing more alarming was heard, first one and then another dropped off to sleep, though the majority sat watching till the cold grey light of the winter's morning dawned; and then, after another glance at the dining-room, now looking more weird than ever as seen by the light streaming through the round, eye-like holes in the window shutters, the party gladly left the house, and doubtless made the best of their way to bed.

Now, I make no defence of this story, for I have placed it upon paper in much the same form that it was told to me. What the noise was that the convivial watchers heard I cannot say, but though I consider my informant worthy of credence, and though it was singular that the impression made on all was the same, yet I cannot help thinking that the best thing to imbibe while sitting up o' night is tea.

## Chapter Twenty Six.
## Caught in his own Trap.

Fancy being almost born a DD, like unto Mr Dagon Dodd, a gentleman who resided, when in what he called his prime, at Number Nine, Inkermann Villas, Balaclava-road, Russiaville—who resided there for the simple reason that he paid his rent and rates with the same punctuality that he did his Income Tax, or it is within the range of probability that Number Nine would soon have possessed another tenant.

Now, although Mr Dagon Dodd had a great right to the letters DD, since they formed his initials; yet he was in no wise related to a celebrated doctor of the same name. Mr Dodd was a bachelor—rather a bald bachelor, with a great deal of very smooth white crown, surrounded by a neat little stubbly fence of very black bristly hair. You never caught Mr DD with his hair brushed in greasy streaks across his head, for the simple reason that his was hair that would not brush, nor yet comb; it grew in a particular way, and stuck to that way most obstinately, besides which what hair existed was so much like a brush itself, that when the well-known toilet appendage came into contact with Mr DD's head there was such violent antagonism that electricity was evolved, and my only wonder is that Mr DD had not brought the powerful current into use in some way.

Mr Dodd was in person slightly stout, slightly asthmatical, and decidedly short; and though a single person, report said that it was not the fault of the gentleman, for he had once proposed to a lady and been rejected. At all events, Mr Dodd was a single gentleman in the popular acceptation of the term, but decidedly not so in appearance, for in addition to his person, which might have been called after the contents of certain brewers' barrels, "Double Stout," he wore double-breasted coats and waistcoats, double-soled shoes, with large black ferret strings, tied in bows, even in snowy weather, while his double chin and double show of importance made the little gentleman do very great credit to Number Nine, Inkermann Villas.

But though a bachelor, Mr Dodd was wedded—wedded to science—science as applied to domestic economy—social science, and he experimentalised largely, greatly to the disgust of his staff of servants—cook, housemaid, and buttons,—who stigmatised him as *messy*. For the fact is, Mr Dodd delighted in patents, and was in himself a little fortune to those men who are for ever trying to perfect that steam-engine which shall draw corks. Though far from sneering at improvements, what a blessing it would be if some ingenious mortal would invent a patent noiseless dressing-machine—a dressing-machine for babies. Oh, *bliss*! bliss!! bliss!!! However such an invention could not be expected from a single gentleman, who had, though, patent locks on all his doors; a patent rotary knife-cleaner polished the knives; a patent boot-cleaner the boots; a patent roasting-jack nearly drove the cook mad, as it basted the meat itself, and all the while splashed the clean hearth and wasted the perquisites. Then there was a patent potato-peeler, a patent potato-masher—egg-beater—carpet-sweeper—cinder-sifter—and prize Kitchener. Patent something with an unpronounceable name covered the hall; patent candles burned in patent lamps; patent enamel saucepans cooked the viands; while Mr Dodd almost fed himself by means of a little chewing thing, which turned with a handle, for teeth and digestion were failing, and in spite of a patent base artificial teeth will prove more ornamental than useful. There was a patent ventilator for regulating the temperature of every room—instruments that were remarkable for their awkward propensities, for, like the greater part of the machinery in Mr Dodd's establishment, these ventilators always made a point of doing the very opposite to what was required of them. For instance, they always stuck and remained open in winter, to give entrance to all the tooth-chattering winds; and as obstinately remained closed when the summer heats prevailed, and a little fresh air would have been a blessing. The patent, or rather to be made patent, coal-scuttle of Mr Dodd's own designing was certainly a noble invention, only that, like Artemus Ward's first novel, it was far from "perfeck," for in consequence of working with a crank the article was cranky, and always put on either too much or too little of the heat-affording mineral, while it had been known to scatter a knubbly shower all over the hearthrug.

But scarcely anything had taken up more of Mr Dodd's attention, than the springs which opened and closed his doors. He very reasonably said that such a trivial matter might easily be worked by machinery sympathising with the approaching feet; but in spite of all his care and trouble, the springs beneath the boards of the floor would not be regulated to the required strength, they would go either too stiffly or too easily. Now this was very often most troublesome, as exemplified upon one occasion, when Mr Dodd was bowing out a lady visitor, taking leave with her husband. The owner of the inventions stood too long upon the spring board, and just in the midst of one of his most profound bows, clap-to came the door, shooting Mr Dodd forward, as if out of a Roman catapult, and making him butt his male friend, ram fashion, right in the region known to us in school days as "the wind," when the effects were most disastrous: the gentleman's watch-glass was broken, and the visitor doubled up in the large umbrella-stand, with his internal inflatable organs in a state of vacuum, while by the recoil, Mr Dodd came down in a sitting posture upon the door mat, where he remained staring at his collapsed friend until he thought better of it, and helped him to rise.

He was often on the very point of becoming a martyr to science was Mr Dodd, and never nearer than upon one dismal, dreary, snowy, scrawmy morning, one of those cheerful times when people are wont to feel put out with everything and everybody—a sort of three-cornered time—a Boxing-day in fact, when, after a little extra jollity on the previous night, there was a strong suspicion of headache and disordered liver. Mr Dodd began the day all askew, by getting out of bed the wrong way, and then felt as if all the skin was off his temper which as naturally became chafed, as that people who have sore places, manage to hit them in preference to other parts of their body however sound. Everything went wrong with Mr Dodd upon that morning. His shaving water was nearly cold, and in spite of the patent guard razor, Mr Dodd cut himself severely; then there was hard water in place of soft, in the ewer, and his face was chapped with the previous day's cutting wind; he felt as if he had taken cold, for the ventilator had not closed when Mr Dodd went to bed, even when he stood upon a chair and hammered it with a poker; while, worse than all, an irritating cough tickled and tormented him, tried as it was by the smoke which ascended the staircase and penetrated his bedroom.

Descending at last through the clouds, like an angry Jove, Mr Dodd encountered Mary, housemaid, with an angry—"Where does all this smoke come from?"

"Oh, it's all that nasty jester, sir, as won't keep up. It's only propped up now by two little deary pieces of firewood, a waiting to be burnt through and let it down again."

Mary's angry master seemed to think the "nasty jester" was no joker; but a little examination soon enabled him to put the register right, and dispense with the "two little deary pieces of firewood;" but directly after Mr Dodd summoned the maiden to the dining-room, by apparently trying to play a tune upon some instrument, whose ivory mouthpiece projected from the wall.

"No stove fire alight in the hall this morning, Mary?" said Mr Dodd, as his attendant brought, in some very badly made dry toast.

"Won't burn a bit, sir," said Mary. "It's wuss than this, and smokes awful."

"Did you turn the little knob by the pipe?"

"No, sir, I didn't, sir."

"Tutt—tutt—tutt," exclaimed Mr Dodd impatiently, as he went to the foot of the well staircase, opened the stove damper, and then stooped down to open the door and see whether a spark yet remained.

It was well for Mr Dodd that he stooped as he did, for with a fearful crash down came a coal-scuttle from the second floor, striking from side to side of the well staircase, and bestowing upon the stooping gentleman's bald head a regular douche of knubbly coals, mingled with dust, while the copper scuttle itself fell upon the stove, and knocked off the pineapple knob which formed its apex.

"Lawk-a-mercy, sir, what a good job as it wasn't the scuttle," exclaimed Mary, as her master shook himself free from the cheerful coal, and gazed up at the skylight at the top of the staircase, to see whence came the fearful shower, but only to find his eyes resting upon the fat, round, inanimate countenance of the page staring over the bannisters, perfectly aghast at the mischief.

The explanation Mr Dodd sought was most simple. Mr Dodd had not yet fitted his house with a hydraulic lift, after the fashion of those used in our Brobdignagian hotels, but had contented himself with a crane and winch for drawing up coals and other loads. This machine, too, was a failure from the ignorance and apathy of the page, who was a regular grit in Mr Dodd's cog-wheels, and who this very morning, from some mismanagement, had nearly offered up his master as a sacrifice upon the altar of science.

Under these untoward circumstances Mr Dodd went and acted in the most sensible of ways, that is to say, he went and washed himself; but it is not surprising that he should afterwards feel more gritty than ever when he sat down to partake of his matutinal coffee, made in a patent pot with an impossible name. He boiled his eggs, too, himself, by means of a small tin affair—patent, of course—in which a certain quantity of spirit of wine was burned, and when extinct the eggs were done.

Mr Dodd finished his breakfast in a very excitable and vicious manner. He felt sore, mentally and bodily sore, for his inventions and patents were his hobby, and they either would not work right, or people would not take the trouble to comprehend them. He suffered terribly; but for all that he persevered, and, being a bachelor, he did as he liked. And, being a bachelor, what wonder that he should have a sewing-machine, and amuse himself with his Wheeler and Lathe in stitching round the half-dozen new table-cloths? But the sewing-machine was useless for buttons, so Mr Dodd set to, to invent one that should meet that want, and so be a blessing for every single man. A week passed—two weeks—three weeks; and then, after no end of brain work and modelling for the new machine, to be called the patent button-fixer, invented by Mr Dagon Dodd, that gentleman didn't do it, and gave up, if not in despair, at all events in despair's first cousin.

But Boxing-day seemed to have set in badly; while Mr Dodd felt ill-disposed to suffer the stings and arrows. According to the old saying, "it never rains but it pours"—in this case coals—and while the hero of these troubles was sternly gazing upon his fire, with a foot planted against each bright cheek of the stove, Mary came to announce the arrival of a tradesman, now in attendance to take certain orders.

Mr Dodd tried to place himself in a less American position, but found that he was a fixture. It was a wet, slushy morning, and Mr D had determined to try the new patent compo-ment-elastical-everlasting-soled boots—a new patent, and one which should have been devoted to the practice of walking upon ceilings, for they were now tightly fixed to the sides of the fireplace, and Mr Dodd in them, to his unutterable discomfort and annoyance. At the first he imagined that it must be owing to the tar he burned upon his fire—a coke fire, whose combustion was aided by the drips from a small vessel behind the register, containing tar; but Mr D soon found that the material of his new impervious boot-soles was alone to blame; and consequently while the man waited he unlaced and set himself at liberty, a culmination at which he did not arrive without slipping off his chair once, and coming into sharp contact with the fender.

Mr Dodd determined in future to stick to his shoes, for it was evident that his boots meant to stick to something else, and they did too so tightly that they had to be flayed off with the carving-knife, and not easily either, for sometimes the knife became a fixture, and at others the sole became again attached, while the heel was set at liberty, and *vice versâ*. So Mr Dodd felt ill-tempered.

"Now, Mr Pouter," said Mr Dodd at last to the tradesman, who had been for some time standing within the door, and smelling very strongly of glue; "now, Mr Pouter, I want the door-springs eased a little, and I want this fixed."

"Certainly, sir," said Mr Pouter, smiling at the recollection of his old friends the spring-doors, which had been quite a little fortune to him, and bade fair to remain so, seeing that they required his ministering hands about once a week.*We* already know how that they would occasionally bang too hard, but they would also bang too softly; when the application of a hand was necessary to make them close, and they might just as well have been common doors. So Mr Pouter smiled.

"What are you laughing at, sir?" exclaimed Mr Dodd, angrily. "I tell you what it is, sir," he continued, rubbing his sore head, for he could not touch his sore temper, "I'll tell you what it is, if you can—not attend to my orders without grinning like a gorilla, I'll—I'll—I'll—employ some one else. Such impudence!"

This was an awful threat for Mr Pouter. It was like saying, "I'll take fifty pounds away from you;" and therefore Mr Pouter, who hated losing a customer, and was much given to cuddling his jobs—that is to say, holding one very tightly till another came in—Mr Pouter looked exceedingly dove-like and mild, ceased smiling, and said appealingly—

"Plee, sir, I didn't laugh."

"Hold your tongue, sir," exclaimed Mr Dodd, "I say you did laugh."

"But plee, sir, I really didn't, sir, and I didn't mean nothin' at all, sir," expostulated Mr Pouter, in a most ill-used tone.

"You laughed at me very rudely, sir," said Mr Dodd, with dignity, "and I now beg that the subject may be dropped. Have you brought your tools?"

"Yes, sir; yes, sir!" exclaimed Mr Pouter, glad enough to have the subject changed, and now looking as solemn and stiff in his features as if his skin were composed of his own shavings.

"Then turn up that carpet, remove the loose boards, and ease the door-spring—not too much, mind; but, there, let that girl pass with the tray."

"That girl" was Mr Dodd's housemaid, Mary, who gave her head a dignified toss; but her step was arrested by the sound of a heavy body falling, followed by an exclamation of pain.

"Dear me, sir—very sorry, sir—wouldn't have had it happen on any account," said Mr Pouter, stooping to pick up the mallet he had dropped upon Mr Dodd's particular corn.

But Mr Dodd did not reply, he only limped about the room with anguish depicted upon every feature, while Mr Pouter tremblingly went on with his work.

"There!" exclaimed Mary, upon reaching the kitchen, "I declare if I'll stop. There's nothing but messing going on from morning till night. It's too bad! for there's that Pouter again, chipping and hammering, and sending the dust a-flying all over the room worse than ever."

"What was all that noise?" croaked Cook, a very red-faced and red-armed lady.

"Carpenter dropped one of his tools on master's toe, and sent him a-hopping about the room like a singed monkey," exclaimed Mary, in a tone of the deepest disgust. And it must be said that this was a very disrespectful and doubtful simile, for the odds were strongly against Mary Housemaid having seen a monkey suffering from the effects of fire.

"What's the carpenter a-doing of?" said Cook, who was busy making paste, and now paused to have her question answered, and to rub her itching nose with the rolling-pin.

"Why," exclaimed Cook's mortal enemy, the Buttons, "master said as old Pouter was to come and fix a jam—something or other."

"There, now, you be off into the hairy and finish them shoes," exclaimed Mrs Cook, fiercely. "Nobody arst your opinion; so come, now, be off!"

Buttons did "be off," for under the circumstances it would have been rash to have stayed, since Mrs Cook was going at him, rolling-pin in hand, with the very evident intention of using it in the same way as her friend Q1866 did his truncheon. But Buttons was not going to be bundled out of the kitchen that way "he knowed," so he took his revenge by flattening his nose against the kitchen-window, just where he would be most in his culinary tyrant's light; and then in pantomimic show he began to deride Mrs Cook's actions, till that lady rushed out at him, when he retreated to his den beneath the pavement, and went on with his work for quite five minutes, then, with a shoe covering one hand and a brush in the other, he made his appearance at the kitchen-door, to deliver the following mystic announcement:—

"It worn't a jam, it were a preserver," but he retreated again with great rapidity to avoid the paste pin launched at his head by the irate cook, but the utensil only struck the closed door, when Master Buttons again inserted his head to howl out a derisive "Boo-o-o," and then disappeared till dinner time.

But matters progressed so satisfactorily up stairs, that by five o'clock Mr Pouter departed, basket on back, with half a yard of saw sticking out, to tickle and scratch those whom he met, to whom on the pavement he was just such an agreeable obstacle to encounter as a British war chariot, with its scythed axletrees, must have been to all concerned. But Mr Dodd was placid, the door worked beautifully, and he determined to have every other door in the house seen to and re-adjusted. So Mr Dodd dined, and at last retired to bed, serene and happy in his expression.

That very night something happened.

It was midnight, and, save when the noise of some cab, conveying the Christmas folk home, could be heard, all was still. But there were voices to be heard in the attic of Number Nine. There was a candle on a chair beside the bed, and Cook and Mary were sitting up, the one listening, while the other slowly waded through the thrilling plot of the "to be continued" tale in the Penny Mystifier.

The night was cold, and shawls thrown over shoulders was the mode, while slowly see-sawing her body backwards and forwards in bed, Mary, after once reading, went back and epitomised the tale for Cook's benefit, that lady not having been very clear upon two or three points.

"Then," said Mary, "when she finds as her par won't let her marry De Belleville, she sits by the open winder, with the snow rivalling her arm's whiteness, and a lamenting of her hard fate, and it's quite dark, and her lover comes and begs of her to fly with him."

"Go in a fly," said Cook, approvingly.

"No! no! go off with him," said Mary.

"Ah! I see," said Cook, "go on."

"And, after being begged and prayed a deal, she says as she will, and he fetches the ladder; and, just as she's done falling on his neck and weeping, a mysterious voice says—"

"Oh!" cried the domestics in horrified tones as they clung together, for in the stillness of the night there was a fearful cry from below stairs, followed by the noise of something heavy falling.

"It's the biler busted, Mary!" shivered and sobbed the cook.

"Oh no, it's master being murdered," gasped Mary; "I know it is. Ennery! Ennery! Ennery!" she cried, banging at the frail partition wall to arouse Buttons, who at last condescended to wake up and knock in answer.

"Oh! do get up and go down; there's something the matter!" cried Mary and Cook together.

"Oh, ah! you go," came back in muffled tones from the sweet youth.

"Oh, do go, there's a good boy!" said Cook sweetly; "do go down and see."

"Ah! I dessay," said Buttons, recalling the morning's treatment.

A compromise was at length effected, and the three domestics stood upon the top of the staircase gazing down, while the moon looked sideways at them through the skylight.

"Ah! I see you!" cried Cook to an imaginary burglar. "You'd better go: here's the perlice a-coming," which was a great fib of Mrs Cook's, for there was not a policeman near; though, from the lady's tones and confident way of speaking, it might have been imagined that there was a police barracks on the roof, just within call.

"Cook!" cried a faint voice.

"There. I know'd it was!" cried Mary. "It's master, half killed."

"Here, help! come down!" came up again faintly.

"Oh! we dussen't, sir!" chorused Mr Dodd's servants.

But at length Buttons was pushed forward, and, a landing at a time, the timid trio slowly descended to the assistance of poor Mr Dodd, whom they found half-stunned and bleeding upon the dining-room door mat; but warm water, diachylon, and half a glass of brandy revived Mr Dodd so that he was able to re-send his servants to bed, and then retire himself, and ponder upon the advisability of having mechanical life-preservers attached to the lower room doors, since the experimental affair fixed that day by Mr Pouter had proved so awkward, when its owner had hurriedly gone down to fetch the letters left upon the dining-room chimney-piece; though if Mr Dodd had been a burglar, the effect would have been most effectual as well as striking.

"No," said Mr Dodd, as he turned his aching head to find an easier spot upon the pillow. "No, I think bells are the best after all."

Next morning Mr Dodd was too ill to rise, and many of his Christmas-boxing friends who had omitted to call the previous day, went away empty. Mr Pouter's bill has decreased yearly, for Mr Dodd's faith has been shaken in patents; while as to spring-guns in grounds, and preservers set with springs on doors, surely it is better to suffer imaginary dangers than to run real risk, for really it cannot be pleasant to be caught in your own trap.